Tortured

Also by

AMANDA McINTYRE

THE DIARY OF COZETTE

Tortured
AMANDA McINTYRE

Spice

TORTURED

ISBN-13: 978-0-373-60533-0

Copyright © 2009 by Pamela Johnson.

Recycling programs
for this product may
not exist in your area.

This is a work of fiction. Names, characters, places and incidents are
either the product of the author's imagination or are used fictitiously,
and any resemblance to actual persons, living or dead, business
establishments, events or locales is entirely coincidental.

www.Spice-Books.com

Printed in U.S.A.

Truth, encouragment and support are three elements of every book that is written. My sincere thanks to Lara, Patti, Pat, Jo and my family for always giving me this and so much more.

The author claims literary license in the writing of this book based in a time when little of the language as we know it existed. The Old English or Anglo-Saxon terms, if used to their authenticity, along with all Gaelic and Roman (Latin) terms, would make reading this book like standing at the Tower of Babel. Therefore, the author has blended the language as well as possible in order to make it digestible for the modern reader while staying true to its intended meaning.

Prologue

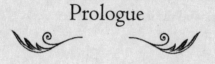

Between ancient Rome and the High Middle Ages, there was a period of chaos and unrest known to the modern world as the Dark Ages. Short of armies, the Romans retreated to their mother country, leaving Britannia on its own to wage war against the brutal Picts and Scots. A Briton king rose up by the name of Vortigern, inviting shrewd Germanic tribes into alliance with Briton to wage battle with these native tribes. However, his greed and brutality, even toward his own people, became his demise. It was not long before the Saxons, Jutes and Anglos—the very armies Vortigern invited in—began to take over, and with a vengeance.

These ruthless Germanic tribes spread across Britannia claiming villages and deserted Roman forts along the way. They pushed the Britons to the farthermost shore, and those who remained either died or became wealas (Welsh)—slaves or foreigners under the reign of the self-proclaimed Saxon lord.

Very little documentation from this time leaves much about

how these people lived to the imagination. Continued unrest among warring tribes meant little choice for the slaves, and daily life became an act of survival in every way imaginable.

Though volatile, this period brought forth a birth of new ideas, new cultures and new nations. For those who lived through it, their stories of courage and daring, passion and pride became the stuff of legends.

This is such a story. One of survival, of passion, courage and hope in a dark and dismal time in history.

—A.M.

Chapter One

Saxon Shore, A.D. 500

"Dunna ever be afraid, Sierra," her mother's voice whispered in her head. "Fear will be your downfall, as it is mine."

Sierra shoved her body against the dungeon's heavy, wooden door. With the dense smoke from the executioner's chamber still clogging her throat, she breathed deeply of the rain-soaked smell of earth and moss. The clouds above were gray and ominous, covering the sun and offering little hope of warmth in this most unholy of places.

Her eyes rose to the hill overlooking the outer wall of the castle. Once occupied by the Romans, the fortress was now home to Britannia's Saxon king, Lord Aeglech. Nine years ago, his tribes had taken over, obliterating all that was once a thriving Britannia. Those who did not accept the new Saxon rule were killed. Those who did became Saxon property. In some ways,

Sierra considered herself lucky to be alive. She owed her life to her mother, and to the threat of a Druid curse that her mother left on Lord Aeglech and his guards in the moments just before she was hanged as a traitor.

More than once over the years, Sierra had wished she had not been allowed to live. Or that her mother had not left her with the gift of sight passed down on the maternal side of her family. She had never wanted the gift, seeing the life of servitude it had enslaved her mother to. Untrained, Sierra was not able to summon her sight at will, but over the years, she had managed to use it well enough to stay alive. And if she could stay alive, perhaps she had a chance of one day finding the brother who had been taken from her the night their mother died.

If nothing else, living in the Saxon fortress had served to strengthen her in odd ways. No longer did she despise the sight of Lord Aeglech or look upon him as a murderous barbarian. Nor did the cries of anguish from Balrogan's torture chamber— where she grew from a young girl to a woman—make her vomit, any longer.

For nine years, she'd lived in this Saxon hell, clinging to her mother's last words, "Dunna fear." It was her first and last thought each day. She had long ago learned to void herself of the things inside of her that could lead to fear. It was all she knew. It was how she survived.

Sierra choked on the cold air that filled her lungs. Blinking the wetness from her eyes, she squinted at the Saxon gallows up on the hill. Placed there for all the village slaves to see, it currently stood empty, gently blowing in the breeze and patiently awaiting its next guest. She absentmindedly touched the lavender wristlet on her arm. Her mother had given it to her once long ago.

"Sierra!"

Careful not to respond too quickly to her birth name, she glanced toward the nearby stable from whence the whisper came.

There beneath the eave, with his arm braced above him, stood Cearl—her lord, her savior—the boy who started as friend and who'd now grown to a handsome man. The one and only boy she had ever given herself to.

Sierra waited a heartbeat and checked around her before she hurried toward him. She gripped the water bucket as it slapped hard against her thigh, and let it tumble to the ground so she could leap into Cearl's waiting arms.

"'Tis good to see you as well, Mouse." He laughed and clamped his mouth down on hers.

She savored his lips, the sharp taste of mead on his tongue, the feel of his arms secure around her. When she was with Cearl, the dark world she lived in faded away, if only for a few moments.

"Is Balrogan expecting you back soon?" he muttered, dropping her to her feet and wrestling with the knotted belt at her waist.

"I have a little time, not much," Sierra replied and turned her head to allow his fervent kisses on her neck. In truth, Sierra did not know what Cearl saw in her. Sentenced to aid the executioner, as his apprentice, she was ordered to keep her hair short and wear men's clothing. It was part of her punishment to have no identity, no gender. Yet Cearl did not seem to mind that she was covered in soot and filth.

"Take care when you call my birth name aloud," she reminded him as his fingers fumbled with the leather knots of her belt. "It is dangerous out here. Someone might suspect that you are familiar with me."

"Is it not true that I am?" He grinned and brought his mouth down hard on hers, before refocusing his efforts on his task. "What shall I call you, then? My wench?" He laughed and grabbed her buttocks through the thin breeches she wore as he pulled her tight against him.

Sierra knew they took a great risk. Lord Aeglech's decree for himself and his guards was that no Saxon was to join with a Briton woman. He did not want the bloodline marred by a Celt bastard; if one of his guards disobeyed his rule, the woman would have to be killed. Though Cearl was not a guard, she feared what would happen to them if they were found out.

"Your wench would imply that I serve only you," she teased.

He stopped, his hands pressing into her upper arms as he studied her face. "Another is pleasing you, then?"

She cupped his unshaven jaw. Cearl was such an innocent. Though his body was that of a man, he often thought like a young boy. "Nay, Cearl, only you do that."

"All right then, let it remain so." He gave her a smile before he captured her mouth. She knew the routine well, and she accepted the rough manner of his tongue delving between her lips.

Sierra's breasts tingled beneath her bindings, and she longed to remove them so she could again feel Cearl's hands on her naked flesh, but today there was not enough time.

She felt safe around him. In all the years of her imprisonment, she had never had reason to fear him. Cearl had not the rules of the other men in her life. He had no need to dominate, perhaps because his place in life was to serve those of higher rank. He was the handsome son of a Saxon villager and helped in the kitchen, in addition to crafting the drums the Saxons used in battle. His hair was a mass of golden curls, the color of the summer sun, and his blue eyes danced with mischief when he was aroused. His smile was the only bright spot in Sierra's dreary existence.

He gave up on removing her tunic and reached beneath instead, yanking her breeches over her hips and pushing them to her ankles. While on bended knee, he leaned forward and pressed his lips against the soft patch of brown curls between her thighs. The brush of his thumb over her moist heat, followed by his eager tongue, prompted her to part her legs, offering him greater access.

He dug his fingers into the flesh of her hips. Sierra lifted her knee to his shoulder and threaded her fingers in his mop of hair, taking pleasure in his adoration. Her body grew tense as he probed deeper.

"Cearl, my need is great." Sierra stared at the thick wooden rafters above as she moved in rhythm to the heated taunting of his tongue.

"It only takes the thought of you, lass, to make me hard." He scrambled to his feet and tugged her close. With a wicked gleam, he captured her face in his hands and crushed his mouth to hers. "See for yerself," he growled.

Cearl grabbed her hand and pressed it against the bulge in his breeches. True it was that his length was firm. She smoothed her hand over the loose fabric, curling her fingers around his rigid shaft.

His strangled gasp pleased Sierra. Neither shared unrealistic notions that their needs were other than carnal. In this place, no one knew from day to day what would become of them. Their moments of stolen passion were not tainted by emotions, but were sparked by the pleasure of their joining.

Sierra pushed Cearl to the pile of hay. He appeared startled— he had not before seen her behave with such dominance. She usually allowed him to do what he would. Today though, something stirred within her. For years, she had gone without the menstrual courses that a woman usually has, but two months ago she had experienced some spotting that had renewed her determination to live. If she was still capable of bearing life, then perhaps she was not entirely as dead inside as she felt.

"This is new." He wiggled his brows as he shoved down his breeches and his cock sprang forth at the ready.

"I daresay a sheep's ass would make you ready, Cearl," Sierra said, planting a foot on either side of his hips. She fisted her hands to her sides and looked down at him.

He smiled and tucked his hands behind his head as he stared up at her, his hungry gaze focused on the prize between her legs. "'Tis your arse, Sierra, and your arse alone, that brings me such heavenly torture."

Once more, she scanned the stable to be sure they were alone. A goat bleated from a nearby pen and her heart tripped with concern.

"Do not worry, we are alone." His fingers found the warm opening between her legs, drawing her attention back to him.

"Balrogan wants one of those birds you have roasting over there and a pint of mead, as well." Sierra closed her eyes to the delicious sensation of his fingers stroking her quiver.

"Very well." He nodded impatiently as he motioned her to sit. "You can have two hens. You can have the whole lot. Come on, the guards will be heading out soon for the night watch. Have mercy, Sierra, I need to be inside you."

She dropped to her knees and pushed his tunic over his hard torso. She leaned forward, brushing her breasts against the rippled muscles of his stomach, enjoying the command she had over him. She loved the sinewy flesh beneath her palms and reveled in his low moan as she ran her tongue over the turgid brown nipples on his chest.

He had told her long ago, when they first met, that she might need a friend from time to time. *Sex* with Cearl had become her escape. *Sex* had become her friend, her sanity in this hellhole.

Slick and ready, Sierra eased onto his hard cock, parting her legs wide to accept him fully. She was fascinated by the changes on his face as he pushed into her. Sierra wondered if this was the expression lovers wore, or if it was merely a reaction to pleasure. For her, the line remained a blur. At one time, she thought she might have real feelings for Cearl. But it didn't take long for her to realize that it was the simple pleasure of joining and little else that drew them together. Emotions had nothing to do with it.

"Ah, yes, yes-s-s, that's my girl," he whispered, his eyes rolling back in ecstasy.

"I am *not* your girl." Anger, like the surly crack of a whip, snapped in Sierra's head, diffusing the hazy fog of lust. She stood up, brutally disengaging her body from his. She would not be anybody's "girl." Since her arrival as a prisoner, Lord Aeglech had delighted in calling her "his little Druid girl" meant to mock the fact that her mother had also acted as his spiritual adviser.

"Ah, come on now, Sierra, you know I do not mean it like that. You have nothing to fear from me, you know that." His eyes pleaded with hers. "Look how you have dominion over me. I am yours, Sierra, your slave. Do with me as you wish."

Her juices glistened on his proud cock. With a warning glance, Sierra relented, knowing well the pleasure that awaited. "Do *not* call me that again."

"Aye, the words shall never again pass my lips."

He wrapped his fingers around the backs of her legs, tugging until her knees buckled and she landed in his lap.

"Tell me you want me inside you, Sierra." He pressed her legs open, inching her back until her dewy quiver kissed his cock. "Do not be so sour. We both need this." He slid his hands along her inner thigh, his thumbs brazenly teasing.

He was right—she did want this. She *needed* this. "To be sure, this does grand things for me, Cearl." Sierra straddled his thighs, rocking against him as he slid deeper.

"Aye, it does, lass." The muscles in his neck bulged as he held her thighs firm, his hips rising to fill her completely.

Sweat broke out over Sierra's flesh. Beaded droplets skittered between her shoulder blades as she rode Cearl hard, their bodies engaged in a frenzied dance.

It was at this moment, when she felt the heat of her climax coursing through her blood, that she sensed a freedom beyond her dismal life.

Cearl clamped his hands over her covered breasts. "I wish we had time…"

She focused on the flexing of his stomach muscles each time he lifted his hips, pushing deep into her.

"Boy, where are you?" The gruff voice of one of Aeglech's kitchen help called from the other side of the stables.

"Piss," Cearl muttered and his body grew still. He scooped up a handful of straw and tossed it through the air.

Sierra grabbed her breeches and rolled behind the haystack, scrambling to get her pants on.

"Cearl, what are you doing, boy?" The man chuckled.

Sierra realized suddenly that he had not had time to pull up his breeches, leaving the cook with but one unspoken explanation.

The cook coughed. "Have you not heard that is bad for your health? Go find you a peasant wench and take care of your needs.

Be quick now, finish up and see to supper. The guards will be coming soon. And Lord Aeglech will need his supper as well."

Sierra peeked around the haystack. The man stood staring at Cearl with a look of keen interest on his face.

"I do not need an audience." Cearl shot an angry look at the man.

The cook muttered something under his breath and stomped away.

As she awaited Cearl's signal to come out from her hiding place, Sierra felt his hand on her shoulder.

"He is gone and I am desperate," he pleaded, staring at her.

"I have wasted enough of Balrogan's time as it is." Sierra scrambled to her feet. "I need to get back or he'll have my head, and yours as well." She bent for the bucket and he grabbed her wrist, yanking her down on his naked lap.

"You know what torment I will suffer if you leave me in this state." He ground his face into the curve of her neck, shifting her hips to prove his point.

"And I know that Balrogan will make short work of your agony if I do not bring him his supper." Unsympathetic to his condition, she could not help but tease him by wiggling her bottom against his semi-hard cock.

"You seductress…I shall not sleep well this night, Sierra." He sighed, tossing her from his lap.

"You could do as the man suggested. Go find a willing Saxon wench to ease your suffering." He should know that sex between them was but a matter of convenience. Sierra had no illusions, nor should Cearl.

He tugged up his breeches and hurried with an awkward gait to the spit where roasting birds sent a mouthwatering aroma throughout the inner ward.

Cearl ripped two bird carcasses from the stick, the tender meat falling off the bones. He plopped them on a wood-plank tray, then gathered a roasted turnip and a pint of mead.

"It smells heavenly, Cearl." Sierra leaned forward to inhale the mingling scents. She knew Cearl liked to reward her with small tokens of affection for having sex with him—a bit of extra meat, an extra pint, a polished apple.

"Here, then. Not that I owe you anything." He shoved the plank filled with food into her hand.

Sneaking a small piece of meat from the plank, Sierra picked up her bucket and gave Cearl a wink. "Perhaps we may meet tomorrow, milord?"

"You love to see me suffer, wench," he pouted.

"It is not my choice, milord." She left him there in the dusky twilight to ponder her meaning.

Days later, Sierra had still not spoken to Cearl. The cook had sent him to the chambers with her and Balrogan's evening meal. But he had barely given Sierra a glance as he left the food and hurried away. She sighed as the guard closed the door behind him and made a mental note to go to Cearl at the earliest opportunity. The hissing sizzle of burning flesh was drowned out by the man's agonizing screams. Sierra sat in the corner and idly wondered how long it would be before another villager was in these chambers, guilty of the same crime.

"Let that be a reminder to those who would follow your footsteps. The king will not again have mercy on you, thief," Balrogan said, then turned away with a shake of his head.

The old man nodded, holding his hand as his body racked with sobs. She was surprised that her master let him live; then again, the man was his kin. Balrogan's uncle had been caught by the village guard and was accused of stealing from Lord Aeglech's supply of grain.

Sierra stuffed a piece of meat in her mouth and washed it down with warm mead. Though she pitied the prisoner's ignorance, she had little concern for his suffering. He had brought it upon himself, this punishment, and she knew that Balrogan had no choice but to carry out his king's orders.

Sierra knew it would be easy to allow the darkness of this place to consume her. But she had to be strong, if only for the strength shown to her by her mother and for the possibility that she might one day be reunited with Torin, her younger brother. She carried the guilt of losing Torin with her every day, not knowing what became of him.

"Get him out of here, Mouse." Balrogan turned his fierce gaze to the old man. "And do not let the king's men bring you back here or I swear your head will find a pole."

The old man nodded, keeping his eyes to the floor as he stumbled to his feet. Sierra unlocked his chains and he fell to his knees.

"Come on, you best be on your way. Balrogan is showing you mercy today." She hauled the man upright, holding on to his skinny arm as she pushed him toward the guard watching over the dungeon entrance.

"This one is free to go. He has confessed to his wrongdoing," she said, wondering how Balrogan was going to explain why he set his thieving uncle free.

"That is not going to make the king happy," the guard grumbled, snatching the man from her grasp.

Sierra knew better than to speak her thoughts openly, so she sidestepped his remark.

"I have duties to attend to. Did you wish to bring up the matter with Balrogan?" Courage prompted Sierra to lift her eyes to the guard, but her pride brought her precariously close to being run through by his sword.

He muttered something indiscernible as he dragged the man up the main stairs to the outside.

A younger guard came down the stairs, pausing to let the two pass by. His mouth set firm, he ignored Sierra as he stomped into the dungeon. He was tall with broad shoulders, and his grimace marred his chiseled features. Sierra followed him into the room, curious at how bold he was in walking straight up to Balrogan. Sierra noticed how the guard touched her master's elbow as he leaned in close to speak to him. She strained to hear their conversation, but they kept their voices too low. She prepared to clean Balrogan's collection of knives, staying well distanced from the two men.

Balrogan turned to her.

"Mouse, Lord Aeglech wishes to see you in his chambers. Leave those until later. Be quick, it's not wise to make him wait."

The guard remained behind, and both men watched her as she eased the door shut. The look in Balrogan's one good eye left a strange feeling in the pit of her stomach. Sierra had seen lust and desire on a man's face, just never before in the company of another man. She harbored no judgment on the two, any more than she faulted herself or Cearl for their need to "escape." But if Aeglech were to discover that his much-feared executioner preferred men, it would be a mark against the Saxon king's pride. It did not take much for the king to exert his power. His pride was fierce and Sierra wondered how long it would be before it caused his downfall. She had seen reckless pride take down great men before, both rulers and warriors.

Sierra's footsteps echoed as she walked through the deserted great hall. Her memory drifted back to when she would come there with her mother. Her mother was first appointed mystic adviser to the Britannia leader Vortigern, and later to Aeglech.

With the Romans gone, abandoning Britannia in lieu of fighting greater battles abroad, the remaining Briton tribes were too busy fighting each other to pay much heed to the mercenaries hired by Vortigern to help fight off the Scots and Picts. And fueled by arrogance and greed, the Briton king chose to ignore Sierra's mother's forewarning of the power of the *adventus saxonum,* the coming of the Saxons.

Not until it was too late.

It did not take long for Aeglech's armies to seize Vortigern's fortress by the sea. From then, it was only a matter of time before they had laid claim to most of the southern regions of Britannia, pushing the Celts farther north.

A flash of light startled Sierra and she paused, blinking, as she waited for it to reappear. The large room was dark, its tables still overturned from the last Saxon celebration of conquest.

A row of narrow windows carved from chalk and stone provided a view of the churning gray-green sea and the sunless sky. Sierra scanned her surroundings, her gaze resting on the deepest shadows of the room. The hairs on the back of her neck stood up. A chill settled across her shoulders and she fully expected to see her mother's ghost by Aeglech's throne where she had always stood.

A quick, dark shadow swept through the window, darting up into the rafters before it swooped low and snatched a mouse from beneath a table. Sierra caught clear sight of the raven only as it sailed out the open window. Something that her mother taught her long ago drifted into her memory. She did not give much credence to the ancient Druid magic that her mother practiced. That magic had not saved her mother, but the curse that she had placed upon Aeglech and his men had saved Sierra, and with any hope, her brother.

It was lore that the presence of a raven was a bad omen, oftentimes the foreshadowing of death. Given her instincts hewn from her grim existence, Sierra knew the scent of death like a second skin.

Though she had seen no vision, her senses crawled with a foreboding so strong that she could not deny it. And unlike what she was used to seeing in the executioner's chambers, this feeling had an aura of destiny to it. As if her mother was trying to reach out to tell her that the time was coming when she would have to show great courage in the face of evil.

Chapter Two

"Lord Dryston, 'tis your turn," the young boy insisted.

Dryston glanced up from tossing stones with the lad and caught the eye of a fetching young maiden carrying a basket of flowers on her hip. Her long dark hair, worn in a braid tossed carelessly over her shoulder, glistened in the late-afternoon sun and her smile appeared to offer more than what she carried in her basket. Perhaps he read too much into it, but for a man who had seen nothing but fighting for many months, her smile was like a refreshing drink from a cool well.

Dryston's gaze followed her until she disappeared amid the street vendors.

"Milord?" the small boy insisted.

"Is it my turn? Then prepare to lose, young man," he teased as he rattled the stones in the cup. With a flick of his wrist, he tossed them atop the wooden barrel that served as their game board. "And I told you that I am *not* a lord." Dryston tapped the boy's nose and he grinned impishly up at him.

"But you fight the Saxons. I heard the blacksmith talking to another man today." His forehead wrinkled. "I thought only great knights fought with such courage."

"True as that may be, it still does not make me a lord," Dryston replied, silently marking his memory to speak to the blacksmith about keeping his identity quiet. They did not need a Saxon spy getting wind of the small militia being gathered for battle.

"Ha! You lose!" The boy's face lit up. "That is two coins you owe me." He stuck out his filthy hand.

"So it is." Dryston reached into his bag and drew out a handful of Roman-Britannia coins. They were useless in terms of the worth they once had, but were still traded for food. "Be off with you now, scoundrel, before I announce you as the cunning thief that you are." He smiled down at the boy and ruffled his sandy-brown locks.

With a loud whoop, the boy climbed off his wooden crate and scurried down the street, ducking into one of the village houses.

The boy reminded Dryston of his adopted younger brother, whom he had found shivering in a hollow log one winter day long ago. The frightened orphan took many months to speak and eventually remembered his name, but had little recollection of a home or family. Despite the mystery surrounding his past, Torin was a quick learner and would come to possess a skill in battle and a charismatic leadership that was rarely seen, even in Rome's most seasoned leaders. That he was a master of military strategy further convinced Dryston that his brother had been put on this earth at this time to serve a greater purpose.

When Dryston and Torin were of age, the Roman army came for them, as many Briton boys were called to serve in the

Roman army. Trained as invincible warriors for the Roman legion, their duty was to Rome alone. They were taught the teachings of the Holy Church, but their mother had seen to instilling in them the Celtic beliefs of her heritage. When their tour of duty was complete, Dryston, Torin and a handful of other soldiers watched as Rome abandoned Britannia, and they could not idly stand by.

They had spent the past few years mobilizing displaced and frightened Celtic villagers who were without leadership and too weak to face the Saxon armies alone. In addition, the great seasoned Roman General Ambrosis, a sympathizer to Britannia's plight, was on his way with his army to meet the grass-roots militia Torin and Dryston had put together.

Dryston gave Torin the credit for convincing a number of the Briton people to join their quest. Many native Britons mistrusted anything that smelt remotely of Rome, blaming the Romans for the downfall of their country. But Torin's steadfast belief in justice had won over many a Briton's heart, and their band of Roman sympathizers and native Britons had already tasted a few defeats of some smaller Germanic tribes.

Dryston walked past the row of vendor carts on his way back to the blacksmith's shop where he had left his swords for sharpening. He snagged an apple from an elderly vendor and tossed him a coin as he kept his eyes open. Saxons were known to send in spies to map out unsuspecting villages so they could return at night to pillage them, burn their houses to the ground and leave nothing behind.

A group of three males stood conversing in the street, watching some lovely young women stack their carts with produce. Even in the rural communities, there was a protocol when a man was interested in a woman, especially one of good repute.

"Ah, there ye be, Dryston," the blacksmith called out as he approached. "Yer blade should slice with precision now." The burley man held up Dryston's sword, eyeing its edge with pride. "Or a Saxon's neck with ease, just the same." He gave him a wink and chuckled. The man's snowy-white beard was spotted with black soot and his blue eyes twinkled as he handed him his blade.

"'Tis fine work, Gareth." Dryston held the blade at eye level, scrutinizing the workmanship. He leaned forward, holding Gareth's inquisitive gaze. "A friendly reminder, sir, that it is not wise to speak ill about the Saxons in public. The streets have ears."

The man's jovial expression faded, and his eyes darted about the marketplace, scanning the crowd.

"Aye, your warning is heeded. But here your quest is favored, Dryston. Our village lives in fear that we may be marked next by the Saxon horde."

Dryston nodded, taking a practice swing of his blade. "Magnificent work, my friend," he stated, purposely changing the subject. He gave Gareth a hearty slap on the shoulder. "What do I owe you, then?"

The blacksmith caught his arm and drew Dryston close, lowering his voice to a whisper. "Death to the filthy intruders. 'Tis payment enough."

Dryston thought he should be able to find a few men in this village to join their army. "With weapons honed as fine as this, we are assured victory." He grinned and looked over the blacksmith's shoulder where he again caught the eye of his mysterious dark-haired beauty. He wondered if she was taken. A woman of such beauty was surely married. Guilt besieged him as he thought of Anne, the young maiden in his village who had pledged herself to him before he joined Torin and his men to prepare for battle. Word came soon after that the Saxons had taken his village, leaving no survivors. Dryston wanted to go back, but Torin advised against it, saying the Saxons would be waiting.

Dryston slid his sword into its sheath and pulled a plump dead rabbit and two squirrels from his hunting bag. "How about these as fair trade for your exceptional work?"

Gareth grabbed the tethers attached to the carcasses and held them high. "Aye, 'tis more than enough, Dryston."

"Fine then, I should be heading back to camp. It grows dark." Dryston put on his red wool cloak, a parting gift from the Roman army.

The man stopped him. "Daughter, come here."

The dark-haired beauty was his daughter? Dryston cleared his throat as she drew near. Her face was fresh as a morning meadow. The scent of the wildflowers in the basket on her shapely hip wafted over him. She reached up and kissed her father's cheek. Dryston suddenly remembered his father's crushing bearlike hugs that gave such security to his children.

"Yes, Father?" The girl swayed her hips gently as she stood awaiting his instruction. Though it appeared her father did not notice, her flirtatiousness was not lost on Dryston.

"Run ahead now and take these to your mother." He handed her the animal carcasses.

"Aye, and shall I also tell her that we will be sharing our meal with a guest?" She slid her dark eyes to Dryston's. Passion lay in their depths; he knew it with every bone in his body. A slap on his shoulder pulled him from his lustful thoughts.

"A grand thought, Cendra." The blacksmith wiped his large hands on his tunic. "Would you do us the honor, Dryston? You said yerself it grows dark. You can sup with us and sleep in the stable. 'Tis not much, but it is warm and dry. Dawn is a much safer time of the day for travel."

"My thanks, friend," Dryston said, his loins stirring with the thought of spending the night in Cendra's company. "If my appetite will not burden your generosity, that is."

"Fine, then." The man slapped Dryston's arm. "Give me a moment to clean up and we'll walk together."

Cendra gave Dryston a broad smile before she disappeared down the main road, holding both his supper and his heart in her hand.

"Daria will be pleased to have the company. It will give her something more than my work to talk about. I dearly love the woman, but she has the need to tell me how I should be running my business." He glanced sideways at Dryston. "Besides, talk of battle and victory gives us hope."

"I doubt my tales of blood and battle would be of much interest to your wife, good friend." Dryston smiled.

"Then apparently you've not met my wife," Gareth replied and gave a hearty laugh. "She would make a good warrior for your cause, for she would talk the enemy to his knees."

It was a meal fit for a king. The rabbit and squirrel were roasted to perfection and the turnips and squash tasted like his mother's used to.

Dryston leaned back and stifled a belch. He caught Cendra's eye. There was no doubt they shared a mutual attraction. Just the same, he had loved and lost one woman in his life and it was enough to caution him about committing his heart too deeply.

"Did ye get enough ta satisfy yer hunger, Dryston?" Daria, the blacksmith's wife, asked.

"It was a lovely meal, more fine food than I have had in a long while." He patted his stomach and grinned with happy satisfaction.

His charm might not have wooed the good lady of the house, but it sure worked well on her daughter. Cendra smiled at him from across the table.

"So, my husband tells me that you are a great warlord," Daria said as she cleared the plates from the table.

He glanced at Gareth, who sheepishly shrugged his shoulders. "I would say, fair lady, that your husband is too kind with his praise. I am an adequate swordsman, when it is necessary."

"Mother, I would think that our guest would like to speak on other matters this evening," Cendra spoke quietly.

Her father wagged a rabbit bone at her. "Yer mother was merely making conversation. You would do well to help her with the dishes."

Cendra rose and began to clear the table. She reached for Dryston's cup. "Perhaps our guest would like some wine? We have a bit left from harvest." She straightened, her gaze going to her father. "Perhaps you would like a cup as well, Father? A toast to Dryston's health?"

"'Tis a fine thought, daughter. Go fetch it in the root cellar. There is a barrel left, if my memory serves."

Cendra winked at him, and he gave her a wink in return, catching the watchful eye of her mother.

He had never had such a sweet, heady wine. Made from blackberries, they said, but its taste better than sweet jam. The comfort and hospitality of their family, along with the drink and Cendra's coy flirtations, lulled Dryston into a blissful relaxation. He had not realized until now how much he missed the good things life had to offer.

He wobbled a bit as he stood to bid them good-night before he made his way to the stable. "Your warmth has touched my heart," he stated to the bleary-eyed blacksmith. They had emptied the entire pitcher of wine betwixt them. Dryston slapped his hand over his heart as he leaned on the table, checking his balance.

The great giant of a man held out his hand and gave him a grin that revealed two missing front teeth. "G'night and pleasant dreams, m'boy." He pumped his hand with gusto.

"I will bid you farewell then, and good night. I must meet with the dawn." The room swam before Dryston's eyes and he laughed at how absurdly light his head felt.

Daria sat in the corner near the hearth busy with her needle-work. Cendra sat opposite her, tying ribbons to small flower bunches. She gave him a glance, and Dryston hoped for another smile, at least, before he retired.

"Go raibh maith 'ad," he proclaimed in broken Gaelic. There were a few words that he could still remember from his childhood. "Forgive my poor use of the old language—" he placed his hand on his heart "—but I offer you my humble thanks."

Daria's dark eyes rose slowly to his. *"Ta'failte romhat,"* she replied with a surprised but warm smile.

"She says you're welcome." Cendra set aside her work. "Do you speak the native tongue, milord?"

Dryston held up his thumb and index finger, squinting to be sure they were aligned just right as he gave his response. Oddly, it appeared he had more than five fingers on his hand. "A wee bit, lass. Enough to get by." He grinned. "If someone would be so kind as to point me in the direction of the stable, I shall go and sleep off this delightful evening." He offered a sloppy bow and heard Daria chuckle under her breath.

A loud snore brought his attention to Gareth, leaning precariously back in his chair, his mouth wide open, slumbering deeply. Daria shook her head and helped her husband to his feet.

"I shall see our guest to the stable. We wouldn't want him to fall into something unpleasant," Cendra called after her mother.

Cendra's hand slipped around his waist and she directed him to the front door. His head felt delightfully unattached to his neck as she opened the door and dragged him into the cool evening air. Just outside their door, the main village road was quiet. The rows of simple straw and wood houses lining both sides of the narrow dirt road appeared dark and quiet. An owl hooted in the trees above. Cendra's lithe frame molded against him as they walked to the side of the house where a small, primitive stable with a lean-to roof provided his bed made of straw. Dryston thought how Cendra kept him erect, in more ways than one.

In his state, it was dangerous to entertain such notions. She was a good woman, sure to please some lucky young farmer one of these days and bless him with scores of babies to bounce on his knees.

"My thanks." Dryston unsuccessfully tried to free himself from her grasp as they entered the stable. The sweet scent of fresh hay tempted him with sleep, but Cendra's arm around his waist tempted him with much greater ideas.

"Are you sure you can find your way in the dark? Perhaps I should accompany you a bit farther in case you stumble and bump your head," Cendra offered.

Her grip on his waist tightened and he glanced back at the house to see if Daria was watching. The moon shone down on the pen built behind the stable. A baby goat scampered in front of him bleating for its mother.

Startled, Dryston stepped back and lost his footing. He and

Cendra fell to the ground, landing on a pile of hay in the corner of the stable. Cendra pushed up on her hands, bracing herself above him, her thighs pressing deliciously against his groin.

"You are a fine man, Dryston," she said as she stared down at him. Her face, in the swath of pale moonlight, took on a magical glimmer, and he could not deny himself the pleasure of touching it.

"And you are a fine woman, Cendra. One who deserves a man who will lie with you every night and be around to raise your bairn." Her skin was smooth as a butterfly's wing, silky against his calloused fingers. Dryston believed entirely what he said and more than anything at this moment wished he could be that fortunate man.

Her small hands found their way beneath his tunic. She slid her hands over his flesh, unleashing a need he had not allowed himself to feel in a very long time.

"'Tis not wise to do such things. It has been some time since I have been in the company of such a beautiful woman. Your charm is intoxicating. You do not understand this dangerous game you play."

"Don't I, now?" she replied, leaning down to speak in a whisper. Her soft breath wafted across his face. It took every ounce of Dryston's determination not to turn her beneath him and satisfy the burning in his loins.

"Just one kiss, milord. Call it one of parting, so you will remember me on your journeys."

Her lips found his. She tasted sweeter than the blackberry wine he'd drunk earlier, and Dryston savored her kisses, holding her face to his.

Her soft moan unleashed a ferocious hunger inside him. He held her at arm's length, trying to find his noble reason.

"Cendra, I fear you do not understand how long it has been." His breathing grew labored as she snuggled her body against his. Dryston's lips found the warm curve of her neck and he breathed in her feminine scent.

"Dunna stop, Dryston. I know what I want. It is my choice," she whispered, turning her face to his. "What I would give to have your mouth on mine each night."

He was lost in the magic of her. Need clawed at his groin, roiling in the pit of his stomach like a fierce storm. "Sweet Cendra," he whispered as she sat upright, her thighs straddling his.

She held his gaze, drawing her dress down over each shoulder, revealing her young, firm breasts.

"Do you like what you see, Dryston?" She drew his hands to her, pushing her soft mounds into his palms.

Dryston groaned and he brushed his thumbs over her pink tips, watching as they pearled at his touch. She held her hands over his, urging his caresses, and closed her eyes in blissful satisfaction.

"That feels good, Dryston," she sighed, and sat her bottom down on his lap. He sensed the dampness between her legs, and his libido soared to new heights when he realized she wore no undergarments.

The twitch of his hardening cock brought home the reality that this was temporary. He was committed to a cause and he could not afford to take a wife until the Saxons were defeated.

"Tell me, Cendra, have you lost your maidenhead?"

"Nay," she sighed. "But I offer you the honor of changing that." She rocked her hips gently over his and Dryston knew her tight, virgin sheath would be like heaven to take.

He swallowed, wanting nothing more than to give in to her, but it was not his honor that stopped him, it was the fear of loving, and losing that love, again.

He turned her to her back, and covered her body with his. Even fully clothed, it pained him to see how well their bodies fit. "Cendra, I cannot take your maidenhead. That is an honor your husband should one day have. But I promise, when you leave, you will remember this night always."

"I have no husband, nor is there one I am hand-fasted to, but that can be arranged." She reached up and pulled him into a fiery kiss. Driven by reckless desire, they matched one another. Dryston wanted nothing more than to sink deep into her and watch her unravel. Instead, he tried to focus on her mouth, the delicate curve of her neck, the sweet fleshy mounds that fit so perfectly in his hands. Desperate with the need to claim her, he fisted her skirt, tugging it over her hips until it bunched at her waist. Pure lust punched him in the gut as he rocked back on his heels and viewed her glistening flower.

"What shall I do, milord?" She rose up on her elbows. "I am told that mating is a man's pleasure."

"Then you have been listening to the wrong yatter." Dryston offered her a grin. Slowly, he grazed his thumb back and forth along the inside of her thigh. She closed her eyes, grasping at the material of her skirt as she smiled. "'Tis most pleasant when you touch me there, Dryston."

"Cendra, a man should give his woman pleasure. His duty is to worship her body."

She hesitated, then coyly asked, "Am I your woman, Dryston?"

He eased his thumb over her slick opening and she jerked slightly. "For tonight, Cendra, I will bring you pleasure, I promise."

She held his gaze and relaxed her legs. "Show me then, Dryston, how you pleasure your lover."

He needed no further encouragement.

"You take my breath with your beauty," he said, stroking her warm, wet quiver, leaning forward to capture her sigh in a soft kiss. "Do you like this?" he whispered.

Her hips began to writhe beneath his hand. "Aye," she said, brushing her hand over his shoulder.

Dryston smiled as he kissed the inside of her thigh, worshipping her velvet skin, captivated by her musky sex. He knew that come the morrow her sensitive skin would bear the blush of his unshaven beard, and the mere thought gave him immense pleasure.

Her teeth worried her sumptuous mouth as he blew across her waiting quiver.

She whimpered. "Dryston, your skills extend far beyond the battlefield."

Teasing her with short flickers of his tongue, he lavished her, enjoying watching her back bow with pleasure each time he found her special spot. He cradled her thighs as she began to moan louder.

He gave a final nip to her bud, and she gasped, fisting her hand in her mouth to muffle a scream. Dryston sucked her sweet honey nectar as her soft thighs rubbed against his face.

"Saints be praised," she muttered, the last waves of her climax coursing through her body. She lay still, her breathing softly labored.

Dryston kissed her stomach and pulled down her skirts. Then he leaned over her to kiss each breast in a fond farewell as he drew her tunic up over her shoulders.

Her arms came around his neck and she kissed him long and hard. He knew if he did not end this now, she would not be a virgin come the morrow. Dryston cupped her chin between his fingers. "I shall not forget you."

She held his face with a look that spoke of the promise of dozens of such nights. "Come back to me, Dryston, when your duty is finished."

He kissed her slowly. "If it is meant to be, then I shall return, Cendra. I give you my word."

He ran his fingertips down her delicate cheek once more, wishing they had more time, wishing he did not have to leave, wishing many things—but none of his wishing changed his fate, or hers.

"*Slan agus beannacht leat.*" She held her hand against his face.

"What does that mean?" he queried.

"Goodbye and blessings go with you," she replied before she kissed him again. "*A ghra' mo chroi,*" she whispered against his mouth.

She disengaged herself from him and began to walk away.

"And what does *that* mean?" he called out in a loud whisper.

She stopped in the full light of the moon and her smile was brighter still. "Love of my heart," she said and hurried back to the house.

Dryston closed his eyes, turning his face to the heavens. "If my life means anything to you, I ask only that you allow me to live long enough to return to this place."

He could hear screams in the distance. A heavy fog swirled around him, obscuring his vision, as he struggled to find his way to the sound. The closer he got, the heavier the mist became. He tried to call out, but the fog prevented his voice from carrying. It was then that he smelled the stench of something burning—

"Dryston!" Cendra's scream jarred him from a deep sleep. The thought occurred to him that the next time he was offered wine, he should be more careful how much he drank.

"Dryston!" This time there was no doubt the cry was real. He opened his eyes, squinting against the smoke that seared his pupils. All around him was a dense layer of smoke, just as in his dream. But this was no dream.

This was a nightmare.

Dryston pushed to his feet, holding his arm over his nose. Through the haze, he could see people lying along the road, in front of their shops and homes. Others wandered aimlessly.

The entire village was under siege.

He choked and stumbled toward Gareth's house. He found a window, but he could not budge it for the latch inside.

He moved forward, and at the front entrance tripped on something blocking the door. He blinked twice and found Gareth's body. The blacksmith's eyes were opened in wide surprise, and his throat was brutally slashed.

"Dryston!" Cendra's voice pierced the din of fire all around him. Spurred on that she was by some miracle alive, with brute force he shoved her father's body away from the door and fought to open it. "Cendra!" he shouted, not caring that one of the Saxons might yet be near. Like the window, the door was either jammed shut or locked from inside. Gareth must have told his family to lock it behind him.

Throwing his body against its weight, Dryston cursed the blacksmith for fashioning such a sturdy door to protect his home from intruders.

Twice more he tried, and finally the door gave way. A rush of heat and flames met him, and Dryston dropped to the floor. He crawled on his belly with his arms outstretched, groping blindly, praying that he was not too late. Cendra had not yet responded, but he dared not open his mouth and allow the smoke to fill his lungs. More than once he wondered if this was his time to die, but he was determined that it would not be before he found Cendra.

His hand touched a foot.

Dryston peered through the heat and saw her curled up in the corner of the room, her face turned to the wall. His fingers grasped the hem of her gown as he crawled to her, but she did not move. Dryston drew to his knees and pulled her into his arms. Her body lay listless—a dead weight.

Outside the screams grew less frequent and the roar of the fire louder as huts began to collapse. Though he did not know how, Dryston managed to get them both outside. The smoke, lifting higher into the night sky, revealed the human carnage the Saxons left behind.

Dryston carried Cendra behind the stable, where the fire had not yet reached. He placed his ear next to her mouth, praying he would feel a breath. Heaviness weighed in his chest as he knelt beside her. She had not moved. In the light of the fire, he looked down at her pale skin, only a few hours ago blushed with the rosy hue of arousal, now blotched with black soot. Her beautiful long, dark hair was singed and hung in uneven lengths. Dryston blinked back angry tears. He wanted to tear apart every Saxon with his bare hands. He shook his head, refusing to accept that she was gone. Placing his fingers alongside her neck, he closed his eyes, willing there to be a pulse.

There was none.

Dryston dropped his head to her breast. There was nothing he could do; she was gone. He held her lifeless body propped against him and rocked her gently, seeking to understand the senselessness of her death.

A strange sound summoned his attention and, picking up his sword, he stood abruptly. The last thing Dryston saw was the face of a sneering Saxon as his ax smacked him in the face and his world went black.

Chapter Three

If ever there was reason to have faith in benevolent deities, Lord Aeglech put to death such notions. He was the embodiment of evil incarnate—of this Sierra was sure, because she lived in his hell.

Sierra hugged her arms. A summons to Aeglech's chambers these days meant he was testing her loyalty.

The rubble of destruction remained as it was at the time the Saxons took claim of the castle. Portions of the walls leading to the second floor had given way, crumbling to rest on the stairs to Lord Aeglech's great chamber. A cool sea breeze blew through a gap in the wall that looked down hundreds of feet below to the sharp rocks and the churning sea.

Sierra picked her way over broken statue remains of Roman gods and goddesses. She believed they were left for Aeglech's enjoyment, a reminder of his conquest. The shell of the once-revered Roman fortress was now a Saxon burke. Stationed strategically next to the sea, it was easy to assume control of supplies and reinforcements from ships of both friends and foe.

At the entrance to the Saxon king's room, two guards, resembling hairy mythical beasts more than men, flanked the ornately carved dual doors leading to his chambers. There was a grunt from one of the guards as they shifted the heavy axes they carried. "Lord Aeglech summons me," Sierra said, folding her arms and waiting impatiently as they assessed her. With a shrewd final glance, one of the guards stepped aside and the other followed suit.

Sierra did not offer her thanks.

"Come here, *wealh,* and fetch me my cup." Lord Aeglech pushed himself upright in bed, his bedcovers pooling at his waist.

Sierra dismissed his degrading name for her. To him it was a sign of power, but it meant nothing to her.

"Milord," she muttered, bowing in homage as was expected.

Lord Aeglech was young and pompous. The leader of one of the most powerful Saxon armies, he exuded strength both physically and mentally. Of average height, he was still an imposing figure built with broad shoulders, a sleek muscular torso and a smile that could charm the devil himself. Unlike his army, he wore his hair and beard cropped short. But his eyes were his most intimidating feature. The color of a blue winter's sky, they shone like ice. To further add to his fierce appearance, he bore a warrior's marking scrolled around his sinewy upper arms. The same circular symbol showing a band of boars that was painted on every Saxon shield.

Balrogan had told Sierra that the boar was a symbol of strength and power to the Saxons.

Sierra cast a glance at the raven-haired woman lying by Aeglech's side. Her cheek was plastered against the bed linens, her nakedness barely covered by them.

"I find that the women of your country are weak. They lack the stamina of the women of my homeland. The ex-

ception being your mother, of course." He gave Sierra a
wicked grin.

She was used to it, the baiting. That, too, was him
wielding his power. Sierra proceeded to pour his mead. It
sickened her still to think of her mother in his bed, but she
knew that whatever her mother had done, it had been to
protect her children. Still, Aeglech delighted in reminding
Sierra of her place, and perhaps his idea of what she could
look forward to.

His frosty eyes met her own as she handed him the cup.
Their fingers touched briefly. She blinked, snatching back her
hand as an unexpected image filled her mind, one of her
mother and him. He smirked, sensing she had seen something
that displeased her.

Sierra's gift of sight was not honed as well as her mother's
had been. Her mother had been of the old ways, Druid in her
upbringing and able to summon her sight at will. Reliance on
magic and spiritual advice was vital to a king's future. The fact
that Sierra had acquired marginal use of her gift was part of
what saved her from his brutality.

She shoved her hands behind her back. "How may I serve
you, milord?" She bowed again. His imposing nature both intrigued and frightened her. She had trouble diverting her attention from the physical appeal of his body. As much as she
detested herself for it, she had wondered more than once what
kind of man he would be in bed.

Aeglech stared at Sierra as he slid his hand slowly down the
slope of his companion's back, then urged it between her thighs
until she stirred. The beautiful woman stretched luxuriously,
smiled at him, and beneath the linens, parted her legs for him.
"Do you find her attractive?" he asked Sierra.

Sierra glanced at the Saxon lord, and he sneered as he jabbed his hand roughly between the strange woman's legs.

"Cunt," he growled, an evil grin splitting his face as he prodded her. There was nothing gentle about him. He was relentless, stroking her deep until at last he drew a helpless shudder from her. With a victorious smile, he yanked his hand away and flopped back on his bay of pillows.

"So easily won," he scoffed, tipping back his goblet and finishing his drink.

"Is that mead?" the woman cooed as she inched up to his side. Her hand disappeared beneath the bed linens, traveling below his waist.

Aeglech grinned and offered her the glass, and when she reached for it, with her free hand, he jerked away, laughing with amusement.

"Do you think I would drink from the same cup as a Briton whore? *Wealhs,* another cup, be quick."

Sierra glanced at the poor woman and realized she had no idea of her fate. Lord Aeglech was very clear in his instructions to his men, and he adhered to his own rules implicitly. One could have as many Briton women as he wanted, but they must not live to carry his seed.

Sierra handed the woman a cup and looked away. With any hope, Aeglech would now dismiss her. Sierra bowed and started for the door.

"No, wait. Let us play a game, the three of us," Aeglech called after her.

She stopped, closing her eyes. He was cunning. Sierra sensed that the game he suggested would not end well for the woman in his bed.

"Drink well, my sweet wench. I have something special

waiting for you." Aeglech's blue eyes narrowed on Sierra. "Come closer, my little Druid girl."

The woman drank her mead, and continued to move her hand under the tented sheet covering the king's lap.

"See how well she tries to please? Come here, cunt." He snapped his fingers and the woman scrambled to his lap, facing him as she straddled his hips.

"Turn around," he snarled.

Her black hair tumbled over her shoulders as she moved with haste to appease him. She glanced at Sierra, standing by the bed. Her large breasts jiggled when she laughed, but Sierra could see the nervousness in her eyes.

"It is comforting to have such loyalty." He squeezed the woman's buttocks and leaned forward, planting a kiss at the base of her spine.

"Over there, *wealh*." He pointed to a table laden with enough food for a banquet feast. "Bring us something to eat."

Sierra had no idea what game he was playing. She did know, however, that Aeglech rarely did anything without a purpose in mind, and that would assure him the victor. She had a feeling he was testing her loyalty.

Sierra held a slice of cheese out to the woman, but the king interceded.

"You feed it to her," he ordered.

His hard gaze met Sierra's as he pushed the sheets from between their bodies.

Sierra's heart began to thud as the strategy of this game began to clarify in her head. She was about to feed this woman her last meal. She stood frozen, wanting no part in this.

Aeglech grabbed the woman's hips, manhandling her until he impaled her on his rigid staff. The woman met Sierra's gaze.

She wanted to warn the woman, but her tongue would not budge, and in her heart, she knew it would not have changed a thing.

"See, *wealh,* how your kind responds to a real man inside them."

He jerked the woman's hips, his fingers digging into her soft flesh.

"You like that, don't you, cunt?" He grinned as he thrust into her again.

"It brings me great pleasure, milord." She licked her parched lips, for the first time darting Sierra a look of concern.

His expression softened. "Of course it does. Your kind does not have men built like me, do you?"

"Nay, milord." She braced her hands on the top of his legs and relief showed on her face as he relaxed his hold on her.

"Eat something! Drink! I don't want my whores to be weak," he snapped, and smacked her backside.

Sierra held up the cheese and she took a small bite, catching a piece that missed her teeth and stuffing it in her mouth before it fell to the sheets.

"Mead! Give her more mead," Aeglech barked, jerking against her hips.

Sierra focused on the woman's face, unable to ignore the familiar smoke of arousal curling inside her. Aeglech was using them both. Taking pleasure in this macabre game where he alone knew the rules.

The woman arched her back, her breasts bobbing as she bounced atop him. A moan slipped from her lips.

"Drink!" Lord Aeglech yelled.

The woman leaned forward and quickly took a sip from the cup Sierra proffered. No sooner than she had done so, she gasped, having choked on the mead, and sent the liquid gurgling from her mouth over her ample breasts. Her hands pawed at her breasts and she bowed her head, her breaths matching Aeglech's forceful thrusting.

The cup fell from Sierra's hands and she stared at the wicked grin on the king's face.

"Lay your hands on her and tell me what you see," he growled through his efforts to hold the woman on his lap.

"But I—I…" Sierra was frozen with fear. What if she saw nothing?

"No, oh-h-h!" the woman cried out as her body neared completion. She had no way of stopping the inevitable. She was Lord Aeglech's now.

"Now," he ordered, compelling Sierra to step forward.

Sierra's hands trembled as she reached out to touch the dark-haired woman. She was going to die anyway, Sierra thought. Why did he want her to use her powers?

She shut her eyes and willed her mind to focus on the woman. Immediately, feelings of fear, lust and terror overtook her and she jerked her hands away from the ferocity of it.

The woman glanced at Sierra, her gaze shrouded by skepticism and arousal.

Sierra inhaled deeply and placed her hands on the woman again.

"Dunna tell him."

The voice was distant, as if trying to break through a fog of emotions.

A vague image appeared in Sierra's mind. She saw a man and a woman. They were meeting in the shadow of darkness. They shared an embrace. He handed her an object that she hid beneath her cloak.

"Tell me what you see!" Aeglech roared and the image immediately dissipated.

The woman uttered a low wailing sound as if she was in pain. She clutched at the bedsheets, fisting them in her hands, then began patting wildly, as if searching for something.

The meaning of her vision suddenly became clear. The woman intended to harm Lord Aeglech and Sierra was caught between warning him and simply allowing it to happen. Considering his odds of surviving the attack, she spoke, "There was a man and a woman. He gave her something."

"She lies," the woman screamed. She started to scramble from his lap, but he held her on her knees, rising to his as he drove roughly into her.

The woman continued to search the sheets in a futile effort to find what she had misplaced. "The two appeared to be lovers," Sierra said, and the woman turned her face to Sierra's, her expression one of surprise.

"We were not lovers!" Too late, the woman realized her mistake. Her release captured her body with a powerful climax that tore a ragged scream from her throat.

"Well done, *wealh*." Lord Aeglech's teeth curled back in a sneer. He turned his face to the heavens and offered a primal yell of conquest. Giving the woman no reprieve, pulled her again to his lap as he flopped back on his pillows. She lay spread atop him, facing the ceiling. Aeglech's hand slipped around her, caressing her breast.

"What were you looking for?" he asked the woman calmly. She shook her head. "Nothing, milord."

Sierra closed her eyes. The woman was a fool. She knew then that Aeglech had baited the woman, all for the game of it. He was simply testing Sierra's loyalty to see if she would concur with what he already knew. He had already found what she'd lost.

Sierra opened her eyes and met the woman's gaze. Her brown eyes glistened with unshed tears. Sierra's face would be the last she would see on this earth.

Aeglech sat straight up in bed, causing Sierra to jump back. He snatched the woman by her throat, thrusting her chin upward.

"You lie, wench! Recognize this?" he roared before he swiped the blade hard across her neck.

The woman's eyes grew wide and turned to Sierra's as she realized her fate. A thin, red line appeared on her creamy-white flesh. Her lifeblood, urged by the last few beats of her heart, burst from the wound spilling out over the sheets.

Aeglech pushed her limp form off his lap and held up the blade. "Is this the object you saw?"

Sierra nodded, not about to tell him that she never actually saw a knife.

"You have done well, like your mother before you. See to it that you do not betray me as she did."

"Guards," he bellowed, and immediately the doors swung open, jarring Sierra from her daze.

"Take this traitor from my sight and hang her from the gallows as an example to all who would challenge me."

"But, milord, she is already dead," Sierra stated.

"Do you wish to follow her, *wealh?*" His voice was cold in its warning.

Sierra dropped to her knee. "No, milord." She silently reprimanded herself for her careless remark. It could have gotten her killed.

The guards plucked the woman's body from the bed and dragged it across the floor, leaving a trail of blood across the stones.

Aeglech flung off the covers and, fully nude, stepped around Sierra to take a piss in his chamber pot. The blade that he'd used and tossed aside lay not more than a foot from where Sierra stood. She eyed it, noting the intricate Celtic carving on its handle. She thought of her mother, her brother and of all the women the Saxon king had used and killed. Her heart pounded against her ribs.

"Wealh." His stern voice broke Sierra from thoughts. "Clean up this mess." He glanced over his shoulder as he went about his business.

"Yes, milord." She stood and tore the sheets from his bed, unable to push away the scene she had just witnessed. Her stomach churned, prompting her to hurry down the stairs with the sheets wadded against her chest. Once at the bottom, she dropped the linens and leaned out a window, emptying the contents of her stomach.

Sierra's head pounded as she fought to catch her breath. She wiped her mouth on her sleeve and lifted her eyes to the full moon cutting a bright path through the dark sea.

It was a full moon just like the night her mother and brother were taken from her.

She closed her eyes, and she could hear her mother's voice. "Dunna ever be afraid."

Nine Years Earlier

Sierra thought she was dreaming, but fear closed its icy fingers around her throat, reminding her that she was awake. Standing in front of the open window stood her mother with her arms raised to the heavens.

Sierra could hear the rumble of thunder rolling through the

night, and in the light of the full moon she saw her mother turn to her.

"Sierra, come quick, there is little time. You must under-stand—and this is very important—it was fear that blocked my sight. What has now been set in motion, I cannot stop. I was afraid, and I am sorry."

She cupped Sierra's young face. "If I have taught you nothing else, remember this. Dunna ever be afraid. It will be your downfall, as it is mine."

"What is it, Mother? What do you mean?" Sierra pushed past her to go to the window to see for herself what was out there, but she saw only the darkness of night and the stars above. Yet the thunder continued to grow increasingly louder.

Her mother plucked Torin from his slumber and steered him toward Sierra. He wobbled in his groggy state, brushing his small hand sleepily over his eyes. He was her half brother and without benefit of either of their fathers, Sierra cared and loved him all the more.

"Quick now, you must hide. And no matter what happens, dunna try to stop fate." She held Sierra's face in her cold, trembling hands.

Tears welled in Sierra's eyes. What use was her mother's gift if it could not protect her? "Mother, what can I do?" she pleaded, sensing danger was imminent and her mother was trying to protect them.

"There is nothing now that can be done. You must think only of your brother and yourself. You must keep each other safe."

Through the window, Sierra caught a glimpse of several Saxon warriors bringing their black horses to a stop outside their small house. Her mother shoved her and her brother into a narrow pantry closet.

"Stay here. Dunna utter a sound." She touched Sierra's cheek and kissed the top of Torin's dark head. "Remember, I love you. Dunna be afraid."

"No! We can run away! Please do not leave us!" Sierra grabbed her mother's hand, but she jerked it away and slammed the pantry door shut. The sound of their front door being forced ajar caused Sierra's heart to falter. Through a crack in the wood, she could barely see around her mother's hip, but she could smell the stench of sweat and filth that clung to the midnight intruders. Her mother spoke as if welcoming guests to their home.

"Welcome, milords. Does Lord Aeglech summon me?"

Laughter followed. "We're here to carry out Lord Aeglech's orders, wench."

There was a brief silence before her mother spoke. "If it's about the boy, he is not here."

"Why should you not lie now, you have kept him a secret all of this time. Aeglech knows of your treason," the guard answered and nodded to the others. "Go round to the back and check for the bastards. Do what you will to the girl, she does not matter, but Aeglech wants the boy dead."

Sierra pulled Torin against her, clamping her trembling hand over his mouth. He struggled at first, but the clatter of pans and plates being knocked to the floor stilled him. Sierra felt his hot tears spilling over her hand.

Through the narrow slit, she watched as a bulk of a man, dressed in warrior's clothing, snatched her mother by the hair and threw her facedown on their table. Her mother's terrified gaze met her own, and Sierra swallowed a scream as the beast lifted her mother's skirts and pushed his hips against her. Tears streamed from her mother's eyes as he grunted and panted,

shoving his lower half against her body. Sierra squeezed her eyes
shut, grateful that her brother could not see. She tried to block
the sound, but the incessant thump of the table on the dirt
floor pounded a sickening cadence in her brain.

When at last she opened her eyes, Sierra met her mother's
gaze again. Her eyes were rimmed red from crying, but she
silently willed Sierra to be strong and to heed her words.

Keep each other safe, just as her mother was protecting them now.
Tears streamed down Sierra's face and she blinked them away to
summon the courage her mother had shown to her and Torin.

The man grabbed her mother's arms, tied them behind her
back and pushed her out the door.

"Set the rope, find the bastards and burn down the house,"
the warrior who had violated Sierra's mother ordered the others.

It did not take the Saxons long to find them.

As Sierra was carried scratching and screaming from the
house, she saw them place a rope around her mother's neck.
Her eyes were wide and fierce, her hair, caught by the wind,
snaked in dark tendrils around her head. She flung her head
back and let out a long, pitiful moan, like that of a wolf. Then
she leveled her gaze on the men holding Sierra and her brother.

"Let the dark curse of a thousand generations fall upon
anyone who should cause harm to these children. The
ancients—the gods and goddesses of the earth, fire, water and
air—bless them. Whoever does them harm shall have his life
and the lives of all his kin brutally taken."

The tall guard holding the knife to Torin's neck looked over
at the man who held Sierra.

"This is Aeglech's doing. He should be the one to kill them."

The leader studied Sierra's mother. "Aye, go on then. Raise
her high and make sure she is dead before you leave." He

mounted his horse, reached down and hauled Sierra up in front of him like a doll. The tall guard followed on a horse behind with her brother. Sierra strained to see her mother's face one last time. But she caught only a glimpse of her lifeless body dangling from the rope. Helpless tears poured from her eyes.

"Druid witch," the guard muttered. "Lesson to ye, child, do not defy the king of the Saxons."

They arrived at the fortress in the dead of night. Sierra had no idea what was to become of them, though she knew that the guards had taken heed of her mother's curse. Perhaps they would be spared, taken as slaves. It was their only hope.

"Do you know why you've been brought here?" Lord Aeglech asked, staring down at Sierra and her brother. His voice was quiet and calm, an unsettling contrast to the cruelty of his reign.

Sierra kept her eyes focused on the gray flagstone. The guards had forced her and Torin to their knees in front of the Saxon king. Twice already, she had been sick en route to the fortress, making the guards even angrier.

"You will answer when I speak," the Saxon lord bellowed.

Sierra raised her eyes, looking at the man who had ordered the hanging of her mother. If she, too, was going to die, she wanted him to be reminded of the curse that would be on his head. "Before my mother died she placed a curse on whoever would show my brother or me harm. Your guards did not have the courage to carry out their task. They brought us instead to you."

His nostrils flared as his hand came down hard on the side of Sierra's face, sending her to the cold floor. Her cheek stung with fury, but she held in her tears.

"Is this true?" Aeglech scanned the faces of his guards.

Sierra kept silent as she righted herself. Her eyes were swollen and dry from crying, her body and mind numb from all that had happened.

The leader stepped forward and knelt. "Milord, we wanted to prove to you that we had captured the boy." His voice cracked from nervousness.

Sierra charged the man, knocking him down, and clawed at his eyes as she screamed curses at him in Gaelic.

"Bloody—" The guard clamped down on her arm and she bit him hard. Sierra's head hit the ground, knocking the wind from her.

"You need to be taught how to treat a man," he spat, starting to tug at his breeches. She looked up at the Saxon king, who stood watching silently, his hands on his hips and his face void of expression.

"I do not see any man in front of me," Sierra challenged.

The man's face darkened with rage and he drew his knife.

Sierra stared at him. "Come here, you coward, and I will dig your eyes out with my bare hands."

He growled as he dropped his breeches and forced her legs apart. He leaned over her, his yellow teeth bared, then he looked up and his eyes suddenly widened. In the next instant, the man dropped beside her to the floor, a small ax protruding from his forehead.

Sierra scrambled to her feet, staring down at the dead man. She glanced over her shoulder and watched as Aeglech summoned another guard to retrieve his weapon.

"Let that be a lesson. When I give an order, I expect it to be carried out." His steely gaze scanned the group in front of him.

"You." He pointed to the guard holding her brother. "Take the boy into the woods and kill him."

"Nay," Sierra cried as she lunged for Torin. Another guard caught her arms, but she jerked away, snatching the blade from his belt. She bolted and brought the knife down, slashing the tall guard's leg. He dropped to his knees uttering a string of curses in his ugly Saxon tongue, but another guard quickly stepped forward and hauled her little brother over his shoulder.

A third guard wrested the knife from her hand and placed her in a stranglehold, the knife poised, awaiting Aeglech's order.

"Do you want to *watch* your brother die?" Lord Aeglech's voice boomed like thunder. "Or just know that it is going to happen? I leave you the choice."

Sierra knew she had been beaten. "I beg you, don't take him. He is a good boy. He would serve you well," she pleaded. "I would see to him—you need never know he was around."

Aeglech stared at her for another moment before he dismissed the guard with a wave of his hand.

"He is only a child." Sierra struggled against the guard and turned back to the Saxon king, falling to her knees to beg. "Please, let me say goodbye. I will do whatever you ask of me."

Renewed interest sparked in Aeglech's icy blue eyes.

"Tell me, girl, do you bear your mother's gift?"

Sierra's mother had tutored both her and Torin in some of the ancient ways. She had told Sierra that one day she would begin to understand the gift she had. The same gift that her grandmother and her grandmother's mother had also possessed. True it was that Sierra had flashes of sight into the past and some into the future, but she was not trained or mature enough yet to harness the power at will. Still, if Aeglech believed she carried the gift and it would save them, then she would make him think it was so.

"Aye, milord," she answered with as much courage as she could muster.

With a jerk, the guard released her. She ran to Torin and grabbed his hands. "Be strong, brother." Though his guard was four times her size and strength, she leveled her gaze at him. "Remember the witch's curse. Whosoever shall place harm on us so shall he and his kin receive the same brutal end," she whispered. "My mother possessed great powers of magic."

He looked at her with eyes cold and dead, but said nothing. With a low grunt, he shoved her aside.

"Sierra!" Torin screamed as he clawed for her.

Her heart twisted as she watched her little brother disappear from her life. It was as if her very soul had been taken from her. She collapsed to her knees, wanting to die.

"Bring the girl to my chambers."

Somewhere in the back of her head, she heard Aeglech bark the order. One of the guards grabbed her shoulder and shoved her in the direction of the departing king. Resigned that she was about to suffer the same fate as her mother, she welcomed death, wanting only to be free of the suffocating pain inside her.

Sierra was thrust into the king's chambers, where she fell to the floor and curled into a ball. She was afraid to look at Aeglech and she hoped her death was quick.

"Your mother served me well with her gift. She was a very...giving woman." His voice was without compassion. "You are not yet a woman, are you?"

She raised her head, hardly able to focus on his face. His eyes were unlike any human eyes she had ever seen. "I am ten and two years."

"Stand," he ordered.

Sierra stumbled to her feet, biting back the tears threatening to break her will. He moved so close she felt the heat from his body.

She lowered her eyes. Though Aeglech had taken everything that was dear to her, she had a spark of hope that if Torin had managed to escape, and if she could survive, she might one day find him.

"You have an aggressive spirit that is rarely seen in a young girl." His fur cloak swished as he circled her. "While it would be easy to kill you, this courage, if trained and nurtured properly, along with your mother's gift, could prove useful to me."

He traced a finger slowly down her cheek. Sierra turned away from his hand and he quietly chuckled.

"You are as beautiful as her," he spoke. "The same color of hair, her pale skin and dark eyes."

Anger roiled inside her as she thought of how he had robbed her of her family. She spat at his feet.

He grabbed her chin and yanked her face to meet his. Above his head, his short blade was poised, ready to strike.

Sierra's eyes held fast to the glint of his blade, preparing to feel its cold bite. Instead, Aeglech spun her around and clamped his hand over her chest, the point of his blade now poised at her throat.

"Your fire amuses me," he whispered in her ear as he lifted her long braid with his knife. "One with the courage of a man should also look like one."

Her head jerked from the motion of his knife as he hacked off her braid, chopping it close to the nape of her neck.

"Your spirit reminds me of myself when I was young."

She whirled to face him. "I am nothing like you!" she screamed, dredging every ounce of anger left inside her. "I would rather die."

His eyes glittered. "That can be arranged, if you do not agree to my terms," he stated with steely calm.

Her body trembled from both fear and anger.

"Your magic is useful to me. Your mother would still be here if she had not betrayed me by keeping your brother a secret."

"What harm can one small boy bring to you?" Sierra's hand shook as she reached up to finger her shorn hair. Her dark braid, the pride of a woman, lay at her feet.

"You will not speak of him again," he stated coldly.

"And what becomes of me? Will you kill me? Will you send me to the dungeon to die, for I would rather you take your blade to me now than prolong my death."

He eyed Sierra steadily. "Such brave words. I have not soldiers with as much courage." He kicked her braid away, sending it across the stone floor. "Guards! Take her to Master Balrogan. Tell him he has a new apprentice."

Fear stabbed Sierra's heart. Balrogan was well-known to the people in the village. No one had ever seen him, but his reputation caused hearts to stand still. He was the feared Saxon executioner.

Two guards escorted her across the great hall and down a winding stair. Her skirts impeded easy movement, and she stumbled, fell and bloodied her lip. The coppery taste of her blood filled her mouth.

She was yanked to her feet.

"Master Balrogan's a busy man. You won't want to keep him waiting," one of the guards growled.

Sierra stared down into the dark oubliette, barely able to see the steps in the dim lighting. She looked back at the guard and considered running herself into his sword.

"Get on, then, I don't have all day." He shoved her shoulder. They continued their descent until finally they stood before a single wooden door. Even closed, the stench of death permeated the air.

Overcome, Sierra bent over and emptied her stomach.

The front guard opened the door. "Master Balrogan, meet your new apprentice."

"Says who?" A man with shoulders broader than the door glanced over his shoulder, then swept a metal rod through the fire pit.

"By Lord Aeglech's decree. She is a fiery sprite. I would not turn your back on her," the guard replied.

Sierra could not control the tremors coursing through her small body. She stood frozen, grasping the door frame. She could not keep from staring at this man named Balrogan. He was dressed entirely in black, his bulging arms free from covering and covered in soot. In her mind, he was the incarnate of all things unholy. He turned to look at her and Sierra thought she would faint.

His head was large, with great jowls that hung over his thick neck. His skin shone an unearthly pale gray, its sheen of sweat mixed with black smudges of filth. One eye was as black as coal and the other had a lifeless, milky-blue haze, the skin sagging over the corner.

"Ugly for a wench," he remarked. "I do not want any wenches in my dungeon," he spoke fiercely, pointing a red-hot flatiron at the guard. Sierra took a step back, ready to run.

The guard behind her pushed Sierra into the room and drew his blade. The other beckoned her to come forward so that Balrogan could inspect her. With an exasperated sigh, he grabbed her dress and pulled her into the dungeon.

"These are your orders, Balrogan. Look here." He snatched up the tartan of a dead Scot and lobbed off a long piece of the cloth with his knife.

"She can fetch you your food, get you clean water from the well. Clean up the blood."

The guard held her still as he wound the cloth around her head, making a turban to conceal her lopped-off hair.

"Just an apprentice. You put breeches on her, she does not even look like a girl."

The one-eyed man grunted.

"Aye, then. Leave her. She can sleep over there." He jerked his head toward a pile of straw tucked like a small nest in the corner of the room.

"I will inform Lord Aeglech that the apprentice has been delivered." The guard stopped at the door. "One more thing, Balrogan."

"What is it now?" The executioner did not look up from his work.

"Aeglech says she's got the gift of sight."

The executioner turned his single-eyed gaze toward her.

The guard said no more and left, closing the door behind him and leaving Sierra inside the belly of hell. She could not move, but she would not cry.

"Go on, over there," he said, nodding to the straw bed. "We start at first light."

In the shadows behind her, Sierra heard a moan. Chained to the wall, his arms stretched out unnaturally behind him, a prisoner knelt on the floor. He sat in his own filth. "Help me," he called to her in a ragged voice.

Balrogan's cat-o'-nine-tails came down lightning-quick on the man's back, slicing open his flesh already striped red. The prisoner screamed in agony. Sierra's mouth opened to echo his painful cry, but no sound emerged as she watched in horror.

Balrogan shoved her toward the straw. Once again, she stumbled on the hem of her dress.

"You'll need some breeches, *wealh,*" he stated. "And you will lose the tartan. I will not have it in my dungeon."

Sierra turned her face to his as she cowered in the corner. "Am I going to die?" she choked through the bile rising in her throat.

The executioner pointed the end of his skelp at her. "Not if you are smart, *wealh*. Not if you are smart."

Sierra let the night breeze from the sea caress her fevered skin. It had been a long while since she had thought of that night.

The Saxons had no idea how they had changed her. She lost her family, but she gained the will to survive. She lost all that she loved, and in return, she learned to close herself off emotionally. If you did not care, there was less pain.

Sierra eased away from the window and thought of the woman who had just died. She was a fool to think that she could kill Aeglech, at least, alone. She had been careless.

As dawn broke through the mist-shrouded hills, Sierra tossed out the last of the buckets of bloody water. She looked at the ghostly shadows of the trees that surrounded the gallows and saw the lone silhouette of a body hanging there.

"Sierra," Cearl called quietly. "I have some fresh goat's milk."

With a parting glance at the woman, Sierra quickly put her from her mind. They called the dungeon an oubliette, *a place of forgetting*. Once you entered, you were likely to become but a memory. Each day, the memories of who she used to be grew

dimmer. The reality of her life was a moment-to-moment existence. It was easier to forget than for her memories to eat her alive.

She ran to Cearl's arms, grateful that—for a few moments—
she could escape from her miserable existence.

Chapter Four

The tickling sensation of something crawling over Dryston's cheek jarred him awake. He lay still realizing that he was on his side and both his hands and feet were bound. He shook his head and watched a spider skitter across the dirt. Dryston shuddered. Give him a battle with a blade any day to a creature bearing eight legs.

"I looked again at his sword—there is no doubt he is Roman," a distinctly Saxon voice said.

Dryston faced away from his captors. He listened carefully, hoping to understand why they had not yet killed him. His head throbbed, and he struggled to remember what had happened in the past few hours.

Suddenly, the memory of Cendra's cries for help penetrated Dryston's head. Grim images of her lifeless body and the entire village engulfed in flames followed. A wave of guilt swept over him that he had not been able to save her.

"Should we kill him?" one of the Saxon asked.

His thoughts were pulled back to the present. If he was going to stay alive, he would have to focus on the present. He turned his head slightly, straining to hear the verdict for his life.

"He might be one of those rebels," another answered. "We should take him back to Lord Aeglech. Let him deal with him."

Dryston silently hoped for that to be the case. Aeglech was the very man he wanted to meet. His men had been responsible for the brutal murders of his family. He turned just enough so he could see the guards from the corner of his eye.

"Are you sure he is Roman?" one asked.

"Did you see his sword? I am certain the man is a rebel spy. Why else would a Roman be scouting around a Celt village?"

Dryston noted three guards total sitting around a roasting spit, and three horses grazing near the trees.

"I say Lord Aeglech will be pleased that we brought him back alive. He will want to question him."

There was a grunt of approval and then the sounds of eating. The aroma of roasted rabbit made his stomach growl.

There was a deep chuckle and one of the guards spoke. "If Aeglech cannot get what he wants out of him, Balrogan will." Another guard agreed, joining in with his laughter.

"Are you implying the king is weak?" the third man roared, and he stood, holding his battle-ax in the air.

A moment went by before the guard responded to the challenge. His voice was deadly calm. "I am no traitor to Lord Aeglech. However, I will gladly challenge you if you are serious. Otherwise you should lower your weapon now, before I cut you off at the knees."

An eerie silence followed, as if the entire wood and every creature in it waited for the warrior's decision. Finally, he lowered his ax and laughed, then slapped the other man on the back. "True it is that Balrogan can coax the confession out of any man," he conceded.

"Aye," the other two responded together. The moment of tension had passed.

"What do you think of Balrogan's apprentice?" The question was posed after a lengthy silence.

"The lad they call Mouse? What of him?"

The man who asked the question shrugged. "They say *he* is a *she*."

One of the others belched loudly. "If that is true, she is ugly. For she looks nothing at all like any woman I have seen."

"Maybe so, but I have heard things."

A bone skimmed past Dryston's ear, smacking against the tree trunk.

"What does it matter, these rumors you have heard? If his apprentice is a girl, Balrogan has her well trained," another guard piped up in response.

"They say she gouged out the eyes of a guard a few years back."

"Gouged? I heard that the man slipped on his blade."

"Nay, I heard it was a witch's spell that got him."

There was another stretch of silence.

"I do not like the thought. Only one of the guards who brought her to Aeglech remains alive and he is barely hanging on. They say that Aeglech favors her."

The first guard nodded. "Has the sight. That is why. You would be wise to keep your concerns to yourself. Spinning such tales among the ranks could find your head on a pole." He tossed an animal bone into the fire. "Do I make my meaning clear?"

The other two glanced at one another and nodded. After that, they ate in silence.

Dryston carefully turned back to his side, staring at the

flickering shadows on the tree trunk. He wondered if it was true. Why would Lord Aeglech allow a girl to apprentice such a gruesome position? Perhaps she was Saxon. He heard Saxon women made fine warriors, often displaying greater courage than their male counterparts, but he had never heard of a female executioner.

"Thelan, you take first watch—the two of us will get some sleep."

As the fire dwindled, the sounds of the night played all around Dryston. He thought of Cendra and her family, and his anger rekindled.

He had to find a way to work from the inside. If somehow Dryston could get word to Aeglech of where he could find the Roman camp, he could set a trap, luring him away from his stolen Roman stronghold and leading him and his army to Badon, where they could launch a surprise attack. It would be a certain victory for Britannia.

Above, a black shadow skittered across the sky, letting out a shriek as it passed between the earth and the full moon. A raven, the ancient omen of death, shrieked again, before disappearing into the dense wood.

Dryston's mother, a Celt who believed in the old ways, often spoke of such superstitions and although he had not before placed much belief in them, he could not shake the raven's significance.

"*A ghra' mo chroi.*" The image of Cendra standing in the moonlight just a few hours ago appeared in his mind. *Love of my heart.*

A tear trickled from his eye as the memory of her voice calling for help haunted him. He thought of her lifeless body where he had left her, of her mother's warm smile as she sat by the fire, and of Gareth's hearty laugh. His heart ached for all the innocent lives that had been taken by the bloodthirsty Saxons.

It made Dryston even more determined to live in order to see that Britannia was won back. In the distance, he heard again the sound of the raven and he prayed that he was not the one to die tonight.

Chapter Five

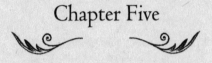

Master Balrogan had had his hands full this week. The heads of dozens of villagers who had not provided Lord Aeglech with his requested amount of grain for the winter lined the road winding to the fortress burke. Sierra wondered how many villagers were left to tend the fields.

It was clear by his moodiness that the king's concern for his security was mounting. Rumors continued to fester about the army gathering against him. His paranoia had spawned more brutality than normal, with sentences of death being handed down for even the smallest of crimes.

Lately, even the guards stayed as far away from Lord Aeglech as possible. The only two whom he did not intimidate were Balrogan and Sierra.

He summoned Sierra into his chambers a few days after murdering the woman in front of her. She found him standing at the window, observing the activity in the ward below. Sitting in front of the great stone fireplace was a wooden bathing tub. She glanced at his naked back and assumed he had just finished bathing.

"Close the door," he ordered, not turning around.

She did as she was told, having no other choice.

"Remove your clothing." He continued to stare out the window. Beyond where he stood she could see the sun trying to break through the clouds. It was just after midday and the heavy scent of rain hung in the air, mingling with the woodsy smell of the fire. Sierra stood motionless, wondering if this was the end for her. Somehow she found the courage to speak. "My clothes, milord?" she asked.

He turned and pinned her with a cold look. "Are you unable to hear now, *wealh?* I ordered you to take off your clothes. And may I remind you I do not like to be kept waiting."

Her fingers found the knot of her belt and she loosened it. With careful ease, she unwrapped it from her waist and let it fall to the floor. His eyes held hers as she shoved her breeches down her legs and stepped out of them. Sierra wore no undergarments; only the heavy linen tunic she had stolen from a dead prisoner remained as partial covering for her body. She pulled it over her head, her body responding to the chill in the air. The head wrap she wore fell off in the process, freeing her short dark hair, grown now to just below her ears. Balrogan was the one who saw to it that it was kept short, but his duties had kept him too busy to do so of late.

"Do you think I should take on a Briton wife?" Aeglech asked, lifting his goblet to his lips as his gaze skimmed over her. Sierra fought the urge to cover herself, as to do so would show her fear. She held her shoulders firm and stared at him.

"Nay, milord, the people are swayed by strength not sympathy." She lied, knowing it was what he wanted to hear.

He smiled. "You have learned much, even for a *wealh*. Balrogan has taught you well."

He circled her, and she felt his eyes taking in every inch of her naked flesh.

"Get into the water," he said.

Sierra did as he asked and climbed gingerly into the still-warm bath.

"Sit," he commanded.

She held the sides of the tub and lowered herself into the water. She closed her eyes to the luxurious feel of it on her flesh. She and Cearl had sometimes sneaked to the cold sea where they'd played in the waves and enjoyed each other's bodies, but it had been a long time since she'd had a warm bath.

"Do you know what to do next, or must I show you how to bathe?" Aeglech offered a mocking grin as he took another sip from his goblet and reached for a bar of lye on the edge of the tub. "This is soap, use it."

He tossed her the bar, and it landed with a *plunk* in the water.

Sierra scooped up water with her hands and poured it over her head, scrubbing her face and hair. She could not remember the last time she had used soap. Though she was taking pleasure in this gift, she had to wonder what Aeglech wanted in return. She knew the king liked his women clean and well groomed. She tried to ignore his heated gaze, and quickly lathered her body, rinsing fast, not taking the time she would have liked.

Sierra glanced briefly at the king. He was perched on the edge of a table, his prize goblet at his side and his arms crossed over his formidable chest.

Her stomach growled unexpectedly.

Aeglech's brow rose.

"Here." He plucked a handful of berries from the tray next to him and walked to the side of the tub. "Open your mouth."

His fingers brushed lightly over her lips as she took the berries from his hand. He let his fingers saunter a moment, resting like a lover would on her jaw.

"You have grown into an attractive woman for a Celt," he stated matter-of-factly.

He trailed his fingers across the back of her neck and a shiver snaked down her spine. The image, still fresh, of his body in the throes of passion caused her flesh to heat.

He was cunning and ruthless—she knew it as well as the back of her hand—and yet she did not recognize this gentleness or understand its reason. It frightened her, not even Cearl had ever shown such tenderness with his touch. Sierra cautioned herself that Aeglech was a shrewd man and no stranger to using his charm when necessary. But what did he want from her?

"There are few of my servants I can trust. Very few have shown me their loyalty over the years. Do you understand what I am saying?"

His fingers continued to sweep languidly between Sierra's shoulder blades, and he knelt behind her, resting his chin on her shoulder.

"I think that you have put your magic on me, *wealh,*" he whispered, his hot breath fanning over her wet flesh.

Sierra's breasts puckered and he chuckled quietly.

"Your body is now most pleasant to look at," he spoke, dipping his hand into the water before he slid it over her breast. "I want to see how you respond to my touch."

Sierra kept her eyes focused before her, willing herself not to be aroused.

"I wonder, *wealh,* have you ever thought of me as you lie in that cold dungeon? Have you ever thought of the warmth of my bed, of my body covering yours, my cock buried deep inside you?"

He twisted the rose tip of her breast, teasing until her fingers dug into the sides of the tub. Nay, lying with the murderous Saxon lord had never crossed her mind. However, *this* was not the touch of such a man. She closed her eyes for a moment, no longer a slave, no longer a prisoner shackled from her emotions. His gentle, caressing touch had challenged Sierra to feel something and as much as her mind fought against it, inside she was like a dry sponge willing to soak up any offering that would make her feel human again.

"Yes, I can see you," he whispered, drawing her from the water. He stood so close that the heat of his body warmed her back. "Your body spread before me like a tempting banquet."

His hands roamed over her body, taking command of her senses, of her reason. Perhaps even now, she was imagining this tender touch. Yet Sierra craved the idea, even if it was a fantasy and nothing more.

"I have need of your gift," he spoke, nuzzling her temple, his hands massaging her breasts, then gliding slowly downward, over her stomach.

"Ah," he breathed against her cheek as his fingers splayed over her damp curls and he found her quiver.

Sierra fisted her hands. "If it is my magic you wish, you need only command it, milord," she spoke as a quiet gasp left her throat.

She swallowed, her resolve weakening. She did not want to feel these heavenly sensations, not from him. She was confused by his gentleness, knowing that at any moment he could snap and end her life without a thought. "What do you need to see, milord?" Sierra asked, trying to keep her head clear.

He turned her in his arms to face him and brought his rough hands to her face. "I need to see my future, *wealh*."

Sierra stared into his crystal-blue eyes, melded fire and ice. "Milord, you understand I have no power over the fates?" She spoke softly so as not to incite him.

His nostrils flared, and she saw his true character flash across his face.

"Do you think me an imbecile?" he growled.

"No, milord," she replied hastily.

He grabbed Sierra's waist and drew her hard against his chest. "I could take you now."

If his words were not proof enough, the hardened length of what lay beneath his breeches was. "Surely you would find greater pleasure with one of the village women who care for their bodies, though their numbers dwindle with your appetite." Sierra offered him a smile.

Aeglech snatched her throat. "You try my patience, *wealh*."

"I speak only the truth, milord," she cast back, careful not to waver from his gaze.

He stared at her, his fingers tight around her neck.

"And what if I no longer care whether you live or die, *wealh*?" He spoke with steely calm, pushing his face close enough that she could smell the wine on his breath. "Your cunt is ready for me. Do you deny it?"

He grinned as he tightened his grasp on her throat. She closed her eyes, pretending he was Cearl as she reached between their bodies and stroked his length. "Nay, I do not, milord," she said quietly.

His hand eased from her throat and slid over her breast. She turned her face away so that his mouth touched her neck instead of her lips.

"You are headstrong and willful despite what you know I could do to you. I have always admired that quality," he whispered against her skin.

His hand and tongue lavished her breasts as she stood straight, her hands stiff at her sides. He stopped suddenly and looked up at her.

"Touch me, *wealh*. Tell me what my future is."

Sierra lifted her trembling hands to his head as he bent to take her nipple between his teeth. A ragged gasp of pleasure stole from her throat.

"I cannot focus, milord."

He pushed her up against the wall. "You will tell me what you see, and if you lie, know your life ends here."

She held her tongue. They both knew he spoke the truth.

Aeglech grabbed her hands and pressed them to his temples. A full head taller, he towered over Sierra, his powerful body dwarfing hers.

"Tell me what you see," he barked.

She struggled with her fear. She had come to be able to dodge Lord Aeglech's temperamental moods. This was different however. He was desperate.

"You will tell me what you see," he yelled, his spit spraying her face.

With a deep breath, she closed her eyes. "I cannot see past your anger, milord." Aware that she might have just uttered her last words, she waited with her heart pounding hard in her chest. Perhaps this was her chance to be free of this place. If she encouraged him and he took her blindly, his pride would give him no choice but to kill her.

And she would be truly free.

Without warning, his grip loosened and she opened her

eyes. For a second, he wore the face of a man tired of war and bloodshed. She stared at him, not believing he could possess even an ounce of vulnerability.

He held her gaze as he drew her arms around his neck. Her breasts pressed against his torso, softness against steel. She could not move. She could not breathe.

"What must I know?" His voice was soft, his breath warm. There was no malice in his voice, only sincerity.

It confused her. "I will try, milord." There was a measure of fear in his desperation, and she thought of her mother's words, *Fear will be your downfall.* Sierra considered the idea that perhaps fate had given her the opportunity to plant a seed of fear in him.

"Empty your mind and I will be better able to see," she offered, placing her hands soothingly on his head.

He rested his forehead on her shoulder, his hands dipping to the small of her back, gliding over her buttocks. He pulled her hips to his.

Passion was blind, she knew that well; it was how she had survived. Aeglech's cock grew firm against her stomach. Sierra swallowed, focusing on the hazy image emerging in her mind.

"There is a battle, milord," she whispered against his warm flesh. The salty taste of his skin and his musky male scent assaulted her senses. She turned her face away from his skin, to clear her head of the traitorous sensations heating her body.

"Go on, *wealh,*" he urged softly.

"There is smoke and fire," she said. "It is very hazy, milord."

"Try, Sierra." He nibbled the sensitive flesh below her ear. "Be my eyes and protect me with your gift. You will be rewarded for your loyalty."

Her own sigh betrayed her as he lifted her legs around his waist and braced himself against the wall.

"Tell me everything," he insisted, coaxing her with slow, thorough strokes to her quiver.

"There are men, many of them, scattered across a large field," she whispered as he ground his cloth-covered phallus against her. She imagined he was Cearl—simple, sweet Cearl, with his infectious smile and his body made for fucking.

"Where is this battle?" Aeglech uttered against Sierra's shoulder. His hips rocked forward, increasing in determination.

"There is a thick mist..." She closed her eyes and tilted her face heavenward, letting her imagination take her from reality. She grew wet as his fingers commanded her, curling into the soft flesh of her inner thighs. She clung to his shoulders, her fingertips numb where she gripped his flesh. Sierra sensed it would not be long before Aeglech would succumb to his passion and take her in a mad fury.

If he killed her, at least she would be free of him, of the torture, the blood and the daily misery. "It is a castle tower, milord, in a field. There is a man on a horse."

"Who?" he muttered, his arousal evidenced by his ragged breathing.

An urgent knock interrupted the moment. The chamber doors flew open and in strode one of Aeglech's guards. Sierra's eyes darted to the man, and he immediately dropped his shocked gaze to the floor.

"Milord, my apologies. I did not know that you were...not alone." The man spoke quietly, his eyes cast to the ground.

"Piss," Lord Aeglech growled, dropping Sierra to her feet.

Brought back to reality, Sierra attempted to cover her nakedness as best she could. Aeglech's cock tented his breeches without shame.

"Leave us," he ordered without looking up.

Sierra and the guard exchanged glances, unsure which of them he was dismissing.

"Leave, *wealh*." Aeglech waved his hand in dismissal.

She nodded, grabbed her clothes and hurried to the door, stealing another glance at the guard. The same guard often visited Balrogan. Curiosity sparkled in his eyes. Curiosity that, if set loose, would cause tongues to wag. Sierra questioned silently what news could be so important as to risk Aeglech's wrath. She tucked herself near the chamber entrance where she could hear their conversation.

"My apologies, milord, but I bring news of great importance."

"For the sake of your neck, it better be," Lord Aeglech roared. He braced his hands on the window ledge, facing away from the man.

"Milord, one of our scouts has returned from the field. He says that they have captured a Roman warrior. They found him in one of the northern Celt villages, and they believe he was gathering support for the rebel cause."

"And what proof do they have that he is Roman?" Aeglech asked, still facing to the window.

"They claim he carries a Roman warrior's sword."

"When are they to arrive?" Aeglech snapped.

"Tomorrow, milord."

"Very well, then we shall see what this Roman knows. Now, guard, about your interruption."

"Yes, milord," the guard responded, fear edging into his voice. "I beg your forgiveness."

From the crack in the door, Sierra could see him standing at attention, facing Aeglech's back.

"My privacy is one of my most treasured possessions, you understand?"

"Yes, milord."

"And yet you chose to barge in here in light of your own belief in the importance of your news."

The guard hesitated before saying, "I am to be punished, milord. I defied your orders."

"Your answer speaks well of your loyalty to me. Still, one cannot be too certain these days. Many spies lurk about, seeking a morsel to undermine my authority. A man of your intelligence understands my meaning, do you not?"

"Yes, milord." The guard snapped his response.

"And so you understand how important it is that you not speak of what you saw here in my chambers."

"Yes, milord."

Lord Aeglech turned and crossed the room, assessing the man as he walked around him. "And you will never again defy my orders?" Aeglech asked, pausing at his grooming table. He fingered several bottles of oils and ointments used for his massages. After a moment, he selected one and held it up to the light, turning it this way and that before deciding to pour the liquid into his palm.

"Never again, milord. I will return now to my post, if that is all, milord?"

The guard was clearly ready to leave the king's chambers, but Sierra sensed Lord Aeglech had other plans for him.

"What is your age?" Aeglech slapped his oily hand over his skin, coating his broad chest and chiseled stomach until he glistened.

"Twenty and two years, milord." The guard held his position.

A wicked smile crept over Lord Aeglech's face.

"Young then, and no doubt still supple," he stated calmly, reaching his hand below his waist of his breeches and sliding his slick hand over his rigid staff. "You can also understand my need to have complete assurance of your loyalty to me."

"I am loyal to you, mighty king," he barked in a practiced military response.

Aeglech stood before the young guard and turned his back to him. Sierra saw the soldier swallow hard.

Lord Aeglech stared straight ahead, clenching his jaw as he continued to move his hand over his cock.

She suddenly understood.

The guard cleared his throat. "Would milord like for me to obtain a woman from the village to appease you, most gracious sire?"

Aeglech smiled, then slipped his breeches over his hips, exposing his firm buttocks.

"That will not be needed, guard. Drop your weapons," he commanded gruffly.

The guard complied without protest.

"Now close the door and drop your breeches." He glanced over his shoulder at the man, whose eyes widened, but only for a moment before he followed his king's orders.

Sierra spoke to no one about the strangled sounds that she heard coming from the other side of the door. The deep sound of Aeglech's groan as the door shook violently against its hinges proved once more to Sierra the king's ruthless power.

Later that evening, the same guard came to the dungeon, and spoke to Balrogan in a hushed voice. Sierra kept her nose to the task of scrubbing the flagstone floor, glancing only briefly at the pair as they spoke in whispers. Her master clenched his great fists as he listened and his expression grew more dim than usual.

"Mouse," Balrogan summoned Sierra with a jerk of his

hand. Over the years, she had put together why Balrogan had never attempted to use her to satisfy his sexual appetite. Although they never spoke about it, she was aware of the unconventional relationship between the two men.

"Yes, milord?" Sierra asked, wiping her hands on her tunic.

"You are to go with this guard. Lord Aeglech has arranged new quarters for you. He says it is in reward for your loyalty."

Sierra's face did not hide her confusion. "I do not understand," she answered.

Balrogan scowled as he nudged the guard's arm. "You would be wise to do exactly as Lord Aeglech instructs, Mouse. These are uncertain times for us all. The king has much weighing on his mind. We are all at his mercy."

Sierra followed silently behind the guard as they wound through the tunnels beneath the fortress. They came to the end of a corridor where there were several rooms used for storage. To the right rose a narrow winding stair, with a swath of light at the top.

"Lord Aeglech's private dining hall is above this room. These stairs lead directly to the back entry of the king's chambers," the guard offered, fiddling with the key to unlock the door.

He opened the door, ushering Sierra inside. She stood motionless, taking in the room before her.

It was more even than what she had had as a child. In the corner, there burned a bright fire in a small stone hearth. Opposite the hearth was placed a simple bed with a straw mattress, tied and covered with linens. On the bedcovers lay an object so exquisitely beautiful that her breath caught at the sight—a gown made of gold brocade and sheer fabric the color of a sunrise. Along the cuffs and hem was intricate embroidery.

Sierra looked at the guard in surprise. "Is this meant for me?"

she asked as she picked it up and ran her fingers over the fine fabric. Her eyes traveled to the floor by the bed, where she spotted a pair of delicate gold slippers.

"By Lord Aeglech's orders." His response was blunt.

At that moment, two servants clambered into the room carrying a small wooden tub filled partially with water. They placed it near the fire.

Behind them appeared Aeglech. They knelt before him and with a single clap of his hands brought them up. He sent the guard and the servants hastening from the room.

"Do you like your new quarters, *wealh? This* is your reward. If you continue this loyalty, I can assure you that I will see that you have all that you need."

Sierra said nothing as he walked farther into the room. He gave her a side glance. She knew in her gut there was more.

"You are of an age now where your skills can be made of better use to me." He pinned her with his gaze. "I have seen how seductive you can be."

Sierra licked her lips. Was she to become his personal wench?

"Balrogan is getting soft. He is not performing his job to my satisfaction. He has set prisoners free on their promise alone. I am becoming a mockery. Torture alone is no longer working."

Aeglech shrugged as he paced in front of her. "To help Balrogan, you will use these skills of your seduction and your sight to glean information from prisoners. If we cannot gain what we need using force, then we will use whatever means necessary. My kingdom depends on your success. Do you understand?"

She was focused on the gown in her hands. Could she do this? Did she have a choice? "What if there are children, milord?" she asked quietly.

"If you are careless and that should become an issue, they will be disposed of. Bastard Celts are not my responsibility."

A cold lump formed in the pit of her stomach.

"Of course, I will have my physician give you plenty of vinegar and cloths, whatever you need. You are shrewd, *wealh,* and bright. By doing this for me, you further prove your loyalty and *that* will be rewarded."

Her gaze followed him as he walked to the door. The vulnerability he'd shown her earlier had been calculated; he'd worn a mask only to test her passion.

"Prepare yourself. Your first prisoner comes soon." He pointed to the shackles on the wall. "We will keep them all in irons. No harm will come to you. Show me what you can do, *wealh,* and if you are successful, as I feel certain you will be, you add to the possibility of your freedom."

She glanced over her shoulder at the small window high above her bed.

"Oh, do not entertain the thought of escape. The door will be guarded at all times and—" he pointed to the ceiling "—I will be watching."

She looked up, and noticed for the first time a square wooden hatch in the ceiling. Aeglech had only to open it from the floor above and he could see her whenever he wanted.

With a nod to the guard to lock the door behind him, he left the room. "See to it that I am informed when the prisoner has arrived," she heard him say to the guard.

There was no time to consider her alternatives, even if there had been any. With the Saxon king, your only option was to obey. Loyalty was now as crucial to her survival as was separating her mind from her body when she did what he asked of her.

Sierra removed her clothes, stepped into the bath and washed her face. As she took a handful of straw and scrubbed the flesh on her knees and elbows, she thought of the Roman captive the guard had earlier spoken of and wondered if he was her first prisoner.

Chapter Six

Dryston did not know how far they had come. Tied to the saddle of one of the Saxon warriors' horses, he had walked miles of uneven terrain. He sensed his feet were blistered and bleeding inside his boots. His protesting stomach had long ago given up the idea of food. Not since his supper with Cendra's family had he had a morsel to eat.

The ropes that bound his wrists rubbed his flesh raw. Twice he stumbled and, having no patience, the guards tugged on his rope, sending him scrambling forward. He kept alert, curious what Aeglech would do with him.

Dryston was not sure if Torin knew yet of his capture. By now, he would have word of the Saxons' rampage in the Celt village and, likely, he had sent out a search party. He prayed that Torin had the good sense not to come for him. Their mission should not be compromised. He would do what he could to lure the Saxon king away from his fortress and into a trap. It was their best hope for victory.

The ropes jerked at his wrists again, and pain shot up both his arms, fanning out like fire over his shoulders. Still, he knew this was a minor discomfort compared to a Saxon interrogation. Dryston had heard the stories. Few lived to tell their tales and those that did bore scars and deformities as a reminder of the torture they had endured.

Dryston's nose caught the scent of a foul odor. He forced his head up and realized they were entering a village. Rumor was that Lord Aeglech enjoyed keeping the bodies of dead Britons where he could smell their stench and so be reminded of the power he had over them. This village bore the mark of the Saxons' dominance.

The huts dotting the muddy road were in disrepair. There were gaping holes in the thatched roofs. Most homes had no windows or doors. It was as if all pride, all life had been sucked from the people who lived there.

Children sat at the side of the road, crying in vain for someone to care for them. The adults he saw did not move from their doorways or walked hunched over, avoiding eye contact with anyone. One or two who accidentally met his gaze possessed eyes filled with terror, and quickly turned away from him. The air was thick with the smell of death and decay, and Dryston fought back the urge to vomit.

"Be quick, Roman. Lord Aeglech is, I'm sure, very anxious to meet you," one of the guards called over his shoulder. There before him stood the remains of one of Rome's first great fortresses. Its north and east walls faced the sea, while the south and west walls were surrounded by a wide moat. To gain entrance to the bailey one first needed to cross a wooden bridge and pass between giant twin bastions. It sickened him to think the fortress was now in the hands of Saxon barbarians.

They paused at the portcullis entrance, and Dryston choked at the sickening stench rising from the moat.

"The murder holes must be full again," said a guard, covering his bulbous nose. "They should put the dead in the pit, not the moat."

Another guard chuckled, seemingly unaffected. "Or Aeglech needs to find something else to pass his time. But it makes intruders think twice, when they have to climb over the dead, eh?"

Dryston held his breath as they crossed the moat. He dared not look into the water at the risk of losing his stomach contents. The sight of decaying heads perched atop the poles lining the road was enough. The black iron portcullis groaned as it was raised to allow passage beneath its pointed teeth.

They emerged into the inner yard. Inside was a bustle of activity. The sound of metal hammering metal came from the blacksmith's alcove. A scurry of goats prompted Dryston and his captors to stop as they passed. Servants carrying yokes and buckets on their shoulders trudged up the outer stairs to what remained of the donjon. Most averted eye contact.

"Cearl," shouted one of the Saxon guards. "Come fetch these horses."

Focused on where he guessed Aeglech's chambers were, Dryston did not notice the body blocking his path and stumbled over it. The poor man, not much older than he, lay at an odd angle, his limbs broken and contorted.

Brought to his knees by his clumsiness, Dryston glanced up, spotting the high window from whence the man might have been tossed. Reminded of his mission again, he had to find a way to be of help to his brethren. Lost in his thoughts, he did not hear, at first, the guard calling for him to get up. Too late, he attempted to stand and without warning, the guard nudged his horse forward, pulling Dryston to his belly. Grass and dirt mashed into his mouth as he tried to hold his face above the ground speeding beneath him.

Spurred on by his comrades, the guard continued his game until he grew bored. Dryston collapsed facedown, his torso on fire. Unsteadily, he brought himself to his feet and narrowed his gaze on the guard, memorizing his face.

"Get a move on." One of the guards grabbed his arm. His knife made quick work of the ropes attached to the horse's saddle. He then sliced the ropes between Dryston's wrists, retying them at his back.

"I will see to the prisoner," the man called Thelan stated. He prodded Dryston in the back.

Dryston caught the eye of the young man tending to the horses. He wore a smile, as if oblivious to the world around him, but it dissolved when he looked up and saw Dryston.

"Move!" Thelan barked, prodding his back again.

Remnants of the grandeur that was once Rome now lay shattered in broken shards along the corridor that led to the fortress's great hall. Once the captains of the strongest armies of Rome had planned their strategy for building their empire inside these very walls.

"In there," the guard ordered and Dryston saw a smirk slide up the corner of his mouth.

Dryston blinked, adjusting his eyes to the dim light within the hall. Everywhere he looked, he saw destruction and filth. Tables lay turned aside, chairs were piled in splintered pieces, hacked up by a Saxon battle-ax. Ornate tapestries, hand-woven likely in Italy, lay in heaps on the floor as if used for sleeping.

"Lord Aeglech." Thelan dropped dutifully to one knee, head bent in homage to his king. "Here is the Roman prisoner. We captured him in our last raid."

At last, Dryston looked into the face of the legendary Saxon warrior, his bloodthirsty reputation known across all of Britannia. He was far less imposing than his reputation touted. Despite the warrior's scrolls on his arms, he was almost unremarkable, except for one unsettling feature—his eyes.

Cold, and without life, his eyes seemed almost transparent. Never before had Dryston seen the pleasure of death so vivid in a man's eyes.

"You are in my kingdom now, Roman." Lord Aeglech spoke with a thick, foreign accent. "Kneel."

"*You* are not my king," Dryston responded flatly.

Aeglech snapped his fingers and an ax handle thwacked the back of Dryston's knees. He fell forward on his face, hearing the snap of his nose as it broke.

The ass would pay for that.

"You should be aware that you likely will die here. Why don't you make this meeting comfortable for the both of us," Aeglech said with an easy smile.

Dryston struggled to his knees, glancing at Thelan, who stood at his side, tapping his ax handle against his palm. Blood from Dryston's nose trickled into his mouth and he wiped it on his shoulder, letting the pain fuel his resolve.

"Do not force my guard to use the other end of his ax, Roman. He will be ordered to do so should you show your defiance to me again."

Dressed in breeches made of smooth animal skins and a vest of rabbit fur, the Saxon leaned back in his stolen throne. He wore no crown, but hundreds of burned and pillaged towns marked his sovereignty. His cold-blooded gaze turned back to Dryston with the self-assuredness of a man well practiced in getting what he wanted, when he wanted it.

A Celtic slave woman sat at Aeglech's feet. He reached down and lifted her to his lap.

"Do you like Briton women, Roman?" He slid his hand over the woman's breasts.

Anger churned in Dryston's stomach. How many women had Aeglech used, then disposed of like refuse? Only a coward would harm a woman or child.

"True, at first their skin is sweet as any woman's. However, where Celtic women pale in comparison to Saxon women is in their passion and stamina. Is that not so?" he asked.

"Aye, milord," the guard responded with a cocky grin.

"Take her away," the Saxon lord growled, shoving the poor woman into Thelan's arms.

The guard did as ordered, hauling her over his shoulder as she kicked and screamed.

"Wait! Take her instead to my chambers and be sure she remains untouched."

Thelan glanced back and Dryston saw a flicker of disappointment cross his face. He nodded in obedience. The woman resumed her fight, her screams fading as he carried her out of the hall.

"We have to take what we have, when we are able. I cannot help that I am a man of insatiable need." Aeglech shrugged.

"I would not know. I have never had to take any woman unwillingly," Dryston responded dryly.

Aeglech reared back his head and laughed aloud. "You liar! It was *Rome* that first took this land, with its men, women and children, and for your own purpose, was it not?"

He could not dispute the Saxon's accusation, although it was generations ago. But Dryston was the product of two cultures—his father Roman, his mother a Celt—and so had loyalties to both. Raised a Celt, trained in the Roman army with Torin at his side, he was appalled when Rome declared that the Britons were on their own against the Scots and Picts. And when the Saxons came, bringing their barbaric ways, he and Torin allied with Ambrosis and swore an oath to end Aeglech's bloody rule.

"My home is Britannia," he answered, his eyes fixed on the king.

Aeglech studied Dryston carefully. He suspected the king was considering whether to dispose of him immediately or keep him around a bit longer. Dryston's one hope was that he had what Aeglech wanted—the location of the rebel camp. That would buy him some time.

"Britannia is dead. It is the dawn of a new age. Even those in Rome are wise enough to see it," the king said with a sneer.

"Britannia will survive by the strength of her people," said Dryston. The king wavered before him, and Dryston realized he was close to losing consciousness.

Aeglech slouched in his throne, perfectly relaxed. His ring-encrusted fingers tapped against the curved arm of the throne. "Britannia's numbers are dwindling. My men are seeing to that. Soon all of Britannia will belong to the Saxons."

"Your men have not yet met all of Britannia's people."

"You seem to know much for one who was found in a Celt village, welding a newly sharpened blade." His eyes narrowed, awaiting Dryston's reply.

Dryston held his tongue. He had to find a way to stay alive and give Torin and his men time to assemble.

The king's attention was diverted when a new woman entered the room. Perhaps she was no more than a figment of his sleep-deprived mind, this angel, dressed in a golden gown, her head covered with a sheer scarf that veiled her features. She looked out of place among the ruins. Without hesitation, she walked straight up to the smitten Saxon king and knelt before him.

Aeglech stepped forward and took the angel's hand, bidding her to rise. She handed him a golden goblet, a cup clearly once belonging to Roman royalty.

"Milord, you summoned me?" she asked.

He blinked as if she had pulled him from his thoughts. On this, he and Aeglech had common ground, for Dryston found her mesmerizing. Who was she? What purpose did she have with the Saxon king? Was she his mistress?

"Ah, yes, of course. You know that the prisoner has arrived. Come, stand here at my side."

Aeglech regarded Dryston with a narrow gaze. "I will give you the opportunity to tell me what you know about the rebellion being gathered against me."

"I know nothing about a rebellion," Dryston lied. One of Aeglech's guards rushed forward and rammed his ax handle into Dryston's gut. He lurched forward, choking for air. Determined he would not let the king break him, Dryston straightened, grinding his teeth against the pain. His eyes were drawn back to the mysterious woman who eyed him steadily.

The Saxon lord took another sip of his drink, leaping from his seat as he hurled the cup across the room. The goblet smacked against the stone and clattered to the floor.

"Who is your king? Where is his kingdom?" he bellowed, the sound of his voice reverberating through the cavernous room.

"I call no man my king. I am free," Dryston responded.

Aeglech started down the steps toward him, and Dryston thought he had drawn his last breath.

"Milord?" the veiled woman spoke.

The Saxon king whirled toward the woman.

"Perhaps I might be able to help?"

Aeglech turned his gaze back to Dryston. A slow curve of his mouth gave way to a satisfied grin.

"A fine idea, *wealh*. Come forward and tell me what you see."

Wealh. The name given to those of native-Briton descent, a degrading term that meant slave. So she was his slave.

She showed no fear as she walked past Aeglech. With a glance over her shoulder, she received his nod and faced Dryston, lifting the veil from her face.

A guard pressed down on his shoulder, bringing him to his knees. She removed the covering from her head. With careful purpose, she used the veil to wipe off the blood from his face. Her touch was as gentle as a mother's, powerful as a seductress's. Dryston's gaze was riveted to her face, but she seemed to look right through him.

"Do you have a name?" he whispered, leaning close as she wiped the blood from above his lip. "Are you a witch?"

"Silence," the king commanded

"What if I refuse your powers?" he asked. Her skin was pale, her hair shorter than most women's, but on her, it seemed to fit. Her cap of soft brown waves barely fell below her ears. She was not beautiful in the way of a noblewoman, but she had a magic about her he could not deny.

The dress, clearly not tailored to her body, offered him a glimpse of her breasts as she leaned forward to place her hands on his head.

A shiver rolled across Dryston's shoulders. He knew of the

ancient Druid teachings. He knew there were some who possessed the ability to see the past or look into the future, but he had never met one before now.

The gentle caress of the woman's hands on his scalp caused his body, weary and sore from his journey, to react in ways he did not expect. As her dark eyes held his, the memory of his night with Cendra appeared in his brain.

"What is it? What do you see?" the king asked impatiently, coming down to kneel at her side.

"There is much passion," she whispered. "There is a woman and a man. They are…" Her voice trailed off as she glanced nervously at him.

"The rebel camp, what of the rebel camp?" the king urged.

Aeglech's fierce gaze met Dryston's as if to intimidate him. Silently defying him, he gave over his mind to that night he'd spent with Cendra, all the pleasure he'd given and received.

The woman splayed her fingers wide over his scalp, and her soft breath caught.

"Can you see the camp?" the frustrated king prodded.

Dryston conjured delightfully lusty images of Cendra in their last moments together. So vivid were they that he began to grow hard.

The witch's eyes flew open and she stared at him. He could not help but smile as she took a step back, studying his face.

"I cannot read this man," she declared quietly.

"What do you mean you cannot read him? You are a seer. This is your gift," the warlord exploded. "What good are you to me if you cannot use your gift when I need it?"

A flash of concern passed through her beautiful, brown eyes.

"His will is strong. It is difficult to read through such a thick head."

Dryston waited for Lord Aeglech to order that he be hanged from the gallows or worse, tossed into the moat.

The woman's dark eyes turned to him. "Master Balrogan will enjoy the chance to break this one."

It was apparent that he had misjudged her.

Aeglech appeared to debate her suggestion, but nodded. He was spared, at least, for now. "Very well, take him to the dungeon and let Balrogan deal with him."

Dryston had a feeling that things had just gone from bad to worse.

Chapter Seven

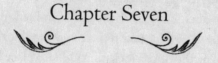

What Sierra had seen when she laid her hands on the Roman frightened her. She'd lied when she said she could not see anything. On the contrary, it was as if *she* had been the woman he'd pleasured. His very thoughts brought forth emotions inside of her that she had fought all of her life to suppress. She had convinced herself that they were not real. No magic on earth, no matter how potent, could conjure such love. The experience left her with a dull ache, an uneasy restlessness that she could not readily dismiss. More so, at one point, there was the fleeting image of a boy's face that she saw. His eyes, in particular, jarred her thoughts and tugged at her soul. She felt a connection to this stranger, and it was more powerful than she knew what to do with.

Sierra could not see the new prisoner's face, but she could tell from his body that he was not much older than Cearl. His chest, broad and darkened by the sun, led to a lean waist. His breeches barely covered his legs they were so tattered, exposing firm, muscular calves sprinkled with dark hair. His head was covered with sackcloth, which suited her fine. He was belligerent even as the guards snapped the shackles over his wrists and ankles, forcing him to kneel on her chamber floor.

"I dunna care what you do to me. I am innocent," he growled, his voice muffled by his covering. With a nod from Balrogan, the guards yanked the man's breeches to his knees.

At that, the man grew strangely quiet.

"He is all yours, Mouse," Balrogan mumbled, ushering the guards out ahead of him before he eased the door shut.

The sound of the door's lock clicking into place brought the prisoner back to life. "I fear no one, not even this *Mouse,*" he called out.

Despite her menial comforts, Sierra was still Aeglech's slave and she had come to the conclusion that she could not guarantee a prisoner's survival, but she could ensure hers.

Sierra kept silent, letting him rant, making him wonder if he was alone. She assessed his body as she finished her apple. She had to admit that the Briton's fiery disposition was as appealing as his strong, lean body. His sinewy strength, like Cearl's, was born of hard labor. A young farmer, perhaps.

A man driven by anger, though, would be filled with passion. And feeding that passion, she could gain the trust she needed for him to admit his guilt for the minimal crime he had performed. Between the strange feelings the Roman had stirred within her and the fact that she had not seen Cearl in days, Sierra's need for sexual escape was eating her alive.

Tension mounted within the castle walls every day. Lord Aeglech was so certain of a conspiracy against him that everyone, even the guards, were susceptible to his wrath. At the king's whimsy, the guards were arresting villagers for the most trivial of crimes. And criminals whom Balrogan might have before punished and set free, were now sentenced to immediate beheading.

Sierra knew the king's paranoia and the number of prisoners was taking its toll on Balrogan. If the executioner's position was in peril, then none of them were safe.

Her eyes drifted back to the man as he jerked against his shackles. He had already spent time hanging upside down in a cage. He had survived the "hole," a place where the sea rushes in and can drown a man. He was a stubborn Celt, and that was fine with her. Every man had a weakness.

She tossed her apple core into the hearth and picked up a bucket of water.

"Who is there?" The prisoner turned his head toward her as she approached.

She did not answer. Instead, she let her gaze travel down his naked body, noting the angry welts of Balrogan's skelp.

"What is your crime?" she asked quietly as she knelt in front of him. Her brow rose, impressed with what lay between his thighs.

"Who are you?" There was the slightest tinge of fear in his voice. "What are you going to do to me?"

"A friend," she replied, reaching into her bucket for a cloth. Her fingers itched to touch the sun-kissed plane of his hard stomach, to let her fingers follow the thin path of coarse hair that led to the dormant prize in his lap.

"A friend? What trickery is this?" he tossed at her.

She would have to be more convincing. "No trickery, I assure you," Sierra replied, touching the cloth to his shoulder.

He flinched away, his tongue gratefully silent. It made her job that much easier.

"Are you a prisoner?" he asked, his voice curious.

"I have been here a long time," she spoke, stroking the cloth gently over his wounds.

"Why do you tend to me? What do you want?"

She slid the cloth over his phallus, stroking him several times, until his hips began to respond. "I want nothing more than you are able to give." She curled the cloth around his staff, gliding her thumb over the velvet head.

"Who are you?" he gasped between clenched teeth.

Already, he grew hard in her hand. "Who I am is not important. I can help you," Sierra said.

"Take off this covering. I want to see you," the man urged, shifting his knees apart to accommodate his hardening erection. His head lolled back as she leaned forward and tugged a stiff nipple between her teeth. He tried to shake the covering from his head, but it was secured with a bit of twine.

"You must trust me." She soothed him with her words and her hands. She glanced down, pleased to see his manhood growing thick and sturdy. Her quiver became wet in anticipation.

"It is a cruel thing you do, woman. I cannot see or touch you." His voice cracked.

Sierra pulled her gown over her head. "You can touch me, Briton," she said as she lifted his head covering only as far as his lips. His was a nice mouth, framed with several days' growth of beard. He had a full lower lip that she imagined would be pleasurable to taste, but she did not want that memory. She leaned forward and guided his chin to her breast. Like a hungry babe, he latched on to her pebbled tip, lavishing her with his tongue expertly.

"Your need grows, as does mine," she sighed, savoring his attention.

"Yes." His hot breath wafted over her skin.

She touched his covered head as she eased her leg over his thigh, sliding over his length, her hand between them. "Do you like me having control over you?" Sierra touched her fingers drenched with her honey to his mouth. He sucked deeply and a low groan escaped from his throat.

She massaged his muscular shoulders.

"What kind of torture is this? Are you a witch, come to place a spell on me?" His breathing grew labored. "Or are you but a temptress of my dreams?"

"My mother was Druid."

"Then you admit, you do this to trick me." His face turned to the heavens as he stretched his body against the chains.

"I offer you no threat." Sierra smoothed her hands over his head covering.

The prisoner leaned forward, resting his beard chin against her breast.

"Save me," he whispered.

"I do not have the power," Sierra sighed. In truth, she was likely the last pleasure he would have on this earth. To that end, she felt they had something to offer each other—she was his pleasure, he was her survival.

"All that matters is now." Sierra eased the covering down over his lips and chin.

"No, please dunna leave me," he pleaded.

The sound of desperation in his voice was what Sierra had been waiting for. She glanced at his cock, jutting firmly between his thighs. "I shall not leave you, Briton. There is more we can share, if it is your desire." She baited him, surprised how easily it came to her.

"Yes, show me, my woman of magic. I am yours."

Sierra stood and grabbed the chains that held his arms to the wall. Astride his thighs, she lowered herself, guiding him inside her. Sierra pressed against his chest as their bodies fused together.

"Wicked sorceress, you tease." He rubbed his covered head against her shoulder.

"I do not tease," Sierra whispered, slowly rotating her hips. "You can tell me anything." She rubbed her breasts against his firm chest.

Her prisoner emitted a groan. His veins bulged beneath the flesh of his neck. Sierra sensed he was fighting the urge to thrust into her. Yet, because of his chains, she possessed control of their joining and they both knew it.

"Tell me, Briton," Sierra coaxed softly. "Did you take water from the king's well?" Her power added a surprising new element to her pleasure. The man's throat bobbed with his deep swallow. She knew he was contemplating his options, few though they were.

A low growl came from beneath the covering.

Sierra smiled.

"I knew this was a trick," he snapped.

Her patience grew short, her need greater. She had no time for games. Grasping the chain, she began to rise.

"No! Wait," he gasped.

With a grin, she slid effortlessly back onto his slick cock. "You can tell me," she whispered as she began to rock against him. This was not like sex with Cearl. She alone was master now.

Only the sound of their breathing permeated the cold silence of the room.

"If I tell you, will you tell them?" He swallowed hard.

Sierra smiled, but her victory had a bittersweet taste. "I will not tell. I make you that promise."

"Your oath?"

"As a Celt," she offered, lifting her hips and using the chains for leverage as she guided him into her ready quiver. She drove her body relentlessly, dizzy with need, blindly pushing toward that moment of mindless bliss—the moment when she was free. Her fingers turned white where she grasped the chains. Sweet escape from her lifeless existence beckoned her. "I am free," she whispered, thrusting her hips hard against him, savoring the pleasure his body offered.

Jarred by the intensity of her own release, she planted her heels firmly against the stone floor and took him deep inside her as she let the life-giving waves wash over her. Through the lust-filled haze in her mind, she heard him speak.

"I took his water, it's true, but it is because the village well is dry," he spoke, gritting his teeth. Her sexual appetite appeased, she opened her eyes to the ceiling above and saw Aeglech looking down at her, a wicked grin splitting his face.

"Well done," she spoke in haste, sliding from his lap before he was complete. She heard the hatch above slam with a thud.

"No-o-o," he groaned, left unsatisfied.

Perched on her knees, Sierra grasped his rigid cock between her hands. His body bucked with his impending release, as he pumped against her grip. His body thrust backward as he gave over to his shuddering climax.

Sierra stood and dipped her hands in the water, glancing down at his heaving chest.

"You will help me escape, then?" he asked, attempting to get his breathing under control.

Sierra pulled her gown over her head. From his anxious manner, she knew he did not possess the skills to plan something as dangerous as an escape. "Do not be misled by your emotions. No one has ever escaped this fortress alive. It is useless to consider it. Even if you did, the guards would hunt you down like rabid dogs. There is the chance that with your admission, you may have saved yourself, but I can give you no promise of that. If you are lucky, perhaps they will just take your hands."

"So that's it then? You fuck me and leave me here to die?" Anger rose in his voice.

"I gave my word to you that I would not *tell* anyone your confession and I will not. Your fate, as it always was, rests with Aeglech, not me." She thought it best not to concern the man even more with the fact that Aeglech had already heard his confession.

"But what about…what about…*us?*" His voice pleaded.

"What do you mean *us?* Did you think that what dangles betwixt your legs is enough to bewitch me? You are no knight, sir, and I am no damsel needing your rescue."

"You are as bad as the rest of these Saxons, you heartless bitch," he growled.

Sierra shook her head. He was no different than most men. Their pride dangled between their legs. "Nay, you men are all the same, believing that a woman's heavenly duty is to serve you night and day, suffer the pangs of labor, raise your bairn, plow the fields, make your bread, and then hike up our skirts and say give me some more, sir."

"*You* seduced me!" he shouted.

"Did I once give you cause to think any emotion was attached to it?" she countered. "Did I fill your head with flowery promises like you would have given me and never kept?" she demanded.

"You're mad!" he shouted.

Sierra would not deny him the pleasure of thinking as much. Perhaps, in fact, she was. She did not blame him for his anger, but she did think him foolish for risking life and limb for a mere bucket of water. Aside from that, she felt nothing for him.

She turned away, ignoring the litany of names that he called her. There was nothing more she could do. He, alone, would have to find the courage to face the truth, and pray Lord Aeglech did not wish to use him as an example to others.

A gurgling sound caught her attention and she squinted through the dark shadows to find the source of it. The prisoner had somehow managed to wrap his chain around his neck.

Sierra sighed and dropped the wood she had been about to toss on the fire. She strode over to him, watching his absurd gyrating, hoping she wasn't too late. Aeglech would have her head if he was cheated out of the pleasure of pronouncing the man's death himself.

She yanked the chain from around his neck. "It may be true that it is better to die at your own hand than to die at the skill of Balrogan, but I shall not have your death on *my* hands."

"Let me die, you traitor, you Saxon whore," he spat, and then collapsed, dropping his chin to his chest.

"No doubt you will be given your chance soon enough," Sierra replied as she picked up another apple and bit into it.

Sierra could not tear her eyes from the sight of the Roman dangling in the cage like a deer after the slaughter. His finely honed body shimmered with sweat as Balrogan tried for the third day to glean information from him.

At his insistence, she had accompanied Aeglech to the torture chamber to review the progress of the new Roman prisoner. Though she had only been in her new chamber for a few days, her stomach lurched from the dungeon's stench.

"Do you have no fear, Roman?" Balrogan pushed his large face close to the cage and shoved the enclosure, causing it to rock back and forth. The prisoner, his eyes a stormy pale gray-green, met the executioner's hardened gaze. Dark hair, black as a moonless night, shrouded his face, but he held his tongue as the cage rocked with him upside down inside.

Lord Aeglech stood at the side, silently watching. The prisoner was either very brave or an eejit. Balrogan glanced over his shoulder, his eyes widening as he took in Sierra's new appearance.

Lord Aeglech gave a nod and Balrogan brought the flame near the prisoner's feet once more. Already, he had singed their bottoms once.

Sierra's eyes were riveted to the Roman's face. He clenched his jaw and endured the pain without a sound. With an exasperated sigh, Balrogan tossed the torch into the pit.

"I will have to think of something else, milord. He is stubborn this one."

Lord Aeglech stared at the prisoner a moment, before he raised his hand. "Take him down," he barked, "and bring him to me."

The Saxon king breezed past Sierra with his guards close behind. He glanced back before ascending the narrow stairs.

"I will have need of you, *wealh*. You know what to do."

"Aye, milord." She lowered her gaze to the floor. Her body trembled at the thought of seducing this man. She feared his power over her emotions she had thought long dead. Carefully, she reached up and swung the cage.

"Be watchful of that one, Mouse, he may spit poison." The executioner chuckled as he prepared his next device. "We'll see if this will persuade him to speak." He raised a handcrafted piece that could slowly sever a man's fingers one at a time.

The Roman's expression remained unchanged as he stared at Sierra from his batlike position. His face was not that of a farmer, or peasant, not as she was used to seeing. He had a warrior's face—proud, rugged, stoic. His eyes, though shadowed from the torture he'd been put through, shone with silent strength. Her gaze drifted to the tight line of his mouth, pursed with determination. A mouth she ventured could command an army as well as a woman in bed. For no reason that she could think of, she spoke aloud. "Lord Aeglech would not want to be kept waiting." She imagined she saw a glint of challenge behind the prisoner's turbulent eyes. He was different, strong, unafraid, her vision of a true warrior. Most men, when faced with Balrogan's forms of persuasion, were eager to offer information and so, too, begged for mercy in the process. In three days, this Roman had endured numerous forms of torture without once having wavered. There was nothing innocent about him, only a powerful resilience seething beneath his warrior's body. A power she was dangerously drawn to.

Balrogan offered a muffled sound under his breath. "Perhaps you are right. He should be intact for whatever the king has in mind for him."

Since the Roman prisoner's arrival, Lord Aeglech had received confirmation that the powerful Roman General Ambrosis was traveling from Rome into the provinces just north of the Saxon stronghold. Given Aeglech's paranoia, combined with the seeds she had managed thus far to plant in his mind, it was clear he was preparing himself for a confrontation. Still, Sierra believed that the Saxon king was bored with the pillaging and conquest of common folk. She believed that he longed for an opponent worthy of a good fight. Perhaps that was why he had not yet ordered the death of the Roman prisoner.

A creak of the cage jarred Sierra from her thoughts. The Roman's gaze met hers and a shiver skittered up her spine. The image of him with the woman appeared in her mind, and she instinctively took a step back. This time she did not imagine seeing the corner of his mouth curve in a wicked smirk. Sierra swallowed a pang of pure desire and sensed that he was able to see deep inside her, as if reading her thoughts.

"I am on my way to the buttery," she said to Balrogan, unable to break from the prisoner's captivating stare.

"See if the blacksmith is finished with my blades, Mouse," Balrogan ordered without looking up. Years of having her around to do his bidding made the request easy. She glanced at the guard, who maintained his post at the dungeon entrance.

"Aye, milord." Tearing her eyes from the Roman, she hurried out, taking the steps with care as she held up the hem of her gown. The image of the woman's face as the Roman pleasured her taunted Sierra. Her sighs were burned in Sierra's memory, the sight of her back arched, knees spread, fingers digging into the Roman's dark hair.

Never had she experienced what she sensed in that Celtic woman's soul, and it both frightened and intrigued her. And ever since she tasted its imagery, her hunger for the same elation grew. The woman in Sierra's mind wore a look of joy on her face that she did not understand. Most disturbing, perhaps, it made her realize her life had become as cold and inhuman as Lord Aeglech.

She heard an anguished male cry rise from the room below. Apparently, Balrogan had changed his mind about letting the Roman keep all of his fingers.

She pushed aside the sound as she hurried across the inner

ward, heading to the only person she knew who could satisfy her frustration.

She found Cearl shucking stalls at the back of the stable. "Be quick, take me. I need to escape." It was a term they used to simplify the need for carnal pleasure, to find release from the tensions around them.

"*Escape,* now? But I am working," he exclaimed with a short laugh. He held his pitchfork at his side and nervously scanned the area. He smiled then, and leaned on the tool. "Your new gown is pretty." He looked her over from head to toe.

Without further discussion, she tugged off the gown Aeglech insisted she wear and stood naked before him. A slight breeze blew across her heated flesh and Sierra closed her eyes trying to imagine feeling for Cearl the way that woman had felt for the Roman. Was she his wife? His lover? Did he still carry the same passion for her?

Where was he, why had he not yet touched her? She opened her eyes and met Cearl's naughty grin. His innocent blue eyes danced as he lowered his gaze to her chest.

"You do make a man forget his duty." He tossed the fork aside and shrugged off his tunic and breeches. "Quick, in here." He motioned Sierra farther into the stall.

"I do like these," he whispered, brushing his fingertips over her breasts. Tingles spread over her flesh, tightening the rosy nubs that Cearl so enjoyed rolling between his fingers.

Even as he teased, causing familiar sensations betwixt her legs, Sierra's gaze remained on the view beyond the knothole in the stable wall in front of her. From where she stood, she could look over Cearl's shoulder and see the dungeon tower rising at the edge of the inner ward. There, in that dark place of forgetting, was a man she wanted to understand, to know in ways that she had never before wanted with anyone.

As she held Cearl's tousled head to her breast, Sierra tried without success to obliterate the sea-green gaze that seemed to look right through her, tormenting her with the life that shone in it as if mocking her own lifelessness.

"I am ready," Sierra spoke without emotion as she stepped around Cearl and leaned her palms against the stable wall, warmed by the afternoon sun. She did not bother to look back as she parted her legs and pressed forward to peer out through the hole.

In her mind, it was not Cearl's fingers that stroked her to wetness, nor Cearl's satisfied groan of pleasure she heard as he took her from behind. Neither was it Cearl's thick cock moving with pleasurable rhythm or his fingers digging into her hips.

Nay, in Sierra's mind it was the Roman prisoner who possessed her both mind and body. As her body broke free, she rose on the balls of her feet, immersed in her dizzying escape. She leaned her cheek against the faded wood as Cearl finished twice more, groaning low as he pressed deep inside her. He snaked his arms around her and teased her tender breasts.

The scent of cedar and sweet straw mingled with their coupling, and Sierra held her breath waiting to feel for Cearl what she had sensed in the Celt woman's spirit.

But she felt nothing, nothing at all. *Saxon whore.* The prisoner's words mocked her.

"I could do it again if you like," Cearl whispered against her neck. "I only need to look upon you to ready me."

Sierra did not want him to poke her again. She had no desire, no interest any longer. In this place of cruelty and death, she had for a moment tasted rebirth, if only in connection with another woman's soul.

She did not know how to tell Cearl things had changed— that she would likely no longer come to visit him. All she knew was that Cearl was no longer enough. Sierra hungered for something he could not give her, something that, in fact, she might not be able to give in return. But it did not quell her yearning.

"Shh," she replied. Her eye on the tower, she pretended that the warm, hard body pressed to her was that of the Roman prisoner.

Chapter Eight

Dryston swore a string of bloody curses as he started awake after blacking out from the pain. Blood, now dried, formed a path down his forearm to his elbow where his finger had bled while he hung upside down.

At least now he was upright, though his situation had not improved much. He found himself chained hands and feet to a dungeon wall, the chains so short he was forced to stand. Without food and water, his knees threatened to buckle. A movement brought his head up, and it was then that he realized he was not in the executioner's dungeon, but in a different place altogether.

He tugged at his memory, trying to recall all he could since he blacked out. He remembered Aeglech's orders that he be taken down from the cage, the strange woman's suggestion that he be spared his fingers, Balrogan's sneer as he severed his fingertip.

It all came back to him now.

Dryston glanced at his right hand, noting the absence of the tip of his small finger and the bloody stub that remained.

"Drink this."

He looked groggily from his wound to the woman standing in front of him. She held a cup of liquid in her hands. He considered the possibility it could be laced with poison or some other witches' potion. He squinted at the coppery-tinted contents and opened his mouth, accepting the drink and whatever the fates brought him. He drank too much, too fast, unable to swallow, his throat swollen and parched from thirst. He coughed, sputtering water down his chin and over his chest. But he did not care. Weariness plagued him, but his instinct cautioned that this was no random act of goodwill. If Aeglech was unsuccessful at extracting information using one method, he was not the type to give up without attempting others. Hedging his gut was right, Dryston hoped he could work that to his advantage. The woman waited patiently as he became more aware of his surroundings. The room could have been a dungeon with the exception of a small rope bed and the fire crackling in the hearth.

She offered him the cup once more and he shook his head. Glancing at him, she returned to her seat by the fire. She wore the same gold gown she had worn the other times he had seen her. It was clear to him that Aeglech was using her, perhaps rewarding her with small tokens of his gratitude. Dryston wondered to what extent the woman offered herself to the Saxon king.

"My thanks for the water," Dryston said aloud. "It was not laced with anything deadly, was it?" He attempted a smile, but his lips were stiff from lack of moisture.

She looked at him over her shoulder and went about her task, stirring the embers in the hearth with a fire iron. He doubted if he had been brought here because the accommodations in the executioner's chambers were full. And he was not the type to sit and wait for whatever was going to happen. He would just get things rolling.

"My finger is in need of care. If the flesh is not sealed soon, I am in danger of losing my arm." Dryston was not entirely sure that he would be able to survive more pain. Already Balrogan had stripped his flesh with a knotted cat-o'-nine-tails. He had hung with his blood rushing to his head for hours on end and had the pads of his feet scorched.

The woman turned to meet his eyes. Despite the misery he had seen in his day, little compared to the lost look in her eyes. She tapped the ash from the end of her fire iron and held it up, its tip white-hot from stirring the flaming wood.

Dryston swallowed. At least she was not squeamish.

She said nothing as she walked over to him, the iron poised like a saber.

"You could just let it get infected. You could just let me die. Why do you help me?" he asked, curious to know who she was.

From a hook on the wall, she pulled a leather-handled skelp— that device he remembered, knowing full well its torturous kiss. Balrogan had introduced it to him his first day and every day since. He prepared to feel its bite again as he watched her roll it over in her hand. She turned the thick, leather-wrapped handle upward and held it to his mouth. In her other hand, the fire iron glowed a deep red, a yellow ember stuck on its end.

He realized then that she was offering him something to bite down on for the pain. He leaned forward and took the handle in his teeth, rolling it back, secure in his mouth.

The woman's dark gaze held his as she brought the fiery end of the iron to his hand. He could feel the heat radiating near his flesh and his eyes watered as his teeth clamped down hard on the handle. Sweat broke out across his forehead and chest. He had no way to prepare for the lightning bolt of pain that shot up his arm and exploded in his brain. He bit down on the handle so hard he thought his teeth would break. The sizzle of his own flesh combined with the sickening smell caused bile to rise rapidly in his throat, but his stomach was void of much to bring up.

Every nerve in his body twitched as once more she pressed the hot tip to his open wound. Dryston heard the sound of his muffled scream over the din of pain rocking his head. He turned his face to the heavens and swore he saw Aeglech's smiling face swimming before him. His thoughts swirled as the world began to pitch and weave. In another moment, he would pass out.

The sound of metal clattering on stone brought him alert, and he realized the woman had dropped the iron. His arm was numb, thankfully; his mind still in shock. She grabbed his hand and he stared at her, unable to speak. He shook his head, pleading with his eyes to do no more.

She drew a strip of cool, wet cloth around his hand, tying it off to cover the newly seared flesh.

Dryston's body continued to tremble yet in the aftershock of the pain. The woman brought his hand to her cheek for the blink of an eye, then let it drop just as fast. Without a word, she crawled into her bed and curled up against the wall, covering her face.

He rolled the handle forward from his aching jaws, and spit it to the floor. Pain pricked his every nerve, but the worst of it was over.

For now.

Dryston licked his lips, bringing his breathing back under control. He took a brief glance above him and saw a wood hatch in the ceiling. Perhaps he had not imagined Aeglech's face, after all.

He returned his attention to the woman. She had not spoken a word since he woke. Yet she was not mute, he'd heard her speak before. He glanced toward the door and saw no movement.

"You are not here of your own will, are you?" he asked.

She did not respond and, for a moment, the image of Cendra's body flashed in his brain. "My thanks for what you did." He waited, wondering what was to happen next. There were no sounds in the corridor.

Finally, she straightened her shoulders and spoke. "My will is to live, as I suspect it is yours, Roman." She eased off the bed, barely giving him a glance.

"Aye, perhaps we could assure that for the both of us, if we work together to make it so," he offered.

She walked to the door and peeked out through the small grid. Facing him, she glanced up at the ceiling and shook her head.

Her sudden willingness to connect made Dryston skeptical, curious at how she could be so easily persuaded. He considered it could be a ruse to garner his trust. Still, it appeared, at present she was his best chance of survival.

The heavy wood door swung open and Balrogan barged in, his milky-eyed gaze fixed on him. "Time to die, Roman scum," he growled, his voice slurred as if he had had too much mead. He raised Dryston's long sword in the air. The blade glinted in the glow of the fire. The giant of a man slashed the blade through the air and gave Dryston a garish smile.

There was no time to protest. Dryston relinquished himself to the fates, bowing his head with honor and thanking God for his life while he still had his head to do so. He thought of his family, of his youth, when his life was free of tyranny and bloodshed. Perhaps the fates were collecting now the sins of his Roman ancestors.

He waited for the touch of cold steel against his neck. Grateful for the blacksmith's work, he knew that the sharper the blade, the swifter and less painful the cut. With any luck, he would have need of only one clean swipe.

But no blade touched his flesh.

Dryston looked up and saw that the woman had wrapped her small hands around Balrogan's mammoth arm.

"Aeglech promised he was mine."

The first words from her lips, and for the second time she had saved his life. He did not know whether to be grateful, afraid of her loyalty to her king or prepared to watch her die before him.

"Do you really think that you can do better than me, Mouse?" The executioner held the sword over his head as if it weighed no more than a feather. His mouth bowed out and sweat drenched his face.

"No, milord." She removed her hands and knelt at his feet. Her dress slid from her shoulder, revealing pale flesh. "But it was Aeglech's express orders that I was to have a turn with the prisoner."

Dryston's gaze bounced from the bulk of the man to the delicate creature kneeling before him. *A turn?*

"Very well, Mouse." The gargantuan man dropped the sword to his side, pouting as he paused to pick up the skelp on the floor. He shook out its leather tendrils, his expression one of melancholy.

"Do not hesitate to use this if necessary. Do you remember where I showed you to strike to achieve the most pain?" he said as if tutoring a student.

"Aye, milord, I remember well all you have taught me," she replied.

"Well done, Mouse." He reached back with a slight smile and patted her on the head. "I will take his sword to Aeglech."

She stood now by the door. Balrogan's giant form hid her from his view.

"Remember what I told you, Mouse. Trust no one but yourself."

As soon as the door shut behind Balrogan, the woman faced Dryston with a hard, scrutinizing look. No longer the meek, subservient student.

"If you lie to me, I will kill you."

Dryston was in no position not to believe her every word.

Chapter Nine

"You play your part well, woman." The prisoner frowned. No doubt, he was trying to determine what her plan was.

Sierra was doing the same.

"Do not mock me, Roman. I have just saved your sorry hide. Even now, I ponder the wisdom of it." She listened at the door a moment and her eyes darted to the hatch above as she approached him.

"You must be the apprentice I have heard about. No one else would dare come up against Balrogan. Should I be grateful then that you want me kept alive for the pleasure of your own interrogation?" he asked, wincing as another shock of pain shot from his finger.

Sierra decided to let him believe that was the reason she'd stopped Balrogan. The truth was, she'd stopped him because she sensed in the Roman a man who possessed the skills and courage to help her escape from this place. But when she had grasped Balrogan's arm, she had seen a glimpse of sorrow in the giant man, mixed liberally with fear. She had never seen him drunk. Sierra sensed that it would not be long before she found out what was his reason.

The Roman's hands hung limp from the shackles that kept him upright. The bandage around the tip of his small finger was soaked now with dried blood. Sierra picked up a bowl of Cearl's rabbit stew that he had brought earlier when the prisoner was still unconscious. It did not please him to see the Roman prisoner shackled to her chamber wall, but she had assured him that she was only doing what Aeglech ordered. It was her duty, and Sierra took no pleasure from it. That seemed to appease him for the moment.

"You are no murderer," the prisoner said in a hoarse whisper.

Not wanting him to misunderstand her intent or her capabilities, Sierra stepped up to him and pointed her finger at his nose. "Then you are more of a fool than I thought. I have slit a man's throat and not thought twice of it," she lied.

He chuckled as if he knew it was not true. Which it was not...*yet*.

Sierra held his eyes a breath longer, her mind gone blank, until a grin threatened his mouth. She shoved the bowl of stew beneath his face. "Are you hungry?"

His dark brow rose. "Your concern overwhelms me."

More of his mocking tongue. Let him ponder his fate then.

"Fine." Sierra marched to the chair by the hearth and began to eat.

"It looks good. What is it?" he asked after a few moments.

She could hear the hunger in his voice. "Rabbit," she replied, taking a hunk of soft bread and soaking it in gravy. "Cearl makes a fine rabbit stew."

"Cearl—that the boy in the stables?" he asked, weariness

slurring his words. At this rate, if he did not get some nourishment, he would be of no help to her at all.

Lord Aeglech would not be pleased with her yatter when she ought to be using her skills. She looked briefly to the hatch above and saw that it was closed. She focused on her meal, her mind reeling with whether to trust this man or not.

"Aye, that is Cearl," she responded finally, stuffing the gravy-sodden bread in her mouth.

"My guess is you are not Saxon?"

"I am the one who will ask the questions, not you." Just who was the master and who was the prisoner here? She needed time to think. Based on what she knew, the Romans were no more trustworthy than the Saxons.

She held up the bowl. Perhaps filling his mouth would silence him. "Do you want some?" she asked, averting her eyes from his.

She needed to find out if the rumors of a rebellion were true. Was the rebel army strong enough to squash the Saxon horde? And who was the boy she had seen? Why had it affected her so? Like it or not, this Roman might well hold the answers to both her future and her past.

Sierra walked up to her prisoner, standing far enough from him that she had to reach forward to offer him a chunk of bread. "Be quick about it. Take it." She held the soggy piece of bread between her fingers.

He snatched the food, closing his eyes as if savoring a royal feast.

"I have not eaten in days," he replied, licking gravy from his lips. "Your Cearl is a good cook—you may tell him I said so."

"He is not my Cearl," she blurted without thinking.

He opened his eyes, regarding her as he swallowed his food. Sierra took a step back even though she knew the chains held him to the wall.

"Why are you loyal to Aeglech?" he asked.

Sierra looked into the bowl, unable to answer him, suddenly seeing her survival as cowardly instead of courageous.

"Do you want for more?" she asked, sensing his eyes on her.

"You did not answer my question."

"I told you I would ask the questions. We are finished for now," she said and turned away.

"It is your eyes that betray you," he called after her.

Sierra faltered. What could he see in the eyes of someone who had no life? She did not turn to face him. "What do you mean?"

"You are not meant to be here. I do not believe you have the heart of a ruthless executioner."

She whirled around to face him. "You have no concept of my life."

He stared at her, and all the air seemed to suck from her lungs. His eyes narrowed, studying her.

She was certain that if she went through with the thoughts swirling in her mind, she would be dead before morning. She reached for his face, brushing the long hair away from his forehead.

His brow furrowed, but he kept silent. Her gaze dropped to his mouth and her fingers gently grazed his face. She held back the urge to touch her mouth to his, to see for herself the passion she sensed inside him.

Brought to her senses by the guarded look in his eye, she dropped her hand.

"Do not think that you know me, Roman," she said, turning away.

"A person's eyes do not lie," he said. "Why do you not follow through with what is in your heart?"

Startled by his bold words, Sierra's gaze darted to his. "What do you mean?"

"You saw something when you laid your hands on me. Do you deny it?" he asked.

"What I saw means nothing to me," Sierra replied.

"Are you certain of that?"

Her heart thudded in her chest. "Images are all I see," she retorted.

"And you felt nothing?" he countered.

"No," she lied, wanting to end this conversation. Not ready yet to trust him with questions of her own.

The corner of his mouth twitched.

"Fine. So what if I did, Roman? Emotions are dangerous things. They can...muddle your thinking, get you killed."

"Or give you extraordinary pleasure, am I right?" he offered with a grin that shot heat to the juncture of Sierra's thighs.

She grabbed the leather skelp in frustration. She would show him how wrong he was and how ruthless she could be when she wanted. Sierra strode toward him. "You are wrong," she spat, caught in a battle between desire and wisdom.

"Am I?" He smiled.

"Yes, you are." She searched his eyes as she rose on tiptoe, bringing her mouth a mere breath from his.

"You're a bad liar," he whispered, his eyes holding hers captive as he lowered his head and fused his mouth to hers.

Sierra dropped the skelp. She threw her arms around the Roman's neck as their mouths crushed together. Fierce. Wanting. Sierra could barely breathe. His mouth commanded hers, promising more.

Sierra wanted more, and she wanted it with this man. Was it possible she had found someone she could trust, someone possessing the skill required to gain their freedom?

His lips touched her closed eyelids, her forehead, giving her a taste of what he would be like as her intimate lover.

"There is so much I can teach you," he whispered against her mouth, capturing it again, coaxing her tongue to dance with his. "Tell me what you want."

Sierra opened her eyes, meeting his sea-green gaze. "Do you think I can be bought, Roman?"

"No more than you think you can seduce information from me, woman." He cocked a dark eyebrow. "Still, the game is quite pleasurable." He gave her a smile.

Furious, she reached again for the skelp.

"You will not use that on me," he spoke calmly. "Help me and I will help you."

"You are mistaken." Sierra leveled her threat, hoping he would relent, and she would not have to go through with a thrashing. Her eyes darted to the welts from Balrogan's previous lashings. She was not yet ready to trust him.

The sound of voices, one of them Aeglech's, brought her attention to the door.

"Dammit," he whispered. He looked at her. "Trust me now and do as I say. You will need to follow through on your threat."

Sierra's surprised gaze shot back to his. Was he daft? "What makes you think it was just a threat?" she lied.

"That kiss. But it doesn't matter. You have no choice. Not if you value your life or mine."

Confused, Sierra's heart pounded hard against her rib cage. She had no time to reconsider; the lock was being turned.

She closed her eyes and swung the skelp high over her head. She gritted her teeth as she brought the leathers down, finding their desired mark with a loud, sickening thwack. Only then did she open her eyes.

The Roman's gut-wrenching cry of anguish met Lord Aeglech as he slammed the door open. The king's gaze changed from interest to glittering pleasure. "Do not let me stop you, *wealh*. Teach this Roman he cannot defeat my powerful Saxon reign!"

Beads of red appeared along the angry red welt on the prisoner's shoulder where the knotted strands had torn at his flesh. Sierra raised the skelp and brought it down once again on his shoulder. The Roman brought his gaze to hers as if to pardon her for the cruelty she inflicted. Her stomach churned.

Tears welled in his eyes. "You cannot break me," he challenged her, although she silently wished he would pass out. She sliced the leather tendrils through the air, cracking them, more for show than anything else. They sliced across his naked chest and his body flinched. Her brain hummed with the din of hundreds of prisoners before him, their screams taunting her, pleading for Sierra to save them.

Then, she had felt nothing. Now, she felt everything.

Brought up short by the sound of clapping behind her, Sierra dropped the skelp to her side.

She wanted to retch.

She held in a silent cry as her eyes beheld the fruits of her labor. The Roman's body sagged against the chains.

"Well done, *wealh*. It is clear that you have learned much from observing your master," he commended her.

She could not tear her gaze away from the blood trickling down the Roman's chest. Lord Aeglech continued his praise without awaiting her response.

"Perhaps my apprentice has, at last, become the master," the king stated.

Bile rose in Sierra's throat.

"You see, even Celts obey me, Roman. I am invincible and

your puny rebel army shall taste the fire of my reign." Aeglech snatched a handful of the Roman's hair and yanked his face up to meet his. Blood trickled from his temple; bruises, pinkish-purple, surrounded one eye.

"Where is the rebel camp?" Lord Aeglech demanded.

Hatred shone from the Roman's good eye as he jerked his head from Aeglech's grasp. He spat at his feet.

Sierra's heart stopped, certain he had gone too far. The king's hand fisted at his side, anger seething on his face. He grabbed the skelp and attacked the Roman in blind anger. He would have killed him had Sierra not stepped in and blocked his hand. "Milord, if he is dead we are no further than before."

The skelp's tendrils swayed as he held it in midair, his gaze darting between the prisoner and Sierra. Her gut roiled with the realization that at any moment he could turn on her.

"Very well, but if he does not confess, then come the morrow he will be hanged as an example to all those who would consider contesting my reign."

She nodded and knelt before him, hoping to appease his anger.

"Break him and we will discuss more freedoms. If you are unsuccessful, we will discuss your death." Aeglech tossed the skelp on the floor and stormed from the room.

Sierra stared after the guards as the door clicked behind them. Aeglech's last words echoed in her mind. She turned, finally, her stomach lurching at what she was capable of inflicting.

The Roman raised his bloodied face to hers. "I was wrong," he spoke, struggling to push the words past his physical pain. "For one so delicate in appearance, you have the skill and courage of a warrior."

Sierra could not help but laugh in response. Of all names

she had been called by disgruntled prisoners in her nine years, "delicate" was not among them.

She grabbed the bucket and cloth, knowing that to care for his wounds, to touch him again, was not wise. "I have made a mess of things," she said as she wrung the water from the cloth and dabbed at his face.

"I am thirsty." His eyes searched hers. Caught in the memory of their heated kiss, she blinked away her desire and lifted the water to his lips. A drop pooled on his lower lip and she brushed it gently away with her thumb. "Did you mean what you said about helping each other?" she whispered, darting a look over her shoulder.

He nodded. "What do you need from me?"

Sierra shook her head, unsure yet of what she had seen, but certain of how strongly it affected her. "You will know when the time comes. For now you must trust me."

He winced as she pressed too hard on a fresh wound.

"Beg my ignorance, woman, but this is a bit one-sided."

He jerked again as she touched the cloth to his chest. His heart beat strong against her palm.

"I can help you, but you have to do something for me," the Roman said quietly.

The soothing sound of his voice almost made her believe that anything he said was possible. "What is it I must do?"

"Tell Aeglech what he wants to know. Tell him where he can find our camp. Make him believe that you seduced this information from me."

Sierra considered the risks involved. With this confession, Aeglech would surely sentence the Roman to the gallows. If she asked to escort the prisoner and they were able to escape, would Aeglech believe the Roman had kidnapped her?

Moreover, could she trust this Roman once he was free and they were alone in the wilderness?

"Come close," he whispered, his eyes checking the hatch above.

She rinsed the cloth again, proceeding to cleanse his wounds, her body responding to being near him.

"There are some castle ruins in a valley not too far from here. If we could find a way to lure Aeglech and his men there, it would make an ambush easier away from the protection of his fortress. The king trusts you. He could listen to what you told him. Could you convince him that this is where the rebel camp is?" the Roman asked.

Castle ruins? Were these the same ones she had seen when she touched Lord Aeglech? "We have no guarantee that this plan will work," she stated quietly, dabbing at his chest.

"Is it better to die in effort to be free, or remain here and die a slave?" he posed.

"What makes you think he trusts me?" She glanced briefly at his face.

"After what you just did? He looked like a proud father. He will listen," the Roman replied.

"And why should I trust you?"

"Because I am all you have."

She stared at his chest, weighing his words. There was great risk involved, the possibility of being caught, the chance she could die.

The very thought of freedom frightened her. What would she do? Where would she go? With no family to turn to—

She narrowed her eyes on him. "I need to lay my hands on you."

"To see if I am telling you the truth? I swear, as long as I have a breath in my body, no harm shall come to you if you help us in this."

"And who is this *we* you are talking about? The band of rebels you belong to?"

His eyes narrowed.

"Our army is far greater than you think. We have gathered many men from all of Britannia, from many clans, and have plans to meet with the Roman General Ambrosis. He and his men are sympathetic to the Britons."

"What if we are not able to get to your camp before Aeglech and his forces reach the ruins? What then?"

He studied her face. "Then our escape must not fail."

"You know it is dangerous to be telling me these things. What if I chose to tell Aeglech about this?" she asked.

He shrugged. "That is a risk I take." He regarded her with gentle eyes. "But my gut tells me that you want out of here as much as I do."

"And what is in this for me?" she asked.

"Aside from your freedom?"

"Assuming we live to escape." She pointed her cloth at him.

"I will see to your safety and make sure you are given food and shelter when we arrive at the camp."

Sierra held the rag between her hands, drawing it taut as she considered her options. "If the king believes me...*if*...then he would be open, I think, to my request for a small favor. I could ask to be one of the escorts to your hanging."

"Does this plan get better?" he asked.

"We could overtake the guards and escape, making it look as though you have taken me prisoner. The guards would be so busy looking for us that Aeglech would not right away make a move to go to the ruins."

"That is an excellent idea," he muttered. "Losing his spiritual advisor would be a great loss to him."

"Except that I do not like that idea."

"Then we hope that we get to the camp to tell my brother of the plan before Aeglech makes his move. That seems plain enough."

"I am glad you think so, Roman. But there is one more thing, something personal I need from you." She lifted her hands, cupping his face, staring into his steady gaze. Her heart thudded against her breast as she tried to use her gift to see his thoughts. She was looking for the image she had seen earlier, the one of the small boy with the eyes that appeared so familiar to her. She knew there was little chance that it could be Torin— perhaps she had only seen what she wanted to see. Still, she wanted to see the image again. Her hands moved along his jaw as she looked deep into his eyes.

"What is it you need?" His voice slid over her like a warm bath.

Her heart all but stopped as she pushed up on her toes and pressed her lips to his. Tentative, she tasted him, taking the edge of his lip between her teeth. A quiet sound from deep in his chest flowed from him as he sought her mouth. Just as she had suspected, his kiss was strong, demanding. He held nothing back.

A flood of images inundated her mind as his emotions broke free. She held her palms firmly to his temples, accepting the ferocity of his mouth. The image, clearer this time, of a small boy tucked inside a log, burst like a brilliant light in her head. Near the boy stood a silver wolf, its gaze resting steadily on her. The boy looked up, and there was no mistaking his coal-colored eyes.

She dropped her hands and the vision vanished as quickly as it had appeared. Her eyes held the Roman's questioning look. She looked at her trembling hands and fisted them.

"What is it?" he asked. "What did you see?"

Sierra shook her head. This was strange. Guilt riddled her, as it had not in many years. Guilt that she had not done enough to protect her brother. So much fear surrounded the image. Was her brother alive or dead? What connection did he have to this Roman stranger? "I cannot talk about this right now." She waved her hand in dismissal.

"Are we going to help each other?" he insisted.

Sierra drew in a deep, shaky breath. She stared at him, weighing his words. Maybe it was time to take back the life that had been stolen from her. It was either that or wait for death from one of Lord Aeglech's tirades.

"You must let me decide the moment of our escape." Sierra's mind raced on.

"Agreed. Will I be given a weapon?"

"No," she responded, considering all the things that could go wrong with this idea.

There was a stretch of silence.

"Your plan is to free me before my execution to fight the guards, then?"

She nodded. "Free you, yes. Fight…maybe, if necessary."

"You *do* realize the danger involved," he said.

"Roman, your only other option is the noose."

"Put that way, I am yours. Whatever the fates may bring," he replied.

"And you are not afraid?"

He gave her a puzzled look. "Fear is a man's undoing. You cannot fear."

Sierra heard the words from his lips, but her mother's words echoed in the stillness at the back of her brain. Perhaps it was a good omen.

★ ★ ★

Sierra awoke with a start, sitting upright in her bed. The images of the Roman with the woman had plagued her sleep, only this time, *she* had been in the woman's place. She swallowed against the dryness in her throat and, though it was pitch black, quickly pulled up the covers, aware the Roman was there, chained to her wall.

"You could not sleep, either?" His voice carried through the darkness.

"Dreams," she responded, dragging her hands through her short hair.

"I have them about my family," he spoke quietly.

"What about the Celt woman?" Sierra blurted. "Was she your wife?"

"No, Cendra was not my wife. So you did see something."

"My sight is not well trained, but it has kept me alive. The king relies heavily on the ancient ways to help him." She hesitated, then asked, "Did you love her?"

"There was not enough time to find out," he said quietly.

Restless from her dream, Sierra swung her legs over the side of the bed and walked boldly up to him.

"So it was the sex you enjoyed with her? She was your wench?"

"Enjoy? Yes, I suppose that's true." Sorrow tinged his voice. "But she possessed many other things that I liked. Things I would like to have had the chance to know more about. Why do you ask?"

She reached out and touched the hard planes of his chest. Taking his silence for approval, she stepped closer and splayed her hands over his firm buttocks. She squeezed the hard muscle, smiling as his breath caught. She slid her hand between their bodies, finding his firm member, and stroked him gently, kissing his wounds.

"I have already given you the information you sought," he said softly.

"Did you find pleasure with that woman? Cendra?" Sierra spoke, touching herself with one hand as she caressed him with the other.

"What are you doing?" he said, his voice strained with arousal.

"I want to give you pleasure," she whispered. She tugged his breeches down his hips and took his smooth cock in her palm. She rubbed her thumb over its tip. "I enjoy sex, Roman. It makes me forget."

His breathing was heavy as she took him in her mouth, coaxing him with her hand.

"Is this how Aeglech uses you, to seduce a man's confession?"

She rocked back on her heels abruptly. "It was obviously not needed on you, Roman." She stood, searching for her gown. His words had stung her pride and that had never happened before.

"Wait, I meant no insult."

Sierra gave a short laugh. "None taken, I assure you."

"And does he appease you?" he asked.

She faced him in the darkness. "I have never given myself to him." Sierra did not like this path of questions. They made her sound like a common whore.

"I am glad to hear that," he responded.

"Why would you be glad?"

"Because I think that you are a remarkable woman, and here against your will. And if you will let me, I can help you."

She forgot about the gown as she reached for his face. He drew her fingers into the warmth of his mouth. She trailed her hand over his chest, careful of the raised welts. "I did not want to use the skelp on you." She placed a soft kiss on the place where his heart beat strong. His cock brushed against her thigh, causing her to grow wet with need.

She touched his lips, craving the taste of his mouth. "I do not want to hurt you again." He captured her mouth in a deep, thorough kiss. She held his face to hers as she took her fill of his strength.

"I want you," she spoke, sampling his lips. Never before had the intimacy of kissing given her as much satisfaction as the act of sex alone.

"Put your arms around my neck," he whispered against her cheek.

"What about your wounds?" she asked, trailing her fingers lightly over his flesh.

"Your touch makes me forget my pain."

Sierra brushed her fingers over his lips. "It is the same for me." She held his shoulder, angling herself over him. Face-to-face, their mouths fused, as he slipped into her with ease.

"Am I hurting you?" she whispered against his chest as their bodies fell into a blissful rhythm.

"The pain is worth the pleasure." He drew a raspy breath.

Lost in the intimate dance of their bodies, Sierra had a sense that this was different from what she had experienced with other men. Perhaps her attraction to him made her want to believe it was more. Whatever it was, it caused a stirring deep inside her, a desire to explore the depths of him. He exuded strength in every way and yet did not act as if he needed to prove it.

She moved with him, her hands clasped around his neck, breasts pressed flat against his solid chest, their hips rocking slowly and steadily. His forehead dropped to her shoulder, his warm breath wafting over her as he left intermittent kisses on her flesh. He lifted his head suddenly and captured her mouth, his groan mingling with her sighs as he drove harder into her, urging her to completion. She wanted him to feel about her the way he spoke about the Celt woman. She wanted to believe that her life could be different, that she could have a future. His body broke free as he clamped his mouth down hard on hers to stifle his groan. Sierra laid her face against his chest, caught up in wave after wave rolling through her.

And then he stilled.

The reality of who she was descended on her. How could she believe that a man like him could find her of the same caliber as the Celt woman he had obvious feelings for? She slid off his body and pulled up his breeches.

"What is your name?" he asked quietly.

"Is it important?" she asked, slipping her gown over her head. There was no need for him to pretend he cared. She had already made up her mind to help him for her own reasons, and she shoved away the possibility that he could care for her.

"It is if we are to work together."

Sierra thought for a moment and relinquished. "It is Sierra."

A moment of silence followed before he spoke. "Sierra. It is a beautiful name."

"And I suggest that you forget it for now, for if you should slip and use it, our partnership will end. In fact, it is better if you do not address me at all in any manner that seems familiar. For appearances' sake, regard me only as your captor. It will be safer for both of us if you do."

"Why did Balrogan call you 'Mouse'?" the Roman asked quietly.

Sierra shrugged as she crawled back into her bed. "It is a name he gave me long ago. The same as you would give a dog or a horse."

They spoke no more after that, and Sierra lay awake for hours thinking about what had happened, thinking of how her life was about to change, provided their escape was successful. Somewhere deep inside, she knew the Roman would do everything possible to keep his word to her. She only hoped she could do her part and convince Lord Aeglech of their plan. Summoning her courage, she tiptoed to the chamber door and tapped on it gently.

"I have to see Lord Aeglech," she said to the guard positioned outside.

The door opened and she stepped into the corridor, casting a backward glance at the sleeping Roman as she did so. All she could do now was hope that the Saxon king believed she was telling him the truth.

Sierra found the king seated alone in the great hall. He sat upon his throne with one leg perched on the arm, his goblet in hand. She knew he had been drinking away his troubles. He did that more and more these days. His gaze turned to her as she entered the room.

"You bring me information?" He took a sloppy sip from his cup, not caring that the dark wine spilled, leaving a deep red trail down his bare chest.

Sierra knelt. "Aye, milord."

He straightened, his attention focused on her. What she was about to do would set in motion events that she could not go back and change. Sierra hesitated. There was the risk she could die, a chance that something would go wrong.

"Out with it! Did he disclose the location of the rebel camp?" His words slurred.

"He mentioned a castle ruin not far from here in the low hills, just before a mountain range."

His eyes narrowed. "Castle ruins, you are certain of this?"

"Aye, milord," Sierra replied.

"Is that not what you told me in your vision?"

"Aye, milord." She did not know what it meant any more now than before, but there was no doubt that it was the same castle tower.

He nodded. "You have done well." He eased back, looking content, exactly as Sierra had hoped. "Where is Balrogan? I want to inform him that we have a hanging later today."

"I do not know, milord. I spoke with him last night. I have not seen him since." Sierra feared Balrogan was with his lover, and worse, that Aeglech would find him. "Shall I go see if I can fetch him for you, milord?"

He shook his head in dismissal. "No, there is time enough to speak to him later." His eyes came back to hers. "I was impressed by your skill with the skelp. Was it enough to gain the information we needed?"

Sierra knew what he meant, but it was best he think she'd had no relations with the prisoner. "It was the fear of your visit, milord. Your way with the skelp exceeded my efforts and Balrogan's, milord."

He studied her.

"I promised you a reward. What would you like? More gowns, more furnishings?"

"I would like permission to escort the Roman to the gallows, milord."

His laughter bounced off the walls of the large room.

"So be it, *wealh*. You shall be given guarded freedom to ride to the gallows. Is there anything else?" He searched her face.

Sierra swallowed and shook her head. "That is most generous, milord. More than I deserve."

"Your loyalty is gratifying. I like to think if I had known any of my daughters, they would be like you. Back to bed, you have a big day ahead of you."

Sierra hurried to her room and huddled beneath the covers. Aeglech had no idea how true were his words. She looked up at the moon shining through her small window. She was about to trust her life to another person, something she had not done since she was a child.

"I swear, as long as I have a breath in my body, no harm shall come to you, if you help me in this." His words came back to her and Sierra made him a silent promise of the same.

Chapter Ten

"Good news, Roman! You are to be hanged today!"

Dryston pried open one eye and squinted at the seductress before him. She wore again that gold gown, covering the lithe, limber body that had been wrapped around him a few hours ago.

Or had that been a dream?

She turned to rekindle the fire, as expert at producing flame within the hearth as in his body. She did not mention what had passed between them in the middle of the night.

"I must find Balrogan and tell him the news. I will return with food and water." She knocked on the door, summoning the guard.

"You need not be quite so elated," he muttered.

She offered him a quick, empty smile telling him that if the passion between them had not been a dream, it certainly had not stayed with her as it had with him. He considered that even if they were able to escape, the way would be treacherous.

There would be Aeglech's men to contend with, as well as mountainous terrain, and wild animals. But all of that paled in comparison to the treachery she had pulled last night, if indeed it was all part of Aeglech's scheme. Physical torture was one thing, emotional torture, as he knew well, was quite another. Her kindness, her seduction, even the ease with which he was able to suggest an escape—it could all be an elaborate trap designed to lead the Saxons straight to the Roman camp. Despite her gentle hands tending to his wounds, she had an un-controlled violent streak in her that he would have to be watchful of.

As he waited for Sierra's return, Dryston drifted in and out of sleep, his body aching from his wounds and exhausted by her passion. And he remembered the winter's day that changed his life, and the life of his family, forever....

Dryston's mother and sisters had been seated by the fire, busy with their needlework. His father, too, sat near the fire, tending to his whittling.

Dryston had decided that today he was going to go hunting, hoping to bring home a rabbit for his mother's stew. When he asked his mother for permission, she glanced at his father, silently asking if it was wise. His two older sisters giggled. They were always mocking his attempts at being a man.

"Ye best watch out for the goblins, Dryston. They like to steal pretty young lads such as you." They enjoyed making life hard for him, their little brother. Dryston looked from his mother to his father.

His father nodded.

"Girls, dinna tease yer brother so," his mother said with a smile, knowing that his sisters loved him too much.

They looked at each other and smiled, then went back to their work.

Dryston's father caught his eye, and gave him a wink.

Outside, the wind howled and though there was little snow in the valley, when he reached the foothills to the mountain, the snow reached his knees.

He tied his horse to a tree and proceeded up the rocky footpath, careful to watch for wild animals. The long, lonely howl of a wolf brought him to a standstill and he waited, listening to the direction of its sound. He knew it was not smart to sit and wait, as wolves traveled in packs. Dryston trudged on, his eyes moving over the winter landscape. A sound from behind halted his steps. His heart pounded as he turned to face the largest wolf he had ever seen. Its thick silvery coat brought out the icy-gray color of its eyes.

Motionless, he tightened his grasp on his sword, prepared for the wolf to charge. Instead, the animal looked at him, then quickly turned tail and headed deeper into the wood.

Both blessed and cursed, as his mother would say, by a curious nature and a taste for adventure, Dryston followed on the wolf's heels, running as fast as the weight of his sword would permit.

He stopped for a moment and rested his hand against a tree, breathing hard. Puffs of his frozen breath punched the cold air. His eyes were cold and numb from squinting into the bitter mountain wind as he ran. Dryston blinked to warm them and realized he did not know where he was.

Tall pines stretched around him as far as his eyes could see. Before him lay a small lake, nearly frozen except for a trickle of water spilling from high over a cliff. He glanced down and, seeing the wolf's prints clearly in the new snow, he followed cautiously, unsure why he felt compelled to take such a risk.

But something about her eyes, the way she'd looked at him, urged him to follow.

The pines absorbed the sounds of the wood. Except for his breathing and the crunch of snow beneath his feet, all was again silent.

The hair on the back of his neck bristled and he turned slowly to find her there, atop a fallen log, not more than a good leap away. She studied him as if waiting for him to make her kill a challenge. He did not know how long they stood there. Dryston wondered if the rest of her pack would show soon. The wolf, looking at him with eyes that seemed almost human, appeared to be assessing him.

She raised her black snout into the air and gave a plaintive howl.

Dryston drew his sword from its sheath, determined that he was not going to be an easy supper for the wolf. To his relief, the animal ducked her head and ran off into the wood.

He looked down, seeing his breeches covered with his own piss. Swallowing with relief that today was not the day he was to meet his maker, Dryston's ears perked to a very faint sound. At first he thought it was only his imagination, but then it came again, a small and pitiful whimper. Not of an animal, but of a human.

Dryston readied his sword as his father had taught him. He moved toward the sound cautiously. His overactive imagination taunted his mind with all manner of things that could make the sound. All the stories that his older sisters had told him of the goblins and fae folk that lived in the woods and stole small children came rushing at him.

Taking a deep breath, Dryston knelt in the snow and peered into the end of a log. As a pair of dark eyes rolled up from a pale blue face, Dryston leaped back, stumbling backward in the snow.

Summoning his courage, Dryston stuck his hand into the

log, grasping an appendage—an arm or leg, he could not discern—and tugged as hard as he could. No goblin or faerie, he thought as he looked at the bluish pasty-colored flesh. No, it was a human child, a small boy with a head of dark hair frosted to his skull and small fingers curled stiff from trying to keep warm. He wore clothes unfit for the weather, and his lips were as purple as twilight.

Dryston had no way of knowing how long the child had been outside. "How did you get here? What is your name?" He shrugged out of his coat and tucked it around the boy.

· "Can you speak?" Dryston asked.

The boy, barely able to keep his eyes open, said nothing.

Dryston followed his footsteps back to the lake, carrying the small boy over his shoulder like a sack of grain. By good fortune, his tracks led him back to his horse.

Back at his house, his mother and sisters assumed care of the boy, seating him first by the fire to warm him, checking to see that his hands and fingers were not frostbit, before they immersed him in a tub of warm water. Still, he did not speak. Days later, after he had slept for many hours at a time, awakening only to eat small bits of food, he still had not spoken.

Dryston's father said it was the trauma of being in the cold that prevented his ability to speak. His mother, a woman who kept her Celtic beliefs quiet around his Roman father, felt sure that his trauma was deeper still.

He shared his pallet with the boy and at night he would awaken to the boy tossing and turning in his sleep, arms flailing, mouth open in a silent scream.

In the months that followed, the boy grew strong physically, but the horrors of whatever happened to him held his voice captive and who he was a mystery.

Dryston's mother believed the gods had led him to the boy that day. That it was the wolf that had led him to the log, that it was Dryston's destiny to find him. He took the boy under his wing, his silent, constant companion, and together they came up with their own form of communicating with each other. It was many years before Dryston finally heard his brother.

The sound of the lock turning in the dungeon door brought Dryston out of his dreamlike state. Sierra swept into the room, wringing her hands with frantic worry.

"What is it?" he asked.

She darted him a look as if debating whether to speak, tell him, whether to trust him. She paced the floor, twisting a small wristlet—the kind his sisters used to make with flowers—in her hand. "Something has happened."

"What?" he urged, fearing that Aeglech was not fully convinced.

"Is everything still going according to our plan?"

She averted her eyes as she continued to pace.

"You remember that we agreed to help each other?"

"Of course I remember. I am thinking." She looked back at the door. "Give me a moment."

Dryston bit back the urge to remind her he was to be hanged and they did not have much time. Then another more disturbing thought crossed his mind. Surely, this was not part of a ruse? She would not think of letting him sway on the gallows as she quietly sneaked away?

She stuffed the wristlet in her pocket and stepped toward him, covering his mouth with her hand.

"I cannot find Master Balrogan," she whispered.

This obviously meant something was not right. Dryston turned his head so he could speak. "And this is not good?"

"No, it is much worse," she whispered. "The guard whom he was close with was killed sometime during the night. His body thrown into the hole, swept out to sea."

"And you think that Balrogan did this?" He was confused why she should care.

"Nay." She worried her lip. "Only by the king's orders would he do such a thing."

"Then perhaps it was an accident?" It was clear she was distraught by the event, though Dryston could not understand why.

Sierra looked at him. "He was his lover," she spoke quietly.

"I can see how that might not please the king. Do you think Balrogan has run off, then?"

Sierra wrung her hands. "No, he would not be so foolish. Lord Aeglech would hunt him down." She shook her head slowly. "No, I fear the fates have more to show us and not all of it will be pleasing."

"Why do you say this?"

"I cannot explain just now and it would not change anything. We must focus on our escape." She held his gaze. "Are you still prepared to help me once we are free?"

"Of course, I gave you my word."

"I suppose that will have to do." She turned away and began to gather a few things in a small satchel. "Flints for fire." She held them up so he could see. She grabbed an apple and a small hunk of stale bread from that morning, stuffing them in the bag.

"Lord Aeglech insists the hanging go as planned." She spoke in hushed tones so the guard outside the door would not hear. Scowling, she searched the room, her short hair standing up in all directions as she pulled a pair of hosen from beneath her bed and added them to the bag. Her eyes caught Dryston's, and for a moment, the expression on her face reminded him of someone familiar.

"The king is allowing me to escort you with the guards to the gallows."

"So he believed you about the ruins?"

"Aye. He did not question it."

"Not even a little?"

She stepped up to him and studied him a moment, as if deciding whether to tell him something. "He believed me, because I saw a vision of him at the ruins when I laid my hands on him."

"You laid hands on him this morning?" Dryston asked.

"I do not have to answer that. Do not get in your head that what happened between us meant anything."

Dryston stared at her. The wall she had built to protect herself was strong. But he had never backed down from a challenge in his entire life. And this woman imposed a challenge from the first moment she'd laid her hands on him. He had to find out more about her and he knew it would not be an easy task.

"Nothing other than it was most pleasurable," he lied. He could still feel her soft body curled against his.

"Good. We do not have to like each other. Our agreement was to help one another."

"Agreed," he conceded for now. "And since you did not ask for my name, it is Dryston." His gaze narrowed as he waited for her response. Her face gave no impression that she heard him.

"You will wait for my signal. Do not try anything before that or I cannot guarantee that you will live. Do you understand?"

Did he have a choice? Dryston nodded. He had little feeling left in his arms. His legs were weary from standing. He longed to stretch out on the ground and ease the ache in his body. Preferably alive. "I will watch for your signal."

"Do you trust me?" she asked, stepping close enough that he could have kissed her had he dared to follow through with the thought.

"Not as far as I can throw you. And pray, then, how do you feel about me?"

"The same," she responded, placing the bag over her shoulder. "I guess we are more alike than we thought. They will be coming soon to prepare you."

"More lashes?" Dryston tossed back.

"Nay, you are to receive a trial."

"For what purpose? Is there any hope that Aeglech will set me free?" he asked, leery of this development. In his days on the battlefield, he had seen fate turn its fickle head at the last moment—sometimes for the better, sometimes for the worse.

"Nay, it is only to give the king the pleasure of pronouncing in front of a crowd your sentence to die."

"Where are you going?" Dryston watched as she tucked a small homemade knife beneath a band tied to her thigh. His gaze rested on her pale flesh.

"Cearl has chosen a special horse for this occasion. I want to thank him," she stated, rapping once to gain the guard's attention. He swung open the heavy door and glanced at Dryston, giving him a sneer.

"Enjoy the next few hours, Roman," Sierra spoke over her shoulder as she left. "They will be your last." The door closed behind her.

He could hope the comment was made for the guard's benefit.

★ ★ ★

Dryston glanced at Sierra riding beside him. Her eyes faced forward, shoulders back. She had barely looked at him since they left the fortress. He hoped that, too, was part of the plan. The day was brisk, proof that winter was approaching. The late afternoon sun hovered over the mountains on the distant horizon.

Dryston counted the days since his capture—seven, if his memory served him well. By now, Torin would have sent the women and children to the mountain caves for safety. He would be preparing his band of common warriors to travel to the spot near the castle ruins where they were to meet General Ambrosis before marching on to Aeglech's fortress. So many lives rested on the success of their plan, and now that they had changed course, it was vital that he get back in time to let Torin know that Aeglech was coming to them, instead. If the escape went as planned, Dryston ought to reach Torin in time, especially if Aeglech decided to come after Sierra, instead of marching directly to the castle ruins. But would the Saxon king believe that Sierra had been kidnapped? Sierra thought he would, and that was the only assurance he had for now. It was a risk, this wobbly plan of theirs, but the alternative was certain and permanent. They had to try.

There was not a great crowd as Dryston had expected. Only a lone farmer with his hay wagon, who barely gave them a glance on the road to the gallows. Dryston glanced at his hands, bound at the wrists. Sierra had been given the honor of holding the other end of the rope as they rode. To his left, the earth gave way to a steep, forested cliff leading to the sea below. To the right, the mountain rose straight up, leaving barely enough room for two riders side by side. It occurred to Dryston that with one yank of the rope, she could send him plunging to his death on the rocks below.

"Where should we send word of your death, Roman?" she asked, staring straight ahead.

She was playing her part well. He answered her, hoping it was part of the plan. "Send it to my brother," he responded. "He is all that remains of my family after the Saxons murdered the rest."

"And your mother told me it was the best she had ever had," one of the guards growled from behind him, causing the others to erupt in laughter.

Dryston's anger seethed as he looked at Sierra and caught her brief glance. She continued, ignoring the guards.

"And what would be your brother's name?" she asked as they emerged from the narrow path onto level ground. The guards from behind galloped around them, one of them smacking Dryston on the back with a battle-ax handle, nearly knocking him off his horse.

Whatever relief Dryston had after leaving the steep cliff behind dissipated as he caught sight of a large man hanging from the gallows.

"Torin," he replied to Sierra's question, but she had leaned forward on her horse and was focusing all her attention on the body. A look of shock registered on her face and she turned to Dryston.

"It's Balrogan," she stated quietly.

The lead guard rode back to her, his face set with a stoic expression. "By orders of the king, it is my duty to inform you that you are now the master executioner of the Lord Aeglech, king of Britannia."

The rope fell slack in Sierra's hand as she looked back at Balrogan's body, twisting and turning from the crossbeam.

"I will ready the prisoner," the guard stated and took the rope from her hand.

Dryston attempted to gain Sierra's attention as they rode past her, but her eyes were still riveted on her former master's body.

The guards from behind were already seeing to the task of removing the body, to prepare the platform for Dryston. At last, Sierra came to life and nudged her horse forward in a gallop, riding up alongside them. "What was Balrogan's crime?"

The guard holding Dryston's rope dismounted and tossed the rope to a guard he remembered as one of those who had captured him. He waited for her signal, but her focus was on finding out about Balrogan.

"The king did not give me details. He was hanged earlier today. I was instructed to inform you of your new duty."

"And so you have," she stated flatly as if she suddenly had found both her tongue and her brain. Her horse neighed and reared up on its hind legs as they placed the noose over Dryston's head.

"Give me his sword, guard. I want to disembowel this Roman before we hang him."

Was it possible he had mistaken their agreement to help each other?

Chapter Eleven

The captain of the guard, who had dismounted, looked for a moment impressed with Sierra's request. Without a word, he drew his sword from his sheath and handed it up to her.

Dryston did not look as impressed as they wrestled him from his horse.

The sword was heavier than Sierra had thought and it slipped from her hand. The guard caught it and handed it to her a second time.

"Are you certain you can handle a blade of that size? Perhaps you would be better off using something smaller?" the guard asked, prodding Dryston up the stairs to the platform.

"Small does not work for me, Captain." She tucked the sword across her lap, giving him a pointed look.

The guard waiting on the platform chuckled.

"Bring him over here," Sierra ordered, raising her voice. She tamped down the fear threatening to weaken her resolve. This was her only chance for escape, and she had to make it work.

"I have to take a piss," the captain called to her.

"Be quick about it, Captain, you have a job to do," she tossed over her shoulder as she followed on horseback Dryston and his guard walking up the platform.

She caught Dryston looking at her, watching for her to give him a signal. Beyond the gallows, she watched the other two guards dragging Balrogan's body toward the cliff. She thought of how he had lived his life and how it had ended so brutally. Perhaps fate demanded recompense for all the lives he'd taken. Sierra wondered if she would meet a similar fate one day— hopefully not this soon.

She swallowed hard as she glanced at the captain who had his back to her. "The captain requests that you go to him," Sierra barked to the guard on the platform with Dryston. "I will see to the prisoner until you return."

The guard looked over his shoulder at his captain. "I did not hear his order."

"Fine, do not go." She shrugged. "It is not my head, although odds are it will be me who delights in taking yours when Aeglech sentences you to die for insubordination."

He scowled at her as he tossed her the rope and tramped down the stairs.

"'Tis now or never, Roman, make it look real," she stated quietly, as she maneuvered her horse close to the platform.

Her gaze riveted to the guard approaching the captain and the other two guards returning from the cliff. They did not have much time. "Now," she whispered through clenched teeth. Her heart beat fiercely in her chest and sweat trickled between her breasts.

The Roman shouted as he leaped onto the back of the horse. Sierra lurched forward and her stomach pressed against the blade in her lap. Caught off guard by an instant pain that shot through her mid-section, she glanced down, to try to see how badly she was wounded.

With his wrists still tied together, Dryston managed to wrestle the blade from her lap and smash the face of an advancing guard with the butt of the sword. Holding one hand to his bloodied nose, the guard grabbed the sword as he stumbled back into the arms of the captain.

Dryston's arms looped over Sierra's head, pulling her close to his chest as his feet prodded the sides of the horse. Sierra held on to the horse's mane as they flew across the field, the king's guards in pursuit on foot.

"Stop, in the name of the king!" She heard the captain's angry shout. She looked over her shoulder and saw them scrambling to get to their horses.

"I should have scattered their horses," she spoke aloud.

"A fine idea, but not one that will do us much good now. We need to put distance and cover between us as quickly as we can."

"I am aware of that!" Sierra shouted. "Which way to your camp?" She pushed his arms lower around her waist so she could assume better control of the horse. His fisted hands jabbed against her wound with every bounce of the horse's gait. Sierra glanced down, saw a thin red line spreading through the fabric of her gown and hoped it was not too deep.

"We will head toward the sun, west into the forest. Do you want me to lead?" Dryston asked.

"You hang on. The way down this mountain is apt to kill a man. You should keep your focus on staying astride the horse."

"And do you trust me not to toss you over the side and leave you here?" he said over her shoulder. "That way they would truly think I used you to escape."

"Trust was not part of our agreement." She pulled her short blade from its sheath on her thigh. "But now that we have escaped, I can assure you that if you have any notions of not fulfilling your part of this agreement, it will be your body that is tossed aside."

His laugh rumbled against her body. In light of their circumstances, a smile tugged at the corner of her mouth.

"Put away your blade, Sierra. You have no need to use it on me. I owe you my life, and just as you made good your oath to me, I, too, will return the favor."

The thunder of hooves roared behind them as they rode deeper into the woods. The tall pines blocked the waning daylight. Their horse whinnied, as the hill began to grow steep. He pranced uncertainly, in spite of Sierra's persistent attempts to move him forward.

"Perhaps I have more experience with horses," the Roman offered.

She glared at him. "Did I not just save you?"

He checked over his shoulder. "Not quite yet."

"Be quiet and let me concentrate on getting us out of here alive," Sierra commanded as she prodded the stubborn horse.

"I do not wish to interfere with that," he remarked. "But I would advise you to get the steed to move along—those guards do not look happy."

After nudging the horse again and patting its neck, the animal stepped reluctantly forward, picking his way cautiously down the wooded hill.

Above them, Sierra heard the captain order the guards to go around and cut them off at the base of the hill. "What now?" she said aloud. The severe angle of the hill pushed her accomplice's crotch relentlessly against her backside, causing her to think of the night before. She scolded herself for having such lusty thoughts at a time when their lives were in such danger. She would do well to remind herself that he likely had not given a single thought to what had happened between them. It had been dark, and she had needs, as did he. That's all there had been to it.

"Do not go to the base of the mountain. Turn the horse about," he ordered calmly.

"Are you daft?" She craned her neck to look back at him. "We seal our fate if we return."

"No," he stated simply. "We will head the other direction and make our way around."

This time he did not ask her permission, when he took the reins in his bound hands and led the horse straight across the steep hill.

"You may have noticed the ground here is soft and unstable?" Sierra asked, gripping the horse's mane.

"There you go," Dryston coaxed the horse, ignoring her. "Get us out of here and I will find you all the apples you can eat."

The hairs on the back of Sierra's neck bristled with his warm breath each time he spoke. Wanting to focus her mind on anything else, she glanced down to check her wound.

"How is it?" he asked her.

"It is nothing, just a flesh wound."

His balance shifted as he tried to see over her shoulder, causing the horse to falter.

"Pay it no mind—or it will not matter if we are dead," she snapped. She did not need anyone to take care of her. She had been doing that on her own for years.

"May I remind you that you are still my prisoner until we reach your camp." She decided that he needed to know that she was keeping her eye on him.

"And here I thought I was a free man," he muttered.

"Do not mock me, Roman."

There was silence as they both watched for the places where the soft earth gave way to the rocky hillside below. One misstep and they would plunge to certain death.

"I have been told that I am a patient man," Dryston stated. "I have been tortured, lost part of a finger and endured a whipping at *your* hand. What more, pray tell me, do I have to do to find favor with you?"

"Which of those did you enjoy most?" she tossed back.

"You know, you remind me of my brother. He, too, has an annoying wit."

They rode in silence and Sierra lost track of how long they had been traveling, until she realized she could no longer hear Saxon voices in the distance.

"You have no need to win my favor," Sierra spoke finally. "We are not on this journey as friends. I trust no one but myself. You would be wise to do the same."

A soft breeze wafted across her face. Sierra tipped her head and listened close, hearing the sound of rushing water.

"The falls," he spoke as if answering her thoughts. "These woods are full of them."

"How is it that you know so much about these woods?" she asked.

He gave no response to her question. Instead, he pointed a finger over her shoulder. "Over there—we will have to climb up to get back to where we want to be."

They emerged into a small clearing. A short distance from where they sat, the earth gave way to the roar of the falls. Sierra edged the horse closer to the ledge and peered over the side. Water rushed over the rocks, cascading down into a billowy mist that rose like a giant white spirit, hovering over the lush green, gold and copper leaves of the trees surrounding the falls.

"This is the way to your camp?"

"A roundabout way, but yes, we should make good time if we have no further distractions." Dryston pulled the reins, turning the horse away from the precarious ledge. "That looks like a good place to make our climb."

Sierra stared up at the moss-covered mountain wall behind them. It was at least thirty to forty hands high. He was right, the spot he'd picked had several places to use as footholds. As his eyes scanned the rock, her memory was jostled by the sound of her brother's voice calling her to hurry.

"Come on, Sierra. 'Tis a shortcut back home. I'll race ya." Torin's small boy grin challenged her as he scurried up the side of the hill.

"Be careful, Torin. The rocks could be slippery!" she called after him, watching as he climbed with the dexterity of a squirrel.

"You can catch me if I fall, Sierra," he called over his shoulder. *"Do not fret, I'll be fine."*

"I'll be fine," Sierra muttered, the memory fading against the roar of the falls. Dryston tapped her shoulder.

"We should get started. We do not want to be on the ledge after dark." He lifted his bound hands over her head and slid off the back of the horse. Sierra lifted her leg over the horse's back, catching her breath as her stomach rubbed against the animal's side.

"You are hurt." He stepped forward and gently touched the tear in her gown. "Let me take a look."

She shook her head and moved so the horse stood between them.

Dryston sighed. "It is not as if I have not seen you."

"But you have not," she retorted. "I am fine. Just as I said."

She passed off his mention of the night before. "Shall we get rid of that noose?"

He gave her a puzzled look, then glanced down at the rope trailing behind him.

"Bloody—I could have hung myself. You might have said something before now!"

"I was a bit preoccupied with Saxon guards," Sierra responded. With his hands yet bound, he wrestled with the rope, drawing it over his head and dropping it as if it were a snake.

She reached for the rope and his boot came down beside her hand. Instinct caused her to grab her blade. She rose slowly, meeting his steady gaze.

"About this business of being your prisoner," he spoke quietly.

He challenged her in many ways, but as she stared into his eyes, she knew how easily she could get lost in them. She had to stay in control. If she relented now, how much liberty would he take with his freedom?

"We may need the rope for the climb," she told him. He relented, and moved his foot.

Sierra coiled the rope over her shoulder and removed the horse's saddle. With a single heave, she tossed it over the cliff, sending it into the misty roar of the falls.

"What in the name of heaven are you doing?"

She tossed him a look. "I do not do it in the name of your heaven, Roman. But in answer to your question, I doubt very much that our horse will be able to climb any farther," she responded calmly. He looked at her as if she had sprouted two heads.

"Do you realize how far it is on foot?" he asked.

"Nay, only that you said it was not very far. Unless you lied to me, in which case I will be forced to kill you now." She slapped the animal on its hind end and it darted off through the woods.

"On horseback! You have just added more time to our journey. Time that we do not have. And that is provided the Saxons do not catch us first."

Sierra tried to reason with him. "Nor will they expect us to be on foot, will they? We can cut across land where their horses cannot go."

He stared at her a moment as if unable to argue that point. "The light is waning. We need to climb while we can."

Sierra nodded. She glanced up at the rocky crag they would need to climb as she twirled her short blade in her hand. Her gown was going to prove too dangerous for climbing. She would have to eliminate some of the fabric. Grabbing her gown, she stabbed her knife through the cloth and proceeded to tear away the fabric until the gown hung just above her knees.

Her eyes rose to Dryston's, quietly watching her. She finished and tossed the fabric remnant into her satchel, her gaze straying back to Dryston's. The look she saw in his eyes made her weak, and she could not afford to be. "Do not look at me like that," she said.

"Like what?" he replied, holding out his hands, still secured at the wrists. "If you will kindly cut these, we can be on our way."

"I am afraid I cannot do that."

"Are you daft, woman? How do you expect me to climb without the use of my hands?" He walked away for a moment and turned to face her with frustration etched on her face. "This is absurd. Untie me this minute."

"Trust me." She took the rope from his noose and drew it around him, tying it off at the waist, then tied it around her own middle. Secured to him now, she started to climb.

"When do you suppose that I will earn your trust?" he asked, still on the ground below her.

"When we reach your camp," she stated simply.

"You are a stubborn woman," he called up to her. "You realize that if one of us falls, we both will die."

Sierra realized that indeed; it was one of the reasons she chose this way. If he chose to take her over the side, then it was his certain fate to follow. "That is why I am ahead of you," she replied and looked down at him. His mouth curled into a grin as his gaze went to her exposed legs.

"This may not be such a bad idea."

"Keep your focus on the climb," she warned. Sierra tugged on the rope, making sure it was tight. She glanced at the last rays of sunlight casting red and orange fingers across the evening sky. Hand over hand, careful with her footing, she moved up the rock wall.

She should have let him go first.

It did not bother her that Dryston was getting an eyeful view as he followed behind her. What bothered her was that she was absurdly aroused by it.

The piece of rock gave way, and she scrambled for a foothold, positioning her legs wide apart.

"Everything looks good from down here," Dryston called up to her. "Still, as much as I am enjoying the breathtaking view, would it not be wise to admit you were wrong, untie me, and allow us to get up this mountainside before dark?"

Sheer determination propelled Sierra to a flat ledge roughly halfway to the top of the cliff. She glanced down and was overcome by the precariousness of her situation.

"Are you ready to untie me yet?" he called up to her.

The deepening shadows were making it more difficult for

Sierra to see what she was doing. One slip and they would both meet certain death on the craggy rocks below. For the sake of both of them, she was wiser to allow him to lead the way. She reached down and took his hand, helping him scramble up on the narrow ledge beside her.

She quickly sawed through his binding. "Do not try anything unwise. I know the place on a man's heel that renders him helpless in a heartbeat."

"Point taken," he muttered and cautiously raised himself to his feet. He navigated his way along the ledge, checking the footholds above before he resumed the climb.

He was at the top in less time than it had taken to untie him.

The rope around her waist jerked and Sierra found herself being hauled up the side of the rock with barely enough time to find a foothold. Dryston sat at the top with his foot braced on a thick, exposed tree root, drawing the rope hand over hand with apparent little effort.

"You do not weigh much," he said as she scampered up the side. She came up over the rim of the cliff and her foot slipped on the edge. The rope jerked once more and she was thrust forward, landing flat atop the Roman.

He smiled.

Sierra pushed herself up. "My thanks," she said, brushing dirt and grass from her clothes. She checked for her seax, but it was not in her leg strap where she kept it. She fell to her knees, patting the ground.

"Looking for this?"

Shite.

"Do not do anything stupid, Roman." She grabbed a large tree branch near her and held it up in case he attacked.

He yanked on the rope, bringing her back to her knees.

"I may be many things, but ungrateful is not one of them. I owe you my life. Perhaps now you will honor me with your trust." He turned the seax in his hand, offering her its handle.

She accepted the knife from him. "I have never known a man I could trust."

He nodded and held out his hand to shake hers. "Then it is your lucky day. You have met me."

She took his hand and shook it. He truly was a man of honor. He had a code that he lived by. It occurred to her suddenly that she did not fully understand him. For her, every day was a matter of surviving, nothing more.

"Ouch!" He tugged at his hand and she realized it was the one with the injured finger. Sierra dropped his hand in haste, a part of her feeling responsible for his injury.

Dryston untied his rope quickly and leaned forward to do the same for her. "We can rest here and get an early start." He drew his tunic over his head and sat on the ground to take off his boots. He stood and stripped off his breeches. He paused for a moment, at the edge of the shallow pool and stretched his arms over his head.

"I have not had a bath in days." He chuckled, glancing at her. "You might have noticed."

Had he smelled of cow dung, it would not have mattered at that moment. She could not take her eyes off his body. She had touched him under the cover of darkness, but seeing him here, in all his glory, Sierra was mesmerized.

She stayed in shadows so she could watch him. His sinewy legs were built like twin oaks, and browned by the sun. Proportioned like the Roman statues at the castle, he was both sleek and powerful. She could not help but gaze admiringly at the prize jutting from between his legs.

And he was without an ounce of modesty.

He dipped his toe in the water and looked over at her, smiling. He took a few steps into the pool, extending his arms out to the sides as the water covered his body. A moment later, he disappeared beneath the surface.

Sierra took in a deep breath, her body coiled tightly between fatigue and desire.

Dryston's head reemerged. "My sisters used to tell me that the pools found near the falls were magical, that they had healing powers. The water would do that flesh wound some good," he called, lifting up his hand to show her his injured finger.

In the twilight, his raven hair clung to his head and neck, exposing his chiseled features.

"Come, the water is still warm."

Sierra could not entertain the thought. Apart from him, she felt in control; next to him, her mind got muddled. "I will start us a fire," she offered instead. She dug into her sack and retrieved the flint. In no time, Sierra had a warm fire going. She purposely kept her eyes from wandering to the pool, and tried not to think about the water gliding like silk over his body.

Her stomach growled and she realized they had not eaten in some time. Earlier, as they rode, they had finished the bread and fed the apple to the horse.

Using the last dredges of light, Sierra wandered into the woods. Among some brush, she found blackberries and raspberries and gathered them in the hem of her now-short gown. Some of the things her mother had taught her about plants and flowers came back to her. She came upon a small patch of mushrooms and marigold root she could use to make a poultice for her wound. She decided that after Dryston fell asleep, she would go in the pool and cleanse the gash. Tomorrow, she would try to find them something more substantial to eat—a rabbit or a woodcock, perhaps.

Dryston was not in the water when she stepped from the woods into the open glen. She cautiously scanned the shadows before going any farther.

She found him stretched out next to the fire, half-naked and fast asleep. He'd used his tunic as a pallet, and his rock-hewn chest rose and fell in rhythm with his steady breathing.

"Dryston?" She spoke loudly enough that it should have jarred him awake. Her gaze traveled to where his breeches lay low on his hips and she remembered how well her body had fit with his. She licked her lips, grateful when her stomach reminded her of its need for food, trumping her desire. Sierra knelt by the pool and washed the berries, then sat against a tree to eat. Her mind wandered, thinking of Cearl and wondering how he was. How different he was in comparison to Dryston. Where Cearl was simpleminded and laughed often, the Roman seemed aware of everything around him—always watching, always thinking.

She noted the welts and bruises where the skelp had eaten at Dryston's flesh. She remembered his cries of pain, real pain, as she reopened wounds that Balrogan had inflicted. She knew that she had done it to impress Aeglech with her skills, to garner his trust so he would believe whatever she told him, but she still felt guilty about it.

A startling realization occurred to her just then. She was no longer a slave. She was free and with this freedom came a sense of loneliness far greater than she'd experienced in the dungeon. There her life had been dictated minute by minute. She knew what was expected, knew what she could and could not do. Out here there were no limits, no rules, no one telling her what to do. And if she was going to survive out here, she was going to have to learn to live like other people, making decisions and living with the outcome of those choices.

Her gaze fell to the slumbering Roman. She remembered the concern in his soft green eyes when he had asked to see her wound. There was a quiet confidence about him and he seemed to fear very little. The firelight flickered on his skin, and she thought about how warm his flesh would be to touch, how he would smell of the fire, the woods and the cool night air.

She looked down at herself, realizing that she, too, had not bathed in days. Moreover, her wound needed to be cleansed and salve applied. Sierra tiptoed over to his sleeping form and watched him for a moment, until she was satisfied that he was sound asleep. Then she went to the bank of the pool and removed her gown. Sounds she had not heard in years called to her, inviting her to join them. Crickets and frogs chirped in the tall grass, and in the distance, the rush of the waterfall lulled the woods to sleep with its steadfast roar.

She stepped to the edge of the water and kicked off her shoes, surprised by the damp, cool grass beneath her feet. Memories of her youth rushed to her mind and she wiggled her toes in the cool, spongy grass. With a quick glance over her shoulder to be sure he was asleep, she reached for the hem of her tunic and drew it over her head. In the light of the moon, she checked the slice across her stomach and found it had stopped bleeding. She ran her finger lightly over the wound. The gash was deep enough that it might leave a scar, but it would heal given time and a well-placed marigold poultice.

With careful steps Sierra tested the bottom of the pool. The moonlight rippled across the water with each movement, and a shiver skated up her spine as she sensed she was being watched.

Sierra scanned the bank, listening for movement, before immersing herself in the pool. The cool water was a welcome balm to her weary body. She took a deep breath, reasoning that it was just her newfound freedom causing her the jitters.

"Whoo-oo." An owl swooped in front of her, skimming the water with its great talons, before soaring up into the night sky. She followed it with her eyes until she could see it no longer. She felt a kinship with the great bird, taking from it the encouragement to explore the feelings she had tucked away when she was not free.

Unlike Dryston, she found it difficult to enjoy life's simple pleasures. The fact that she grappled with how to relax enough to float in water—something she used to do as a child—made her realize how much had been stripped from her. The past nine years had taken their toll. Even now, part of her feared she would awaken again in Aeglech's hell.

Beyond the tall reeds, the firelight flickered, illuminating the darkness. She thought of Dryston asleep, completely relaxed, his grand body shimmering in the fire's glow. The mere thought caused her body to respond and she closed her eyes, aware of the water gently lapping against her breasts.

Sierra took a deep breath and dipped below the surface. In the dark silence, she found a measure of comfort. She raked her fingers through her short hair and bobbed to the surface.

Perhaps Dryston was right. Maybe there was magic in this place. Her senses were alive, her mind aware of the beauty around her. This was a startling change from how she'd been living. By comparison, this place was paradise, and the fact that she was able to notice that was, indeed, a form of magic.

"Is it real, Mother?" she whispered to the stars sprinkled across the velvet night sky. She wondered if her mother heard her and if she was a fool to think it possible.

Possible. The word could change everything. But she was not yet ready. Instead, she released herself to the water's gentle arms and tried not to think at all.

Chapter Twelve

The sound of water splashing awoke Dryston from a much-needed deep sleep. It took him a moment to remember where he was and with whom.

He was pleased that Sierra had gone into the water. Her wound needed to be cleansed. He had heard once that Saxons rubbed the oil of poison fish on their blades. So that if the blade itself did not kill you, the poison would finish the job.

He lay on his back and stared up at the blanket of stars. Damn, it felt good to be free again. For a moment he was reminded of his childhood when he and Torin would go camping in the woods. If they were lucky they'd find a group of maidens bathing in a pond. He realized then that he had not heard Sierra splashing.

He opened his mouth to call out to her when his eyes caught some movement near the bank. From the depths of the dark water, the watery siren emerged, pushing her cap of dark hair back from her face. Lithe and delicate, her pale skin shimmered in the flickering firelight.

She turned her face to the sky and Dryston's eyes followed the gentle slope of her neck and around to the white globes of her breasts. She was a goddess, a flesh-and-blood woman...a Saxon executioner's apprentice, he reminded himself.

Dryston could not tear his eyes from her.

She glanced at him as she bent for her clothes. Dryston held her gaze.

"I see you are awake." She spoke as if she did not realize the effect she had on him. Either that or she was torturing him purposely.

She tugged her gown over her head and plucked at her hair. "Who cut your hair?" he asked as she walked toward him.

If the pool was magical, he did not know, but she looked radiant, even more than she had at the fortress.

"Aeglech," she responded. "He did not think I needed to have any identity, any gender."

She dropped to her knees and lay a few mushrooms before her. Then she took a small, flat stone and proceeded to mash the roots.

"I thought of tying you to the tree so you would not try to leave."

"Do you really think I would?" He watched as she ground at the roots.

She ignored his question. "I am making a poultice. I need to place it on my wound. It should help it heal."

He nodded, noticing she did not answer him. Trust was still an issue.

"What do you want me to do?" he asked, kneeling beside her.

She kept her gaze down as she added mushrooms to the marigold paste.

"There is nothing. For the moment, go ahead and eat." She nodded to a pile of berries atop a bed of autumn leaves. "It's not much, but it's food. Tomorrow we can try to find something more. It will be easier in the light of day."

"I just have two requests."

"What is that?" she asked as she started to tug her gown up over her hips.

Dryston glanced away.

"Surely you are not overwhelmed by the sight of a woman's body?" she asked with a curious smile.

Dryston looked at her. "Perhaps you should lie flat?"

She handed him a stone smeared liberally with the green paste she had created and lay back on the grass. Her eyes watched him as she pulled the gown up over her stomach. "Can you see the length of the wound?" she asked, rising up on her elbows. She winced and flopped back on the ground.

A shallow wound would not cause such pain, he thought. Still, the poultice would help to ward off infection. Dryston tried valiantly to focus on the wound. There was a thin slit in her tender flesh between her navel and the soft triangle of dark curls between her legs. She held her gown high on her torso, her hands placed just below her breasts.

"What is it you wanted?" she asked.

Dryston caked his fingers with the herbal paste and dabbed it on her gash. There was no reason he should be aroused.

But he was.

"What?" Dryston's voice caught and he frowned.

"You said you had two requests."

"Ah, yes."

A soft whimper escaped from her mouth and she arched her back. Dryston closed his eyes. It was far too easy to remember how her body fit to his. To remember her forehead on his shoulder, her heated breath against his skin as their hips found a mutual rhythm.

Dryston swallowed. "Did I hurt you?" He leaned down and placed a kiss to the flesh above her belly.

Her fingers curled over the top of his head.

"You did nothing. You have a gentle touch for a warrior."

He could not help himself as he muzzled her soft, warm skin. He left another kiss slightly higher, then another. He finished applying the salve and wiped his hand on the grass. When he turned his attention back to her, she had removed her gown and lay on the grass staring up at him.

"I do not wish to hurt you."

"Dryston, you could not hurt me if you tried." She reached for him and brought his lips to hers in a searing kiss.

Careful not to brush against her wound, he hovered over her, pressing his hands against the cool grass. She was a seductive blend of innocence and sin, encouraging him with her hands, stroking him until he ached to join with her.

"Those two things," he spoke, sampling her mouth as he caressed her breasts. Still tender, he winced as he adjusted to the injury on his hand.

"We should wrap that well with a clean cloth." She took his wounded hand and brought it to her lips, kissing his knuckles.

More than he understood, Dryston wanted to free her from her emotional bondage. He nuzzled the warmth of her neck. "First thing…" He touched the pulse of her throat with the tip of his tongue, delighted when she sighed, stretching languidly beneath him.

"Yes," she breathed against his mouth before kissing him again.

"You need never tie me up. Unless it is for pleasure." She nipped at his lip, teasing him.

"Agreed," she whispered, curling her fingers over his ear. "Your second request?" she asked.

He kissed her deeply as he slid his hand gently between her thighs. This attraction was unexpected. The more he tried to avoid it, the more he wanted her. Her hips rose, meeting his insistent stroke.

Her eyes drifted shut as he sensed her body coiling tight. "That second request." Dryston leaned down, whispering in her ear, pushing deep two fingers into her hot quiver. "Come for me."

Sierra grabbed his face in a searing kiss as her body unraveled beneath him. He would have taken her had it not been for her wound. His body trembled with need and he kissed her once more before rocking back to his knees. With a quick glance, he was relieved to see the poultice still in place.

Sierra lay on the grass, looking up at him, the firelight shimmering in her eyes. "Why did you not take me?" she asked.

Dryston directed her hand to his tented breeches. "I want you. There is no question, Sierra." He had a strong desire to pull her into his arms and hold her as she slept, but already she was pulling her gown over her head. "Your wound… I—"

His voice trailed off as she glanced at him with a slight nod. She lay down on her side, tucking her hands under her cheek.

"I think I will take another swim," he said aloud. The ache between his legs was uncomfortable and he swaggered awkwardly to the pool. In haste, he shoved off his breeches and braved the chill, clenching his teeth. The water felt even cooler now as he glided through its velvet hands. He thought of her eyes—guarded, yet beckoning for more. He wondered what her life might have been like when she was younger. Was her dark hair once long and falling in soft waves to her waist? He had never heard her laugh, never seen her give a full smile. Dryston knew that he had to bear in mind where she came from.

He emerged from the pool and dressed quickly, noting that she had not moved. He crept to the other side of the fire, sensing she needed the distance. He lay down and she opened her eyes to look at him.

"Thank you for finding some food," he said. She sat up and scooped a handful of berries in her hand. She reached around the fire, offering them to him.

He took the berries and inspected them. "No elderberries?"

She shook her head. "Nay, blackberries and raspberries only."

Dryston nodded. He had once had a bad reaction to elder-berries as a child. His throat had swelled, and would have suf-focated him, had it not been for one of his mother's herbal cures. Dryston stuffed a handful of berries in his mouth, de-lighting in the tart burst of flavor on his tongue. "Perhaps tomorrow we can find something more substantial by light of day—a rabbit perhaps. Do you like roasted rabbit?"

She nodded, eating the berries one by one.

"Are you Celt, then?" he asked, hoping to find out more about her.

"What concern is my past to you?"

"I am interested," he said simply. And that was the truth of it. Twice now he had experienced her pleasure and still he knew nothing about her. "You and I are not so different, you know."

She glanced at him. "I do not remember asking about your family."

Dryston shrugged and tossed a stick into the flames. "I thought since we—"

She interrupted him. "Because we were intimate, you feel you need to know my past, or that I should know yours?"

Dryston would not give up that easily. "Perhaps you can tell me how you came to have the gift of sight."

She lay on her back and tucked her arm beneath her head. "It runs on my mother's side of the family. That is all I know."

She offered no more. The woman was prickly as a thistle, to be sure. Dryston lay down, frustrated in more ways than one. "You know my family was killed by the Saxons."

An owl hooted in the trees.

"Many Britons have lost their families," she replied. "You are not the first, nor, sadly, will you be the last."

"Then you understand what it is like to lose a loved one?" he prodded her gently.

She did not respond, and for a moment he thought she had fallen asleep.

"And where is your family?" he asked.

"Dead."

"I am sorry." Dryston rose up on his elbow and looked at her through the flames.

"Was she special to you, this woman?" she asked.

Her question came from out of nowhere. "What woman?"

"The woman I saw when I laid my hands on you."

Memories of Cendra flooded his mind. "What did you see?"

She sat up, her dark eyes sparkling in the firelight. "The two of you were together in the straw. Not unlike what we were doing moments ago. Who was she?" she asked.

"Cendra?" He spoke her name for the first time since the night she died. He was not interested in reliving those memories at the moment. Guilt washed over him anew.

"If it eases your mind," she stated quietly. "She was not violated before you found her. She died without much pain."

Dryston stared at his companion. A lump formed in his throat.

"There were too many Saxons that night. You should not torture yourself with guilt. There is nothing more you could have done."

Dryston blinked back the tears prickling at the backs of his eyes.

"Tell me what happened to the boy," she said suddenly.

"There was a small boy in the village. I did not see him after we ended our game."

"No, the boy in the hollow log."

Dryston pushed upright. "How do you know about him?"

"It was an image only, very quick. Nothing more," she stated.

"Why is he of interest to you?"

"I am curious only as to what became of him." She turned on her side then, facing away from him.

"Does he seem familiar?" Dryston asked. Even now, though Torin could speak and remembered bits of what happened to him, most of his memories remained locked away, perhaps never to be revealed.

"I lived in a village where there was a story of a woman killed by Lord Aeglech. They took her son away to be killed and no one ever heard of the daughter again. They assumed she, too, had been murdered." She shrugged. "Still, it is not uncommon for the Saxon king to invent such stories to keep the villagers afraid."

"Do you know her name?" Dryston asked.

She was silent. He wondered again if she had fallen asleep.

"Sierra?" he prompted.

"I am tired and do not want to talk about it. It is an old story, best forgotten."

Dryston lay back and put his arm under his head. He wasn't sleepy. His mind went over their conversation. He could not imagine what horrors she had seen in her life.

"Dryston?" she spoke sleepily. "Make no mistake about it, I saved your sorry arse from that living hell and you owe it to me to take me to your camp."

"I know, Sierra," he said quietly. Dryston watched her until the fire grew dim and the morning light began to brighten the eastern sky. She was a remarkable woman to have survived the torture she must have seen. Few were the scars on her flesh, but he suspected she bore many on the inside.

Chapter Thirteen

"Piss," Sierra muttered, eyeing the log she had seen the rabbit disappear into. The sun was high in the sky and still the Roman slept like the dead. She straightened, glancing over at his slumbering body, and wondered for a moment if he was truly still alive.

A flash seen from the corner of her eye snatched her attention, and she held the branch high as she chased after the frustrating creature. She came close, once or twice, smashing the branch on the ground, only to miss the rabbit as he darted off in another direction. Sierra was beginning to think that berries and mushrooms would be their breakfast, as well.

She spied his silver-gray tail from across the glen and charged at him, missing the fact that Dryston's feet were in her path.

"Oomph!" The branch flew from her hand and the rabbit escaped into the woods. She slammed her fist to the ground, spewing a string of curses. Pain from her belly, wound tightly with strips of cloth made from the discarded hem of her gown, caused her eyes to water.

"You lost him," Dryston said from above her. Sierra glanced over her shoulder. She grabbed another nearby branch and hurled it at him.

He was not as fast as the rabbit and the branch bounced off his head with a resounding thwack.

"Has anyone pointed out you have a reckless temper?" he offered.

"Then do not insist on telling me what I already know," Sierra spat. "If you are so much the better hunter, why do you not catch our food instead of sleeping the day away?"

"Fine, I will show you how it is done." He motioned her to follow as he walked over to a small dirt mound hidden beneath a bramble bush.

"Your blade?" He held out his hand.

"Do you think me daft?"

"Do you wish to eat this morning?"

Sierra's stomach growled in protest. "Fine." She handed him her seax blade.

He knelt in front of the mound, chopping at the dirt until he had dug a deep hole. Sierra's frustration turned to curiosity when he tugged off his tunic to attack his task with greater insistence.

Sweat glistened on his shoulders and back, the muscles in his arms bunching with each movement. He reached into the hole, measuring its depth by the length of his arm. Apparently satisfied, he placed the blade in the bottom, its sharp point facing upward.

"Now we cover this hole with leaves and twigs. Be careful not to cover it with too much. We want the weight of the animal to spring the trap."

Her gaze rested on his mouth as he explained the principle.

"Are you listening?" he asked.

"Yes, I am." Mostly, she thought, offering him a pointed look. The man was annoying, and 'twas a good thing he was nice to look at. "I heard your every word, Dryston." She forced out his name. This business of using birth names was far more intimate than she liked.

The grin he shot her caused her cheeks to warm. She turned away, busying herself with gathering up leaves. Why was she blushing like a scatterbrained maiden? He had no need to have his ego built up.

"What do we do now?" Sierra asked, throwing a few twigs on top of the trap.

"We wait."

"Wait? For how long?"

"Until we catch the rabbit." He spoke to her calmly.

She opened her mouth to warn him about the danger of mocking her. That, and the fact that they did not have all day to wait.

Dryston leaned toward her and placed a finger on her lips.

"It is important to be very quiet." He scanned the area and looked back at her.

"I have to piss." He jumped to his feet. "Wait for me over there." He pointed to a tree.

"You said to be quiet!" Sierra stared at him disbelievingly.

He strode back to her and shoved his face in hers. "That was to get you to stop asking so many damn questions."

"How do I know that you won't run off?" she countered.

He flashed a smile. "I do not know nearly enough yet about you."

She watched him trot off into the woods. Irritated by his ego, but impressed by his honesty, she complied, going to wait by the tree as he asked.

She smiled when she caught sight of his finely shaped arse, pale with the morning sun glinting off it. Sierra could not remember the last time she had truly smiled, nor the reason for it. Today she would remember both with pleasure.

Dryston rolled his shoulders, and a brief spark of yearning snaked up Sierra's spine at the sight of his broad back. His focus returned to his waist and she looked at the trap.

"Have you seen anything?" Dryston whispered as he knelt back down beside her.

She shrugged and shook her head. "Look, I know what you are trying to do. It's just that I do not want to think of you in those terms." She kept her eyes on the trap. *Come on, you damn rabbit.*

"What terms would that be?" he spoke quietly. His attention, too, was on the trap, but she pictured him staring at her with those pale green eyes.

"Lord Aeglech will not stop until he finds me," she responded, ignoring his question. "His need to know his future has grown relentless. He told me that he trusted few people. I was one of them. Balrogan, the other."

"That didn't turn out well for him." Dryston gave her a sideways glance. "But he wouldn't harm you if he thought I had kidnapped you."

She shrugged. "'Tis difficult to say. He might not, but he might just as well stick my head on a pole and parade it through the village."

"Sierra?" Dryston spoke her name softly.

"What?" Sierra grew restless with his constant yatter, his trying to get her to open up, to trust him, rely on him. She simply wasn't capable of such things. Why didn't he understand?

Dryston studied her face, his eyes softening.

"Just say what is on your mind. You will, anyway." She turned toward him.

Dryston appeared to be carefully mulling over his words. Whatever he was about to say weighed heavy on his mind.

"There is yet another reason he might come after you." He held her gaze.

Sierra waited a moment, then raised her eyebrows, tired of the delay. "Speak your mind. I've told you that I was his spiritual advisor and that he trusts…trusted me. Is that not enough?"

"Yes, it could be and probably is. But—"

"Out with it, Roman."

"What if he suspected we were working together and allowed our escape so that he could follow us?"

Sierra stared at him. "Are you implying that you think I said something to him?"

"No, but he may have suspected something when you asked to escort me to the gallows."

"But isn't that what we wanted? To get him away from the castle?"

"Yes, but it bothers me that our escape was far too easy. And why didn't he come to the hanging?"

Sierra shrugged. "In all the time I lived there he never went to a single hanging. He prefers beheadings."

Dryston frowned and glanced away.

As they waited, watching for the rabbit and lost in their private thoughts, a disturbing realization sent a chill over Sierra's shoulders.

She had gone in search of Master Balrogan that morning, concerned about his strange behavior the night before and what she had sensed when she touched him.

"Mouse?" a faceless voice had called out to her as she

hurried from Balrogan's torture chamber back to hers. Distraught that he had not been there, her concern was growing by the minute. She stopped, cautiously searching the shadows, thinking it might be her master. Sierra had sensed Aeglech was on the verge of madness when she'd spoken to him earlier that morning. Although Balrogan had committed many unspeakable acts, he had always treated her well. For a man of his station, he could have taken advantage of the situation many times, but instead he had cared for her in his own way. His absence gravely concerned her.

A Saxon guard stepped from the shadows. "Come with me." He stared down the dimly lit catacomb of tunnels that snaked beneath the outer walls of the castle. Sierra hesitated, wondering if it was wise to go with him, but her instincts spoke to her that the man could be trusted. She hurried to keep pace with him as he slipped around corners quickly in the curving underground hallways.

"This way, hurry," he called over his shoulder, then motioned her into a cubicle of a room. It had no door, only a jutting wall that prevented the view from the main corridor. There was a small makeshift bed and a table with a candle inside. A man lay in bed, aged in years and, she suspected, by illness. His face was wrinkled and he wore a scraggly beard of white. At first she did not recognize him, but as she moved nearer, the candlelight illuminated her sight and so, too, her memory. It was the man who had been the one ordered to take Torin into the woods. She stood at his bedside and wondered what was wrong with him, not that she had it in her heart to care. Still, she was curious about what he had to say.

"I am dying," he croaked out in a low whisper.

"And why should that be of interest to me?" She glanced up

at the guard who had brought her there. Beneath a guard's cloak, the man wore the garments of the clergy. As monks were forbidden within the fortress's walls, Sierra looked from one man to the other, questioning what strange game they were playing. "How did you get past the guards?" she addressed the monk.

"This man is dying of infection, but he sent word to me by way of special contact that he wished to be absolved of his sins and be converted, so that he may see the face of God. I am sorry for the deception, but these are dangerous times, and we do what we must to serve God's calling." The monk's eyes darted toward the room's entrance.

Sierra chuckled. "And what makes you think that I have any mercy for this man? Further, what makes you think that I won't leave here and go straight to Lord Aeglech and expose you both?"

"Because you will want to hear what this man has to say," the monk replied calmly.

"Let me save you both time and trouble. May your soul be damned to hell," Sierra said to the bedridden man as she turned to leave the room. "And you would be wise not to waste your time on this man." She glanced back at the man dressed in the dark brown robe.

"It is about Torin," the old guard spoke, his voice weakening.

Sierra's steps halted at the sound of her brother's name. Her eyes darted to the monk, holding his massive wood crucifix over the man. His eyes were closed, his lips moving in silent prayer. "What about him?" she asked.

The dying man lifted a trembling hand, covered in open sores, to take the book from the monk. His feeble hands shook as he rifled through its pages until he found what he'd been looking for. He lifted a lavender wristlet and held it out to her.

Sierra stepped to his bedside and stared at the token. It was exactly like the one she wore. Their mother had made them for her and Torin to protect them from harm.

She took the delicate wristlet, the flowers miraculously still intact. "Where did you get this?" she asked.

"I took it from your brother when I left him in the woods," the guard replied.

Sierra's gaze fell to the man on his deathbed. He yattered on, but she did not hear his words for the hate seething inside her.

"I dropped your brother off in the mountains and took another route back to the castle," he explained.

"You left my little brother—only a wee bairn—alone in the woods in the dead of winter? If I had my skelp, I would enjoy you a thousand lashings until you begged for mercy." Her hand trembled as she stared at the man.

"I deserve no pity for what I did. I was under orders, and to defy them meant certain death."

Sierra raised her hand to strike him, but the monk grabbed her arm, holding her back.

The man's eyes drifted shut as if he did not care what she did to him. "When I left him, he was alive. I hoped that he would be able to find shelter—a cave perhaps, or a village nearby."

Her voice shook as she stared down at the man. "Why…why tell me this now? What more pain can you inflict on me?"

The guard sighed. "I feared your mother's curse. I thought if I carried the wristlet with me, I would have its protection."

"Did you go back later to see if he was alive?" she asked.

"Nay, I took the wristlet and kept my disobedience a secret. I have carried it with me all these years," he admitted, squeezing his eyes shut. "I am sorry."

"I am capable of much worse than Aeglech," Sierra reminded him. She had only to tell the Saxon king about the man's deceit and he would be dead. The monk, if he stayed, would be an unfortunate casualty.

"What can anyone do to me now? In a few days, maybe hours, I will be dead," the guard said weakly.

"What do you want from me?" Sierra asked. "If it is safe passage from this place, you can be assured that I will not help you."

"Forgiveness," he stated weakly.

Sierra gave a short laugh. "Doubtful, Saxon. Since I neither worship the Roman God nor believe entirely in the ancient Celtic ways."

He nodded. "Already this day God has taken *my* son in payment for my sin."

The man was talking gibberish. Sierra had no mercy and little tolerance for the two men before her. "What is it and be quick. I do not have all day."

"There is something else." He coughed, spitting up blood, causing the monk to rush forward with a towel.

The sound of voices coming down the corridor brought up the monk's head. He clenched his cross tightly as he held it protectively over the man's body. His lips moved fervently in prayer, although his eyes were wide with fear.

"Take the wristlet. Perhaps one day you can forgive me." The old guard coughed again, his face grimacing in pain. "If your brother is alive—" He coughed again. "He would be—"

She could wait no longer if she did not want to risk being caught. Sierra fisted the wristlet in her hand and quickly left, ducking around the corner of the dark hall just as three guards and Lord Aeglech swept into the room.

She heard the monk scream.

Aeglech's voice was filled with anger as he spoke to the dying man. "Why would you summon a Christian to your bedside? You are a disgrace to your Saxon lineage."

The man uttered a few words but Sierra could not hear them clearly. She waited breathlessly for the man to mention that she had visited him, but he did not. The thought crossed her mind that perhaps he had spoken the truth to her and was sorry. But it did not change how she felt. All the apologies and all the forgiveness in the world could not bring her brother back.

"You imbecile!" Aeglech roared, and the dull sound of a neck being broken followed. The king strode from the room.

It was after that that she had learned of Balrogan's lover's death—the son of the old man. She had feared telling the Roman what had happened, concerned that he might change his mind and not help her, thinking that Aeglech had sent her to lead them to the Roman camp. She had chosen to keep it to herself, wondering what the boy in the log and the guard's confession might have to do with one another.

Sierra touched her satchel, where the wristlet lay. Had Aeglech coerced the confession about Torin from the guard before he killed him? Sierra wondered whether to trust Dryston yet with such news.

"You look like you are far from here." Dryston took her chin between his fingers. "What is it?"

Sierra blinked away the memory and focused on the present. "I was only thinking of all we'd been through. It did not seem to be so easy of an escape, in my view."

"Shh." He grabbed her leg and yanked her down. She fell on him and splayed across his lap. He cupped her face between his hands. There was a plump rabbit sniffing about.

Sierra watched the little beast in fascination, the very same one she'd chased out of the hole, his nose in the air, sniffing for signs of danger.

She held her breath. *One more step…*

One moment he was staring at them, and the next, he had disappeared.

"We got him!" Sierra leaped from Dryston's lap and rushed to the hole. At the bottom, lay the plump rabbit, her blade stuck clean through him.

"No need to thank me," Dryston said confidently.

She stood to face him. "Aye, 'tis true. It is deserved. Thank you." She stuck out her hand to grasp his in friendship.

He held up his palm. "No, a kiss, right here." He pointed to his cheek and tapped it with his finger.

"You want me to *kiss* your cheek?" she asked.

"Or my ass. It is an old Roman custom."

Sierra dropped her hand from his. "Shite," she muttered and gave him a quick peck.

"Go stoke the fire. I'll clean the rabbit." He grinned.

Sierra looked at Dryston as she sucked the succulent rabbit meat off the bone. He was acting as if they were on some grand adventure. "We should be moving on. Aeglech and his guards will not give up so easily."

"You called him Aeglech."

"Yes, it is his name," she responded.

"No, you did not call him *Lord* Aeglech. I think that is a good sign. You are embracing your freedom." Dryston tossed a bone into the fire and licked his fingers.

"You are reading things too closely." She pointed a bone at him.

"Perhaps, but I prefer to see it as progress." He walked to the pool, washed his hands and cupped them to get a drink.

Sierra watched him, bothered by the fact that he found her a work in progress. Something that was broken, perhaps. "So, you think of me as something that needs mending, then?"

He glanced over his shoulder and shrugged. "It's not something to be ashamed of, Sierra. You have been a prisoner for a long time. It is bound to take a while to adjust to a normal life." He walked back and stood over her, looking down.

Sierra knew that once they reached the camp—if they reached the camp—they would go their separate ways. She did not entertain thoughts of anything more than what might happen along the journey. Still, his view of her bothered Sierra for reasons she was not able to understand.

A rumble of thunder rolled across the sky as Sierra pushed dirt over the fire. "We should look for a cave tonight."

He glanced up at the sky. "There should be something once we reach the base of the mountain." He offered his hand to help her up, but she refused it.

"I am fine," she responded. She had checked the wound after taking a predawn swim. Unable to sleep, she had made another poultice as Dryston had slept and smeared it over her midsection, carefully binding the area with fresh strips of her gown remnant.

"You're sure that you can walk?"

"I can keep up. Don't worry about me." She squinted at the sky, the scant bit of sunlight being consumed by dark rain clouds. Sierra walked on ahead and, after a moment, realized that she was alone. She turned around. He was standing where she'd left him.

"West is this way." Dryston pointed in another direction.

"May I remind you my mother was a Druid witch. I know these things in my gut."

"And may I remind you that you have a slash across your gut. Perhaps it is affecting your senses?" He stood his ground.

"You think you know the best way?"

"I know that I know the best way. I also know that we haven't got time to bicker like an old couple every time we have a decision to make between us."

She shook her head.

"Look, I meant nothing unkind when I mentioned you were making progress."

She tossed him the rope. "I hadn't thought about it, Roman. In truth, I cannot recall much of what has happened between us at all since we escaped," she lied. "Perhaps it's best left as is? Now, we had better stop this yatter. We are up against time."

He looked at her a moment longer and nodded.

The had walked for what seemed like hours. Sierra, lost in her thoughts, had not spoken a word, and it seemed her companion was equally absorbed in his own thoughts. They were still picking their way through the forest and had not yet arrived to where their descent would begin.

"You are sure you know the way?" she called over her shoulder to him. To make matters worse, it had rained on and off for the past hour. The ground was sodden, as were Sierra's clothes. Rain trickled into her eyes as she trudged through the dense woods.

"Are you still angry about what I said?" Dryston asked.

Sierra stopped and faced him, grasping the long stick she was using for walking that she'd found lying at the base of an old oak. Her mother had told her that oak trees had great power. Certainly, it couldn't hurt to have it along if she needed it. Like now, she mused as she entertained thoughts of using it over Dryston's head.

"Get this through that thick head, Roman—"

"The name is Dryston," he stated quietly.

She ignored him. "I do not care what you think of me, only that you keep your promise. Are we clear?" She resumed walking.

"You think I have a thick head? Your head is as thick as the tree you got that from," he called to her.

She sighed. If he was looking for a fight, she was in no mood to give him one.

"Is there anything…anything at all you care about?"

His remark smacked her between the shoulders with the impact of a well-thrown knife. She shut her eyes to the pain of it. Had she expected him to see any more in her than the obvious? The women he was used to were soft, demure and able to inflate a man's ego with their charms. Up to now, she had not had to deal with the part of her that was emotional, and suddenly here she was facing a rush of emotions so foreign to her. She was certain that if she took the time to sort through them all, she could pinpoint very specific things she cared about—but now wasn't the time.

She continued to walk, refusing to answer him. The storm above began to subside, but the turbulence inside her continued to rumble.

"You have no reason to fear me, you know."

Sierra glanced over her shoulder, brushing away the rain dripping into her eyes. "I do not fear you."

"Then talk to me. Let me help you."

She fought the image of running into his arms and being held in his safe embrace. Sierra shook her head. "It is better, Dryston, if we do not become close. You and I are from vastly different worlds. I have lived a lifetime of guarding against the things that most people take for granted about themselves." She waited as he caught up to her.

He did not touch her, though he stood close enough that the heat from his body warmed her chilled flesh. "Stop trying to see something in me, Roman. There is nothing to see."

His hair lay plastered against his unshaven cheeks as he studied her. Carefully, he raised his hand to touch her face and Sierra flinched, turning away. "Don't pity me," she said, backing away a step. He reached for her arm and held her in place as he brushed the rain from her cheek.

"I do not pity you, Sierra. I only want to show you that I want to be your friend. I want to help you."

She stared at the ground, unable to look at the compassion in his eyes. She did not want to rely on someone else. She did not want to let her emotions run free for fear they would consume her and she might never be in control again.

"I do not want, nor do I need your friendship." She glared at him, hoping he would not see the truth that she hid. "We need to go." Sierra tore from his grasp but was immediately jerked back against him.

"I don't believe that you've forgotten everything that has happened between us, Sierra."

He gave her no time to respond as his mouth came crushing down on hers, seeking—demanding—a response.

Sierra's moan was stifled by his persistence. Her head spun with the intensity of emotion that invaded her. She fisted his tunic in her hands, holding it tightly as she selfishly took all that he offered.

"We don't have time for this," he uttered breathlessly as he held her close and scanned the area around them.

"'Twas not my doing," she remarked, looking up at him. Her lips still felt the pressure of his on them.

"Had we the time, Sierra, I would silence that mouth of yours, except for the pleasure of hearing you call out my name." His pale green eyes, ignited with lust, bore down on her.

She smiled. "And what makes you think it is *your* name I would call?"

He grinned and captured her mouth in a heated kiss that left her dizzy with need. She dropped her walking stick and leaped into his arms, winding her legs around his waist. He grasped her bottom, holding her to him as he backed her against a tree. Their mouths fused urgently to one another's as he worked at his breeches, freeing himself. He entered her swiftly, holding his head up and silently watching her as he pushed deep. Sierra held tightly to his neck, forcing herself to ignore the pain in her lower belly where he brushed against her wound.

He held her eyes with his as he drove into her, and though she felt pieces of the wall guarding her heart begin to fall away, her resolve was still strong. "This does not change anything." Her breath caught as her body teetered on the edge of her climax.

Dryston clenched his jaw and his eyes glittered with the ferocity of his actions. He thrust into her twice more, a groan ripping from his throat as she came undone.

He quickly dropped her to her feet, leaning his head against the tree as he caught his breath and adjusted his breeches.

"That should ease the tension between us," Sierra said, swallowing against the dryness in her throat.

He looked up, meeting her eyes. "Do you smell something?"

Taken aback at his question, Sierra blinked. "What?"

"Smoke, I smell a fire. Don't you?" Dryston lifted his face to the sky. He turned full circle as he sniffed the air. "Over there, come on."

He grabbed her walking stick and her hand, tugging her in the direction of the scent.

He led her to a small clearing surrounded by large boulders and a few trees. Sure enough, a thin plume of smoke rose from the clearing. A burly man sat on a log in front of a small fire. He had several woodcocks strung to a nearby tree. Though dressed as a villager, it was likely his job was as a hunter for the Saxon king.

"Stay here, and when I have him distracted, get his horse," she whispered. He grabbed her arm as she started to leave.

"Are you sure about this?" His eyes searched hers.

"I will be fine. We need that horse."

He nodded and released her arm.

Leaving her walking stick behind, she grabbed her arms as if warding off the cold and stumbled into the man's camp.

"Help me," she spoke weakly, weaving and then dropping to her knees in front of the man. He reared back on the log, his bearded face shocked as his eyes quickly scanned for other intruders.

"I have managed to escape. I was taken by a Roman prisoner and held against my will. I'm cold, so cold, and I've been walking so far. Please I beg you, help me."

Sierra was aware how his gaze dropped to her exposed thighs. She leaned forward, bracing her hands on his knees. He licked his lips, taking in the view where her gown gaped. "Could you hold me for just a moment? I need to get warm."

The hunter's expression changed from guarded to greedy as he spread his arms wide. "Poor girl, come here now and let me warm you," he soothed in a low voice.

Sierra crawled into the man's embrace and snuggled against his chest. "You are kind, milord. I have been through a terrible ordeal." She rubbed her hand over his tunic. "Are you hunting for Lord Aeglech?" she asked.

"I am one of his prime hunters, milady," he stated with puffed-up pride.

"Then you will see me safely back to the castle?" She twirled the end of his red beard between her fingers.

"'Tis my pleasure, but why don't we stay here a while until you are warm enough to travel?" His fingers ran down the side of her cheek, trailing over her shoulder, his palm covering her breast.

Sierra smiled and saw Dryston approaching from the corner of her eye. She grabbed the man's face and kissed him hard. Jarred by a jolt, she opened her eyes and saw the hunter's eyes roll back into his head just before he slumped to his side.

Dryston held her walking stick in his hand. "This does indeed have purpose. Come on, he won't be out long."

He climbed on the horse and reached down for her. Sierra glanced at the hunter—out cold—and grabbed one of the birds. "No need in these going to waste," she said as she climbed up behind Dryston.

Sierra clung to Dryston's waist, resting her cheek against his back. Her eyes drifted shut as she struggled to stay awake. Between the pelting cold rain and her fatigue, she felt as if the very life was being sucked from her body.

Some time later, Dryston's voice caused her to open her eyes.

"See those foothills?" he called over his shoulder. "We will make camp there tonight."

He had been relentless, driving the horse as far from Saxon territory as possible. Having to take the unplanned route to avoid the Saxon guards without benefit of a horse had cost them more time, time that Sierra sensed in Dryston they did not have.

"Not much farther, Sierra," Dryston spoke in a gentle tone.

She dozed off again, time meaning nothing, as she settled against the comfort of his rain-scented tunic.

When she opened her eyes, they were perched on a ledge overlooking a small spring. He helped her from the horse and, void of strength, she let him. A sharp pain cut across her stomach and she doubled over.

"You are shivering." He braced his arm around her waist.

"Something is not right…" Her voice trailed off and she felt herself being lifted, her body cradled in his arms. The light grew dim and when her eyes fluttered open she saw that they were inside the mouth of a shallow cave. Dryston was digging in her sack, probably for her flints.

"I need to look at your wound. I fear you may have an infection."

She nodded. "It came to me," she said, struggling with her words. "Balrogan told me once that Saxons rub their blades with the oil of poison fish." Her tongue felt swollen.

He reached for the hem of her gown. She batted his hand away. "If this is true, then it is in my blood. It may be too late."

His face blurred as he reached for her.

"Look at me, Sierra." His voice was fiercely quiet. "What would you do if it was me in your position?"

She tried to force a smile, but it took too much effort. "How do you know that I would do anything?"

Her eyes drifted shut.

"Because I know," he replied, his lips resting on her forehead. Her mind drifted in and out of consciousness as she tried to think. "Springwater. My mother spoke of its healing powers."

He stood to leave.

"If near a hawthorn tree, 'tis all the better," she called to him, her voice weak.

"Will you be all right here alone?" he asked.

"No worse, to be sure. Hurry, I am not certain how much time we have. Wait, take my blade." She reached for her calf strap and found it empty.

He drew it from beneath his tunic. "I kept it after I cleaned the rabbit."

"'Tis a good thing I didn't need it for that hunter. Be quick," she whispered. Her last coherent thought was that she hoped that she would live long enough to ask if he liked rabbit or venison best.

She felt herself falling into a dark abyss. Like the oubliette, the black hole yawned wide, waiting to devour her. Her mother's face and Torin's—small and boyish—rushed at her. Balrogan's milky stare engulfed her. And then, there was only darkness.

"Sierra."

She turned her head toward the voice she knew so well. Cearl lay on his side, looking at her, his golden curls shining bright as the sun, his blue eyes dancing with life. He gave her a boyish grin, the one she had come to depend on, just as she had come to depend on his body.

"Cearl," she said, "why are you here?" Sierra touched his smooth face. He was so young in many ways, yet so strong. He could carry bales of hay on one shoulder, yet he was afraid of the dark. "I am glad you are safe," she said as he bent to capture her mouth with urgency. Sierra held his face, accepting his kisses. He knew little of how to pleasure a woman, always in a hurry to satisfy his need. But she could not deny his body or the way she was drawn to it. His passion, unbridled and unrefined, excited her.

Sierra lay in a patch of lush, cool grass. Above, the leaves in the trees glittered in the sunlight, sparkling like stars.

"You are beautiful," another man's soothing voice whispered near her ear. His was deeper than Cearl's—gentle, unhurried. His touch commanded her body, coaxing her to surrender to her pleasure. Mature hands that seemed to know what to do without her asking. Long fingers stroked her deeply, giving way to a mouth and tongue between her thighs, offering her a glimpse of heaven.

Cearl's voice sounded in her ears as he offered praise for her body. "I like these, Sierra," he stated honestly as he teased her taut nipples.

Her body coiled tightly as the other man continued to feast on her quiver, his large hands caressing her thighs, urging her to release herself to him.

Cearl squeezed her breast, and took its pebbled tip in his mouth, grabbing her hand and guiding her to his phallus. Sierra wrapped her fingers around him and slid his length up and down with her palm, just as Cearl liked. She heard his soft sounds of appreciation as her hips began to rise from the attention being lavished on her quiver.

Cearl's staff grew hard and she felt the jerk of his body as he prepared for his release.

"I want you, Sierra. I have always been the one you run to. The one who could make you smile. Think of all the years we have shared together. How could there be anyone else? How could you want for anything more than what we have?"

Sierra could not think straight for the sweet ministrations between her legs. "It does not feel the same as with you, Cearl," she said, one hand pumping hard his phallus, the other holding his face, hoping he understood what she herself did not.

Cearl's blue eyes looked down at her, appearing lost. Sorrow shimmered in them. He pushed against her hand and held her gaze as he spent himself, then laid his head upon her breast. "I am finished for now, Sierra," he told her softly. "But I can try again later, if you want me to."

On the verge of her own release, Sierra opened her eyes and Cearl was gone, replaced with Dryston, who moved within her with slow purpose and determination. "Let go, Sierra. Come to me." He spoke gently, soothing her weary soul. "No one can steal your life from you again. It is yours to give to whomever you wish. To whomever you find worthy of all the beauty inside you."

She reached for the dark-haired man, his gray-green eyes filled with compassion and desire. Beckoning her to step away from the past and surrender freely to her future.

Warmth fused in her blood, heating her flesh, her heart, the cold recesses of her soul. A brightening invaded her chest as she reached for the Roman and let go, her body shattering in a million particles of light.

Exhausted, Sierra collapsed and looked up at the sunlight shining through the trees. Her mind was tired, her body spent.

She frowned at the sound of her mother's voice. Appearing at first as a shimmering light, the image of her mother took shape.

"Get up, Sierra," she commanded. At her side, a silver wolf waited, its ice-blue eyes staring at her.

"I am tired, Mother. I want to stay here with you."

"Nay, daughter. You are not ready yet to be with me," she spoke.

"When, Mother? When will I see you again?"

"I canna answer these things, my child."

"Will it be soon?" The light faded, and her mother's watery image began to disappear.

"Wake, daughter, and face your destiny."

Chapter Fourteen

"When, Mother?" Sierra mumbled. Dryston pressed his hand to her forehead, her cheek, and to her hand—she burned with a fever. His meager offering of springwater was not going to be enough. He had to get the fever down and to do that he would need to get her to the spring.

Her eyes fluttered open. "You are still here, Roman?"

He was pleased to hear that she could still recognize him. "I am happy to say the same to you. Your fever is worse. We need to bring it down.

"Forgive me, Sierra. But I see no other way." He peeled off his tunic to use later as a covering for her, and lifted her into his lap. She leaned against him as he struggled to remove her gown. Her fevered skin was hot against his flesh. Her limbs were listless and when her head dropped to his shoulder, his heart all but stopped. He cautiously placed his palm over her breast, waiting to feel her heartbeat. It was weak, but consistent.

"Mother," she moaned softly in her delirious state.

"Stay with me, Sierra," he muttered. Her body slumped forward and Dryston silently cursed Aeglech and his men. He eased her into the cradle of his arm and slipped his hand under her knees, glancing at her wound as he brought her out of the cave. He could not deny that he felt something for her. Whether it was a protective instinct, or something greater, Dryston wanted the time to find out. He shifted her in his arms and she curled into him. Her sweet breasts brushed against his chest as he carried her down the winding path to the spring below. The way was narrow. He picked along carefully so as not to slip and take them both over the edge. If the ancients believed in the healing magic of the springs, then Dryston decided that at this moment, he would, too. He said a silent prayer to Mother Earth and hoped her ear was not turned from him.

The rainstorm had left behind the strong scent of autumn leaves and moss. Dryston took a deep breath as he looked out over the newly drenched wood. If such a place of magic and healing truly existed, it had to be here. He glanced down at Sierra's frail body. Her pale skin, untouched by the sun, reminded him of the beautiful statues of the goddesses of old Rome.

When he reached the spring, Dryston trod slowly into the water, watching his balance. His memory flashed back to their escape when he had jumped on the horse's back and she had fallen forward. In the chaos of the moment, he hadn't realized she had been injured.

But she'd never once complained.

He strode deeper into the pool, letting the water cover Sierra up to her neck. Her body jerked as the cool water slid over it. Across from them, a small waterfall pushed through the thick brush and rock above, spilling into the secluded cove. The heavy scent of sweetgrass and lilies permeated the air.

Fireflies blinked among the reeds and the chirping crickets were joined by a deep-throated toad. He moved with Sierra, drawing her body through the still waters. "I am here for you and as long as there is a breath in my body, I shall not leave you," he said, looking down at her. It was because of her courage that they were now free. He knew no chants, no charms nor spells to speak, like those his mother would have used at this moment.

Her deep brown hair dipped in the water as her head lolled over his arm. Dryston drew her close, aware of his heart pounding in his chest. "Be strong, Sierra," he whispered as he continued pacing through the water.

He walked doggedly back and forth in the pool. For a time, he held her beneath the gentle falls and let the healing water splash over both of them. As dusk gave way to night, his arms began to ache. He could no longer feel his legs due to the cold water. If he stayed any longer, he might not be able to carry her back up the hill. Reluctantly, Dryston waded out of the pool, his breeches clinging to his skin. He laid her on his tunic inside the cave and covered her with her gown, then using her flint, he breathed a sigh of relief when the spark caught, igniting a warm fire. Dryston now had no choice but to wait. Her wound itself did not appear as angry and swollen as when he had applied the poultice. He tucked her gown around her body, covering her legs with leaves to keep off the chill. He owed her his life, but more than that, he realized, he had found a kinship with her. A kinship unlike any he had ever had with a woman. She was indeed beautiful. There was a raw honesty about her. She possessed a determination, independence and courage that touched him in a way that he had not expected.

Her sack lay on the ground where he had tossed it in his haste. Maybe she still had the makings for her poultice inside.

He dumped the contents of bag on the ground and sifted through the torn pieces of fabric. Nestled inside the cloth were a few berries, a mushroom, some marigold roots and a lavender wristlet similar to the one Sierra wore. He placed it aside carefully, sensing it might be important to her.

Dryston recalled how Sierra had made the poultice before and used the flower and water from the spring to make more. Carefully, he dabbed the root paste on her wound.

"Stay with me," she whispered. She tried to raise her hand to touch his arm, but it fell to her side as she lost consciousness.

He looked down at her, this fierce woman who possessed as much, if not more, courage than most men he knew. Knowing he had done all he could, he sat by the fire and picked up a piece of hawthorn branch he had found. Using her small blade, he whittled a bowl for her to drink from. He tried not to think about the idea that he somehow cursed the women he cared about. Each one had suffered a cruel death, and he was determined not to let the same thing happen to Sierra.

His heart twisted at the hand that he had in her current situation. Had he not leaned against her quite so hard, had he not talked her into helping him escape, would she be fighting for her life? Frustrated that he could not think of more to do for her, he set the bowl aside.

With a sigh, he cut a piece of his breeches, snatched the bowl and walked again to the spring. He crouched at the water's edge, dipping the bowl and drinking deeply, quenching his parched throat. What he would give for a pint of mead and a warm bed. He filled the bowl once more, soaked the torn cloth and glanced up to the heavens. He wondered if there would ever be a time when he could look up in thanks, rather than in frustration.

He hurried back to Sierra, hoping she might be awake, but her eyes remained closed, her skin deathly pale. He dropped to his knees, questioning the fates, trying to make sense of why she would gain her freedom, only to die a few hours after.

He inspected the poultice and rewet it, giving it moisture. She tossed and turned, mumbling gibberish that he could not grasp. He feared for a moment that the poultice might be doing more harm than good.

"Dryston?" she whispered in her semiconscious state.

"It is well, I am here." Dryston took her hand and suddenly it seemed so small.

"She says no, I can't go with her." Her lips white, and cracked, moved slowly as she forced out her words.

Dryston knew it was the fever talking. She wouldn't likely remember what she'd said. He lifted her head, placing the crude bowl to her lips. "Drink, Sierra, as much as you can. You have to fight this."

Beads of sweat broke out on Sierra's forehead. She sputtered, spewing out the water, as her eyes fell closed and she went limp.

Dryston lay her back on the pallet and placed the torn fabric on her forehead. She shifted and reached for his hand.

"Burning," she muttered. Sweat trickled down the bridge of her nose and over the curve of her cheek. Her hand covered his, moving the cloth down the slope of her neck. Wrestling with fever, she had pushed off her covering, and now moved the cloth wherever she felt warm. Dryston's thumb accidentally grazed her nipple, and she sighed as the rosy-brown tip puckered with arousal.

He drew back his hand. When she was well and strong again, he wanted to show her what pleasures awaited a man and woman when emotions were allowed to be a part. For now, he hoped her feisty attitude would be enough to see her through this.

"Stay," she whispered, touching his arm.

Complying with her request, he lay down at her side and pulled her gown up, covering her. He did not trust his temptation to offer her respite from her pain. She curled her body next to his, as he spooned her back and curved his arm over her waist. For most of the night he stared at their shadows on the cave wall. He forced his mind to other things. Would she have the strength to travel tomorrow? How soon would Torin be leaving to meet with Ambrosis? Had Aeglech sent *more* men after them?

Sierra's soft backside pressed against him. He rested his chin on top of her soft cap of hair, and shut his eyes.

Dryston's mind wandered to the last time he and Torin had time to speak of things other than battles…

"You have the gift, Dryston, of finding hearts in need of rescuing." Torin poured another glass of the fine whiskey that they shared to celebrate another of Rome's battles won.

"You say I have a soft heart, then? How can that be when it beats with the fierceness of a lion?" Dryston roared, and they both fell into laughter. He held up his glass and, with a smile, swallowed down the only magic potent enough to erase the bloody images of war.

Torin wiped his mouth and glanced over at a young girl who had more than once winked at him. She had a mane of fiery hair and eyes the color of a spring meadow.

"Nay, my brother. I do believe that your heart is strong, true as you say. But you—" he pointed at Dryston "—you see a rose where most people only see its prickly thorns."

"And that is a bad thing?" Dryston asked.

Torin shrugged and took a sip of his drink, then narrowed his gaze on him.

"Nay, it is not, my brother. But it may be danger to that heart of yours."

Dryston snorted at his brother's words. "And you should talk, my dear brother, for you fight, even now, the lust that burns you inside."

"We are not discussing me," he responded, glancing again at the red-haired beauty attempting to gain his attention.

"Word of warning. Be wise, Dryston. Keep your eyes open so that the thorns do not scratch you in your noble pursuit of the rose."

"You are just envious, brother, that I am betrothed to Anne." Dryston smiled and raised his glass. He wondered where his bride-to-be was tonight, if she was thinking of him as fondly as Dryston was of her.

Torin's gaze rested with interest on the copper-haired maiden. "She is a lovely flower, your Anne. Indeed, you are a lucky man."

Something about his brother's words had stuck in Dryston's gut. He had not slept well that night. Two weeks later, Dryston heard that Anne had slept with another while he was away in battle. Another week later, the Saxons invaded Dryston's family home and the village where he had grown up. When they were done, there was nothing left. Dryston never had the chance to hear from Anne's lips if the rumors were true.

He considered Sierra realistically. True, she was a pixie devil with a sharp tongue, and a prickly nature—and he grew hard just thinking of her. "I fear I am in trouble, Torin," Dryston spoke aloud in the darkness of the cave.

The morning brought the threat of rain yet again. He fueled the fire and, after checking on Sierra, went out to find them some food. With as little as she had eaten, she was sure to be ravenous when she woke. Though he had tried unsuccessfully to get her to eat, he wound up eating the whole woodcock in one sitting.

Dryston moved farther into the foothills and the wind grew cold. There would likely be snow on the mountains by nightfall. Prompted by the concern of losing his way back, Dryston headed back down the hill, resigned that he was not to find a deer today. The lonely howl of a wolf stopped him in his tracks. At this time of year, it was likely desperate.

He held his blade at the ready, moving quietly down the mountain path. His eyes skirted the woods. Ahead in the clearing he needed to cross to get back to the cave lay a freshly killed deer. Three wolves with brown-gray coats circled the feast, snapping and snarling at one another, trying to determine which one should take the first bite. Dryston crouched behind a boulder, watching in the hopes that when they were satisfied they might leave him some scraps. There was a rustle in the trees, and his gaze briefly captured a silver flash darting toward the wolf pack. Caught off guard, the unsuspecting wolves stumbled off in all directions.

Dryston kept still, praying the large silver wolf would not catch his scent, for he sensed he was a dead man if she found him. The bitch raised her black nose in the air and Dryston squeezed his blade, securing his grip. She was a stunning thing to see. Her full winter coat would have made an exquisite pelt. But there was something vaguely familiar about her. Her crystalline-blue eyes turned toward him as if the boulder he hid behind was transparent. Her gaze held his captive. Sweat trickled between his shoulder blades, and he could scarcely breathe. She lowered her head, nuzzled the deer carcass, tore off a hunk, and with a glance bolted into the mist.

Dryston rested for a moment behind the rock, letting his

heartbeat return to normal. He had not understood the territorial significance of what had just happened, but there was one thing he was certain of, although he could not explain it. She was the same wolf he had seen many years before when he had rescued Torin from the log.

Chapter Fifteen

He was the first thing Sierra saw when she opened her eyes. How long had she slept? Was it the same day? She had drifted in and out of sleep. Sometimes, Dryston was there and other times he was not.

"Shorter strokes, Roman," she offered in a whisper, coughing through the strange, dry sensation in her throat.

His eyes, always reminding her of the changing sea, looked up with interest, eyeing her a moment before he went back to his work.

Sierra blinked, trying to focus. Her head felt groggy. The reality of what had happened began to take shape in her head.

"How long was I asleep?" she asked. Her torn gown, lying atop her like a blanket, pooled at her waist as she attempted to sit up. She gave Dryston a questioning look.

"You've been in and out of consciousness for the past several hours. I had to undress you to carry you into the spring," he spoke, stroking the flint as he tried to make fire, not looking up.

"And for that you needed to remove my clothes?" she asked.

"I wanted your clothes to dry before I dressed you again." He smiled as the brush caught fire.

"You carried me into the spring?" She vaguely remembered being curled against his broad chest. A shiver danced across her shoulders at the thought of him carrying her down the path to the spring, in an attempt to save her life. He was the epitome of all that was good. There were some men who would have taken advantage of such a situation. "I do not remember much…"

As if reading her mind he spoke. "I did not take advantage of the circumstances, if that is your concern."

Sierra nodded. The fact that he was kind enough to quell her concerns said a lot about the man.

Outside the cave, she heard the sound of rain pelting the ground. The air was cool, fragrant with wet leaves. "I think this is yours." She held his tunic out to him, her eyes straying to the sinewy flesh of his chest.

She looked down at her wound and noticed a dried yellow paste. If he had taken her into the spring, then he must have applied a fresh poultice. "You made a salve?" she asked, rising to her knees so she could pull the gown down over her hips.

"I found the marigold in your pouch. My mother used to make a similar paste. I hope I got the portions correct."

"Whatever you did must be working. It is not nearly as sore. Your mother was Druid then?" Sierra asked.

"My father did not believe in her ways."

"Were they happy?"

Dryston looked up briefly as he stirred the fire. "I never

thought about it. I guess they were." He cleared his throat as if wanting to discuss something else. "I found a deer killed by a pack of wolves. I am sure you must be hungry. I have a small piece here that I will roast for us. There are some nuts and berries in your pouch that should appease you until the meat is ready."

"I owe you a great deal for all you have done." She tried to stand, wobbling a bit as she held her hand out for balance.

"Still a bit weak?" he asked, taking her hand.

"A little. It will help to walk. Do you have my pouch?"

He handed it to her and she dumped a handful of berries into her palm, and shoved them in her mouth all at once. She chewed as she watched him prepare the deer meat on a stick. "I am going to go down to the spring and get a drink. Perhaps take a swim to wash off the fever."

"Do you need me to come with you?"

"No, I am fine. You have done so much and I give you my thanks, but I can take care of myself now." She stepped into the rain, coming down in a steady torrent.

"To the right, there is a path. Watch your footing, it could be slick," he called after her.

"Spoken like a dutiful brother, Roman. I will," she replied over her shoulder. She picked her way down the sodden path carefully, breathing in the mossy air.

Dots of rain tapped the water, leaving rings on its surface. Sierra stepped out of her gown and into the water. Beneath the surface the water was warmer and she dived in, letting the water slip over her body. She swam to the falls and stood on the ledge, letting the cascade wash away the residue of fever that seemed to coat her skin. A snap of a twig brought her head around, and there standing on the bank was Cearl. Her gaze scanned the area, expecting Aeglech and his men to appear.

Thankfully, Cearl seemed to be alone, although he carried a Roman sword that she suspected was Dryston's.

"I have searched everywhere for you, Mouse."

Sierra swallowed, glancing quickly to the cave above. Smoke from the roasting meat rolled from its opening.

"Whatever that is, it sure smells good. I have not eaten in days." Cearl smiled, then his face grew somber. "Is the Roman with you, Mouse?"

When she was sure he was alone, she waded through the water to meet him, countering his question with her own. "Why are you here, Cearl? Have you brought Aeglech's men with you?" She searched the bank, her gaze darting back to the sword on his belt. She needed to find a way to get it from him.

"Nay, I separated from them days ago. I told them I was going back to the fort, but as I passed through here, I smelled the meat cooking and hoped to get some food. I guess it's lucky I found you. Did he do that to you?" He pointed at her wound, where there was still an angry red welt on her flesh.

Sierra sensed he was not telling her the truth, not completely. But they had shared years of comforting one another and she believed he was sincere about her welfare. "No, that was an accident. He's been very kind to me, Cearl." She hoped to reason with him so that he would not confront Dryston.

"How kind, Sierra?" he asked, pressing his brows together. He glanced up at the ledge. "Let me take you away now, before he knows." He pulled off his tunic and handed it to her. "You can put this on."

Her gown lay on a bush, but he hadn't seen it. Sierra smiled as she took it from him. She had to find out how far away the guards were. "You are so brave. It might not have been me you found," she said, moving toward him. Sierra stepped onto the bank and his eyes raked over her body in their usual de-lighted way. "What if you'd found someone who might have done you harm?"

"I am glad it was you, Sierra." He removed the sword and dropped it to the ground, offering her a wicked grin. He hadn't changed. "I have been concerned about you out here with that Roman." His eyes darted to the ledge.

"He's taking a nap," she lied, hoping to ease his mind. Sierra trailed her fingers down his chest, flicking his turgid nipple with the tips of her nails. His hands covered her breasts as he sighed against the top of her head. "How have you been, Cearl?" Sierra slid her hand over his crotch, summoning his arousal.

"Lonely." He pouted.

"Poor boy." With him it was always about sex. She did not have to worry about what he was thinking. She checked again the ledge. Dryston had not appeared. Smoke curled in her lower belly as her eyes drifted below Cearl's waist and took in his desire.

"Sierra," he whispered against her neck as he pulled his breeches down over his hips.

The understanding between them was direct. They both wanted one thing and there was no need to pretend otherwise. He sat down on the bank and pulled her astride his lap, holding himself erect as she positioned herself over him.

"Not today, Cearl," a voice boomed from behind her.

Dryston grabbed Cearl by the shoulders and tossed him through the air. He landed with a resounding splash in the spring.

"The stable boy, Sierra?" Dryston's face was dark with fury. "Did you stop to think that Aeglech's men could be close by?"

"I asked. He said he was alone."

Dryston searched the heavens as if he would find the right words there.

"Well, then, as long as you have the word of your Saxon lover. It seems you could hardly wait to get him between your legs," he snarled.

Sierra stared at the venom coming from him. This was a different side to Dryston that she had not seen. She had not cried in years, but his scathing humiliation cut her to the quick. She jumped up and grabbed her gown, fisting it to her chest as she faced him.

"You are not my keeper. And further, *Roman,* 'tis not true that you have taken a woman for pleasure before?"

He grabbed her arm and whirled her to face him.

"That is not the same."

She jerked her arm from his grasp. "Of course it is not." She glanced at Cearl, tugging up his breeches as he sloshed from the pool.

"You dare touch a hair on his head and you will have me to answer for it." Sierra charged naked up the hill, not caring that her white arse was out there for both men to see.

There were no sounds but the rain splattering against the rocks outside and the occasional snap of fire as they ate their roasted deer.

Sierra glanced at Dryston, who had taken back his sword and also taken Cearl's seax blade from him. Had she not been there, Dryston would have him tied up as well.

Cearl worked on his meat, seemingly content and unaffected by the Roman's distrust. For the first time, Sierra regarded Cearl's simplicity with respect. Chances were that he'd already forgotten that he was part of a search party.

Dryston, who had not said a word since the encounter, threw Sierra a harsh glance.

"Cearl," she said, turning to face him, purposely ignoring the Roman. "What happened to Balrogan?"

Cearl shook his head softly and his blond curls reminded her of a little boy. Except for the unshaven stubble on his jaw, he appeared every bit as innocent. "It is not good."

She had had her suspicions, but she wanted them confirmed. "Tell me anyhow, Cearl. He was my master." She refused to acknowledge Dryston's low-timbered grunt.

Cearl sighed and wiped his fingers on his breeches. His gaze darted to where Dryston was seated near the entrance, keeping guard.

"They say they got caught."

"They?"

"Aye, Master Balrogan and one of the guards."

Sierra pretended to be surprised. "And what happened to the guard?" she asked.

Cearl grimaced. "Aeglech made Balrogan behead the guard, then toss him into the hole. It was sad. That guard's father died just after, the same morning. Isn't that odd?"

Dryston glanced over his shoulder. "Filthy beast got what he deserved," he said, adding, "as should all Saxons."

"And who are you to judge what is right and wrong?" Sierra countered. "Romans killed thousands of my people for not believing in your precious God."

"That was not me." He raised his voice as he stood.

"But it wasn't right."

"We will take back the land that was stolen by these barbarians." Dryston strode back to her, his face intent.

Cearl watched in silence.

"And for whose benefit? The Celts? The Britons? All of Rome?"

He stared at her. "You do not understand. You became accepting of *them*." He cast a glance at Cearl. "You do not care any more for Britannia than do the Saxons. You care only for one thing—what is good for Sierra, nothing more."

He grabbed his sword as he strode out of the cave into twilight. "Do not let me ruin your happy reunion," he called over his shoulder.

Guilt and anger muddied her thoughts. "He is no better than Aeglech when it comes to taking," she muttered. What made her nauseous was that Dryston might be right. She had never known a man who gave so much, when she had done little but *take* most of her life.

Cearl smiled. "Do you think he will be gone for a while?"

Sierra looked at Cearl. "Do you think of nothing but sex?"

His eyebrows shot up in surprise and he shrugged. "Did you want me to think of something else?"

She sighed. "Sleep well, Cearl. He will have us up before the sunrise."

She awoke some time later when only the embers of the fire glowed in the dark cave. Cearl had fallen asleep, but only after she had insisted that she did not want him to get infected with the poison from her wound. It was not entirely the truth. However, he would not have been able to accept well the truth.

Moving her hands along the wall, she paused at the cave opening and looked up at the bright moon.

"Did you enjoy some time with your stable boy?"

His voice issued in the dark. Sierra steadied her heart and turned to find Dryston sitting a few feet from the cave.

"One of us needed to keep watch for Aeglech's guards," he snapped quietly.

"What if I did lie with him? What concern is it of yours?" she responded, bristling at the tone of judgment in his voice.

"It is of no concern to me whom you spread your legs for," he responded, not bothering to look at her when he spoke the biting words.

"Is that what you told *Cendra?*" Sierra asked, challenging him.

"You have no right to speak of her like that. She was nothing like you. She was a lady."

His arrow hit her straight and deep. Its poison sank into Sierra's bones as he intended, but she would not back away. It was not in her to do so. "You have spoken the truth and perhaps it makes you feel better to do so. It is no secret that I am no lady, but at least I do not pretend to be something I am not. You, on the other hand, wear your piety on your sleeve for all to see, when inside you are just as prone to lust and cruelty as the rest of us."

"That is enough," he stated flatly.

"People like me and Cearl, we're nothing in your eyes. You are not able to see past your preconceived judgments of me. You see a filthy face, tattered clothes and the life I did not choose, and still you judge me for what I must do to survive."

"This conversation is over." He glanced at her, then turned away.

"I do not fit into your idea of a lady," she continued, "because my hair is not long. Because I do not wear the clothes of a proper maiden, or act helpless and in need of a big strapping arse like yourself."

He looked at her then and his gaze narrowed.

"Maybe you are so put off by me because you know I do not need you to survive. I have lived through hell without your help and I can certainly continue to live without you."

"I said, enough!" Dryston jumped to his feet and grabbed her hard by the shoulders.

"Go ahead, toss me over the ledge, and then you can do the same with Cearl. Rid yourself of our useless existence."

Her words were stopped as his mouth came crushing down on hers. He gave her no time to breathe, fusing his lips to hers and pulling her into the heat of his desire.

Reckless anger fueled his passion and she welcomed it, wrapping her arms around his neck as she leaped into his embrace. Her world spun as he turned her back to a moss-covered boulder, pressing his body to hers.

He shoved her gown upward, caressing her flesh as he ran his fingers lightly over her breasts. Shivers skittered over her body as he bent to take her turgid nipple in his mouth. Her fingers threaded his hair, cradling his head to her as he lavished each breast, pulling each pearled tip gently between his teeth.

"How is it that you can have such disdain for me, but cause me to want you at this moment as if you are the air I need to breathe?"

He planted kisses across her stomach, pausing at her wound, his hands moving and caressing, her need building with each breath.

He stood, grabbing her face, his gaze intent on her. "I do not disdain you. On the contrary, I am infatuated with you completely."

"You are thinking with your cock," she cautioned as he trailed heated kisses along the curve of her neck.

"If that is so, then the rest of me agrees." His hot breath seared her flesh. "I want to make you forget, Sierra. Forget everything that has happened to you and make you see the passionate woman that you are."

Her thoughts turned back to the first night as his hands had touched her in ways that turned her bones to liquid. He placed her on her feet, lifting her gown over her head, and removed his breeches. Taking her face in his hands, he captured her mouth in a deep, thorough kiss. A small whimper broke from her throat as fire raged through her body.

He picked her up in his strong arms and leaned her against the cool moss, wrapping her legs around him as he bore into her. Driven to mindless ecstasy, she surrendered her control, letting him command her body even as he threatened to break the wall she had built around her heart.

As his thrusts grew more urgent, tears trickled from the corners of her eyes.

No words were spoken, no promises uttered, blind need took control of their bodies, pushing them toward release. Sierra's thoughts swirled in a dizzying haze. Deep inside, she knew that somehow he had managed to find a way to touch a part of her lost years ago.

"Face your destiny." Her mother's voice echoed in her head.

Dryston's warm chest brushed against her breasts with each fervent thrust. He kissed her softly on the shoulder, whispering against her cheek. "I am not hurting you, am I?"

The intimacy of his question cracked her protective wall. Tears flowed down her cheeks.

"Nay." She gave her simple reply and hugged his neck tightly. Part of her never wanted to let go, and yet she knew they would not speak of this moment again.

He uttered a quiet groan and drove into her twice more, filling her with his hot seed.

He rested his forehead against her shoulder. "I promise next time—"

She pushed at his shoulders, forcing him to put her down. She fished in the dark for her gown. "Do not make any promises," she said with a short laugh, wiping the wetness from her face.

"Are you crying?" he asked quietly.

"Aye, Dryston. But do not think that it means anything," she responded. Sierra found her gown and hurried to the cave's entrance. He did not call to her, or ask her to stay. Why should he? They had both satisfied their need. She sneaked back into the cave, unsure whether to cry or empty her stomach. Something strange was happening to her and it was his fault. Around him, her thoughts became muddled. She yearned for things she had never before thought of, impossible notions of a home and children. These were not things that a woman like her should entertain. In her way, she, too, was a warrior. But the battles she fought were not of flesh and blood, but images of her past.

"Where did you go?" Cearl's voice asked sleepily.

"To take care of business. Go back to sleep."

"You are welcome to sleep here by me, Sierra."

The sound of her name caused her heart to twist. "Nay, Cearl, I am not feeling altogether well. It might be wise for me to be on my own." The truth would hurt his pride. She curled up on her bed of leaves and wondered how she would face Dryston come the light of day. Each time he touched her, another piece of her finely crafted facade chipped away.

Sierra shut her eyes but her mind continued to spin. How would the other Celts in the Roman camp treat her? Was her fate there the same as it would be if she returned to the Saxons? She had no home, no family that she knew of. And if, by some miracle, Torin was still alive, how would he feel about her, given the life she had lead? Would it be best if she left now and tried to begin anew on her own somewhere else? Her thoughts went back to the look on Dryston's face when he'd grabbed her shoulders. There had been torment flashing in his pale green eyes and she knew he fought against the very thing he hated to admit. For it was the same feeling that she shoved aside now.

He had felt something just as she did, but was the risk worth the price of finding out what it was?

Chapter Sixteen

Dryston hated himself. He squinted against the brightness of the sun coming through the trees. His first waking thought was of his mouth pressed against the slope of her smooth neck as he came into her. By all that was holy, he had barely slept the rest of the night thinking of her, thinking how much of an idiot he was. He had lost control of his senses, pushed to the edge of reason by her barbed tongue.

He closed his eyes to the throbbing beginning in his head. He was now caught in a web of his own making. *Shite.*

What happened between them, whatever it could be labeled, was not the stuff of poetry and sonnets. Nay, it was animalistic, fierce and desperate. The most incredible night of his life.

Dryston moved his head from side to side, sighing as his neck popped back into place. He struggled to stand, stiff and sore by his own doing. He glanced at the moss-covered cavern wall in the light of day. The hell if it was that amid all the confusion and passion, as he had looked into her eyes, he had seen her challenge. He had sensed it with every pore of his body. But it was not one that beckoned him to break her will. Nay, it was a challenge that begged him to free her from her self-imposed prison, to make her feel something again.

If Dryston would admit it, last night he had felt something shift inside himself. It frightened him that he might truly have feelings for this strange woman. During the night, he had tossed and turned, thinking of the past few days. The fighting, the quibbling, her serpentlike tongue, her headstrong ways…the look of passion on her face as she had matched him thrust for thrust.

Piss. He was growing hard again.

Dryston put his lustful thoughts in check. He needed to decide what to do about Cearl. He was not yet convinced that the Saxon stable boy was as innocent as Sierra claimed he was.

Cearl awoke as Dryston entered the dimly lit cave, holding his sword safely at his side.

"Was it cold outside?" the boy asked, rubbing his eyes and grinning.

"I was keeping watch for Aeglech's men. You would not have any thoughts about that, would you?" he asked, poking the end of the sword in the smoldering embers of the fire.

Cearl glanced nervously at the sword, his gaze rising to meet Dryston's. For a moment, Dryston thought he was about to admit that he had been sent by the Saxon guards to find them. He gripped his weapon.

"The guards think I returned to the burke, as I told you before."

"So you did," Dryston replied, making it clear that he did not believe his story as easily as Sierra did. He shoved the thought of Cearl with Sierra from his restless thoughts.

"Leave him be," Sierra spoke from within the recesses of the cave. She emerged, looking tousled and unkempt and her sumptuous mouth still swollen from the passion they had shared.

Dryston pretended not to notice the slow thud that started in his chest.

"Cearl can be trusted," she said quietly, bending to the fire and gently blowing across the embers, sparking a flame.

He dragged his gaze from Sierra's face and focused on Cearl. "We need to move on," he suggested, keeping his eye on Cearl's reaction.

"Fine, he can come with us." She looked up at him with a friendly smile.

"But I want to go back, Sierra," Cearl said. "It is my home. If I do not show up at the burke, they will know you have captured me. If I return, saying that I found your dead bodies at the bottom of a ravine, your throats torn wide open by wolves, then they will call off the search."

His bright gaze bounced from Sierra to Dryston.

"Quite a tale you came up with, Cearl. It seems you have thought it out carefully," Dryston offered, ignoring the disapproving look on Sierra's face.

Cearl fished out some deer meat being kept warm over the fire. Dryston spied the rope tossed to one side and an idea began to form in his head.

Though he suspected that Sierra was not going to like it, she was just going to have to get used to it.

"I agree, Cearl. I think it's best if you do not join us." He picked up the rope with the tip of his sword, sliced it in half and dropped it at Sierra's feet. If they were going to get out of there alive now, he would have to take the reins.

"Are you daft? This is not the way. It is not needed. I swear that to you," she said, shoving the rope away.

He pushed it back to her. "It is not your permission I am asking," he stated, his eyes intent on hers. "It is an order."

The moment he uttered the word *order,* her face clouded with fury. Her lips, so sweet and giving last night, formed into a firm line. He did not give her the choice to protest. "Do not challenge me on this," he stated, making it clear that he was taking over from here. From the look she gave him, he figured he should sleep with one eye open tonight.

She stared at him for a moment more and snatched the rope from the dirt.

"I am sorry, Cearl. He gives me no choice," she spoke.

"I venture it will not take them long to find you, if my suspicions are correct," Dryston said as he snuffed out the fire and shoved dirt on it with his boot. "Make sure the fastenings are tight."

Sierra worked on the ropes. Cearl just sat there and smiled, a silly expression on his boyish face. Cearl lived in his simple world, but there was something about the complete ease with which he allowed her to tie him up that raised Dryston's suspicions. Still, there was no time to explain all of that to her now, and he doubted she would have listened anyway.

"They are tight, but, Roman, I ask you to re—"

"Listen to me. We have no time to waste. Now, are you coming with me, or do you wish to stay here and play nursemaid?"

She stood, and for a moment Dryston thought he had lost her.

"Sierra?" He stated her name calmly. The thought of leaving her here frightened him more than the prospect of facing the guards alone.

"I am coming."

Dryston released a quiet sigh, realizing he had been holding his breath.

She leaned down and kissed Cearl on the top of the head as if she were his mother.

"Please do not leave me here," he said, imploring Sierra with his eyes.

Her steps faltered. Dryston grabbed Sierra's arm. "No matter what has happened, trust my instincts on this." He stared down at her, fighting the urge to kiss her.

The hesitation in her eyes was strong, but with a sigh she went to retrieve the horse where they had hidden it in a clump of trees. She was quiet as he helped her mount behind him, but he had a strong feeling that she was even now debating her decision.

Dryston ripped a piece of his tunic and left it hanging on a bush. A bit farther, he reached out and snapped a tree branch part way. He'd been doing this since they left Cearl back at the cave.

"What are you doing?"

"Proving my point," he replied calmly.

"And is that so important?"

He looked over her shoulder and offered her a smile. He liked the way the wind blew her short wisps of hair over her curious and beautiful eyes. "This is a military tactic. You purposely leave clues, so that the enemy can follow you into your trap."

"And you plan on taking on the Saxons alone?"

"If it comes down to that, Sierra, I will just send you before me and you can slash them with your mighty tongue."

"You best sleep with one eye open tonight," she warned in a cold voice.

"Aye, I had already thought of that," he replied.

"You truly think the guards will come for Cearl?"

"I'd stake my military career on it," Dryston replied. "I'm

taking us the back way into the camp. It is a way less traveled by the Saxons. We'll be safer taking that route."

"Dryston, I am tired, my stomach protests and my arse is numb. How much farther is it before we stop for the night?" Sierra asked.

The sun, high overhead when they'd started out, was now dipping into the western sky.

"Where we are staying is not far," he told her.

"You seem to know these woods well. Where can we find some food for our evening meal?"

She yawned long and loud and it brought a smile to his lips. The more he was with her, the more he realized how much he liked her. "These woods are not far from the camp, but the village where I grew up is not far, either. I spent a great deal of time in these woods as a child."

They rode on in silence as they had done most of the day. She apparently did not want to discuss what happened between them last night and he was just as happy to comply. He was still trying to figure it out himself.

"Do you miss them?"

"My family? Every day."

"I wish—"

"What do you wish?" he asked, checking over his shoulder, sensing she was on the verge of revealing something about herself. She had spoken once or twice of her mother, but not of any other family members.

"Nothing," she replied, slipping back into her silence.

Perhaps it was too painful to remember, and like Torin, she had blocked the darkest parts of her life. He was anxious for her to meet his half brother. In some ways, especially in temperament, they were very much alike.

"A woodcock—stop," she whispered, tapping his shoulder. "I need my blade, quick." She slipped off the horse and fell on her backside.

"Piss, I told you I could not feel my legs."

Dryston laughed, and it felt good. It seemed like ages since he had laughed out loud. He glanced at her as he climbed off the horse. From the scowl on her face he deduced she did not share his mirth.

"It was amusing," he muttered as he searched the leaves, looking for the bird. The thought of a plump woodcock roasting on a stick made his mouth water. "Where did it run to?"

"My blade, if you please." She punched out each word.

She held out her hand, and he grabbed it to help her to stand.

"My thanks for keeping watch over the sword while I was ill, but I am able to carry it now."

She stood barely to his chest, one hand shielding her eyes from the sun, the other extended, palm up.

He pulled the short blade from his boot where he had carried it for the past day or two. Begrudgingly, he handed it to her.

"Mine is bigger, anyway." He winked, tapping the sword he carried in a sheath made from one of the arms of his tunic.

"Have you always been this full of yourself, or is the show just for me? For if conceit were gold, Roman, you would be a wealthy man." She tucked her blade in the strap attached to her leg.

"And if your tongue were an arrow, we might have our supper by now." He grinned.

She offered him an impatient look.

"I saw the bird over there in that thicket of berries. Perhaps it is hiding among the thorns for safety," she offered as she moved toward the bush.

"Then perhaps you should chatter some more and the confused bird will think you are his thorny safe haven?"

She pulled the blade from her leg with lightning speed and flashed it before his chest. He stepped back, barely missing its wicked bite.

"It is your tongue I shall cut up for my supper if your yattering makes us lose this bird. Now help me, or stay out of my way," she warned.

She was captivating when she took charge. He supposed that was part of what he admired about her. In a vain effort to appease her, he followed her signal to go around behind the bush. He held his sword high above his head, watching her from the corner of his eye. She looked like a mighty huntress with her determined expression, her blade poised as her gaze darted amongst the leaves, watching for movement.

Dryston licked his lips and blinked, realizing that his throat had gone dry. He swallowed, and his throat felt tight, as if someone had him about the neck. His eyes began to water, then burn as he rubbed them to quell the itching. A sneeze began to build and he could not have stopped it any more than he could a sunrise. He motioned to her, trying to gain her attention, but she dismissed him with a wave of her hand.

He rubbed his hand over his nose in a final attempt at stopping the sneeze. Unfortunately, it only made matters worse. His gaze met hers over the bush. Her eyes widened when she realized something was wrong.

Dryston took a deep breath. His eyes blurred, as he tried to stay focused. The sneeze broke free, echoing through the quiet forest. A flock of birds nesting in an oak rose in one great mass to fly to another tree, escaping the sound.

The fat woodcock raced by him and he swung at it like a blind man, chopping at the brush with his sword. Another sneeze came then, more powerful than the first, sending the frantic creature in circles before it disappeared into the dense thicket.

Dryston peered at the scant few blossoms left on the underbrush where he hid, and realized with a sinking feeling that it was an elderberry patch. "Elderberries," he muttered, sniffing as he backed away from the offending bush. He had not noticed its bloom before, too preoccupied with watching Sierra. But his reaction to them was quick and severe and he had to find relief. He trotted down a small incline to a creek that gurgled through the leaves. He dropped to his knees, splashing the cool water over his face and neck, sipping handfuls of water. After a moment or two, he was again able to draw a full breath.

"Bloody eejit!"

He cast a weary gaze to the heavens. "You cannot cast blame on me for this," he tossed back. "I have no control over my body's reaction to that plant."

It was foolish not to check the thicket first, but she had distracted him. He glanced over his shoulder, seeing her stomping down the hill with the fury of hell on her face. He wiped his hands and turned toward her, pulling his sword and tossing it to the ground—behind him. If this got ugly, he did not want anyone hurt.

"You lost my supper." She came at him, her fists raised. He caught her arms midair and easily turned her in a choke hold, one of the first hand-to-hand battle moves he ever learned.

Her heel came down on the top of his foot and his hold loosened. Long enough for her to swing her foot and snag his ankles, dropping him to the ground.

"You need to learn to control that temper," he warned, dodging the swipes to his head.

"And you need to learn that just because you possess a cock, you are not always right." She managed to find his jaw, meeting it with a loud thwack.

Dryston determined they were no longer talking about the lost bird. "Fine, woman, you want to talk pride? I see a woman too proud and too angry to ask for help." He grabbed her wrist and held it tight.

"And I see a man too blind to see what is before him."

She jerked her arm, but Dryston held it in a firm grip. "You are a stubborn, prickly thorn." He studied her face. Her mouth spoke one thing, but her eyes spoke something entirely different.

"I have discovered I am that way only around you, Roman," she retorted, pushing back her hair from her face.

"You know, Sierra, this journey would be much easier if you did not constantly feel the need to prove yourself better than me."

Her mouth dropped open in surprise. "I do not have anything to prove to you."

He nodded. "Which is why you spend your every waking moment trying to undermine me."

"That is absurd."

"It is true," he replied.

"It is a lie," she spat.

She was so predictable. It aroused him that he knew her so well. He smiled.

She narrowed her gaze. "You do that to me," she stated.

"What do I do to you, Sierra?" He held her gaze, and circled his fingers around her wrist, unwilling to let her go. He was determined to hear from her lips that she felt something between them.

"You turn things around. Make everything muddled. It makes my head hurt."

Dryston leaned forward cautiously, hesitating a moment when she snapped her eyes to his. He placed a soft kiss on her forehead. "Does that help?"

"Nay." She tried to pull away from him. "You make me ache all over. I do not like it." She held her free hand to her head, keeping her eyes averted from his.

"Perhaps the ache is something else. Is it painful?" he asked, bringing her wrist to his lips.

Her dark eyes turned to his. "When I think too much about it, yes."

He curled his hand around her neck, tugging her close, until her face was inches from his. "Then perhaps we should not think." She searched his face, her brown eyes showing the struggle going on inside her.

"If that were possible, I would welcome it," she said.

He knelt, drawing her to the ground with him.

Unlike the blind fury of the night before, he took his time pleasuring her, giving her body time to respond, to want more, to need him.

He drew her gown over her head, and placed it under her as a pillow. "Has anyone ever told you how beautiful you are?" He reached for her face and she turned to her side, away from him. He lay down beside her, cautious not to move too fast. The scars she bore from her imprisonment were even deeper than he realized. "Let me hold you, Sierra," he spoke. He sensed it was a crucial moment for her, coming to grips with the fact that she might feel something for him. He brushed his fingers gently over the edge of her wound, healing well with the treatments and spring water. He rose up on his elbow and kissed it gently.

She turned to her back, placing her hand aside his cheek as

he kissed a trail over her stomach. Her soft sighs humbled him and he cupped her supple breasts. Would she at last allow another person into her life? Someone who could help her find her way? And was he that person? He wanted more than anything for her to find the emotions she had buried long ago. For only then would she be free to give wholly of herself to anyone.

It was a dangerous game he played with his heart, Dryston knew. Every woman he had ever loved had been taken from him.

Sierra cupped his face, and traced his brow with her fingers, studying him carefully as if seeing him for the first time. She sat up to meet his mouth in a searing kiss, as she pushed his breeches past his hips.

The chill caused him to breathe deeply. She wrapped her fingers around him and stroked him long and slow, then took him in her sweet mouth. His hand found her face, aroused by the movement of her jaw as she pleasured him. He had no idea when exactly it happened, but at some point on this journey, he had come to truly care for this woman.

She took his face, and tentatively touched her mouth to his, the tangy taste of him still on her tongue. Then, she turned on her hands and knees in the autumn leaves and looked at him over her shoulder. "I want you inside me, Dryston."

He held her thighs, sliding effortlessly into her warm, slick glove. Hot and tight, she moved back against him, urging him deeper. He wrapped his arms around her, weighing her breasts, caressing them in his palms. She bowed her head and abandoned herself to her pleasure. He waited, holding himself back from driving mindlessly into her warmth, listening, waiting for her to acknowledge that it was him she wanted and not just a faceless cock.

She had not spoken, but her moans fueled the fierce need

building inside him. In a few moments, they would both find their release and then it would be over and everything would go back as it was before.

Not this time.

He pulled from her and brought her to his lap, impaling her on his ready cock. He grabbed her chin, forcing her face to his. Her eyes, glazed with arousal, met his. "Look at me," he insisted, determined that this time she would not forget who gave her pleasure. "This is me, Sierra," he ground through his teeth as he moved within her, slow and determined. Her eyes fluttered shut and he grabbed her face more roughly than he meant to. "No, you will look at me. You will know the man that has endured your barbed tongue, who barely slept when you were ill, who cannot seem to rid you from his mind."

Her mouth parted, and she rocked her hips to meet his in perfect rhythm. "Tell me, Sierra, that you know who this man is," Dryston gasped, teetering on the verge of his release. But he would not allow himself the pleasure of it until she said his name. His heart beat fierce against his ribs. "Sierra, say my name. Say you want *me*—not just—" His mouth opened as she tightened once more around him, her climax caressing him, drawing him closer.

"Say my name." He pushed out the words, his body trembling with the force of his impending release.

"I—" she began as another wave of pleasure crashed through her body.

"Fuck me," he cursed quietly as his body shattered. He squeezed his eyes shut to the explosion of stars in his head, the need for release consuming all else. His heart twisted as he heard her pleasured scream and emptied his hot seed into her.

He turned away from her not saying a word. His heart

pounded fiercely, whether from arousal or frustration he couldn't tell, nor did he care. It came down to a matter of trust, and he had to face the fact that she might never be able to trust him, not because she did not want to, but because she was not capable of trusting anyone but herself.

Awkwardly, he fumbled with his clothes and she, with hers. Several times, Dryston started to speak, but none of the words he strung together in his head made sense. He had attempted to free her and had only imprisoned himself in the quest to do so.

Chapter Seventeen

He had changed everything. Sierra did not want to face the idea that he could feel anything for her. Why he did was yet a mystery to her—even with her uneducated view of the world she could see they were as unlikely a pair as ever lived. Yet when he touched her, she felt more alive than she had ever been. He made her want to hope for, to believe in something better.

Still, what had she to offer him in return? She was not like the maidens he had chosen before, the women he had given his heart to and made plans of home and hearth with. He offered her passion and nothing more. She could not, dared not want for more. It was all that she could offer. And she knew that passion alone would not be enough for him.

Letting the horse rest, they walked in silence. Dryston, ahead a few yards, held the reins, and Sierra was glad for the distance so she could think. He wanted something from her, but she could not give what she did not have to give. A wayward tear trickled down her cheek and she wiped it away.

"It is not much farther," he called over his shoulder.

Sierra nodded, swallowing the lump in her throat. How was it that in such a short time this man could have such an effect on her?

"Here, under these vines, there is an overhang with a sheltered spot below. We should be safe there." He tossed her the sack with the flint. "See this creek." He pointed to a narrow stream. "If you follow this to the source, there is a spring. I will take the horse and water him. You start us a fire." He tramped off through the trees, his face grim.

Sierra wanted to call out to him and tell him not to give up on her, but pride stopped her. She assembled the makings for a fire, and in no time, she had flame.

As she waited for him to return, she scanned her surroundings. Here, in the valley, the leaves and vines grew lush and green, as if the summer still lived in this place. As a precaution, she checked closely at the underbrush surrounding the cave for any elderberry plants.

Sierra wandered the area, gathering here and there a few clumps of vine to make a pallet. Still Dryston had not returned. She began to wonder if he had abandoned her, or if the Saxons had found him. She left the vines near their camp and followed the creek in the direction he had left her. Along the way, she picked up a stick and trailed it alongside her, listening for any sounds.

The stream gurgled as it played over the stones and she picked her way through the bushes and trees, following its path. The whinny of a horse caught her ear, and she tiptoed ahead with caution. Peering between two bushes, she spotted the horse preoccupied with nibbling the grass on the bank of the spring. It was more like a small lake, actually, protected on three sides by high cliffs covered with ivy and shimmering bright green moss.

She stepped from the bushes and paused to stroke the horse's nose. A splash caught her attention and she turned toward the sound. There she found him. His broad shoulders glistened in the waning sunlight as he dived headfirst into the water. A moment later he broke through the surface. He turned his face toward her.

"You have not seen any fish, have you?" She shaded her eyes to better see his expression.

"Why not find out for yourself?" he called, moving his arms back and forth in the water.

Though tempted, her insides were still in turmoil from earlier. And were she to oblige his invitation, she knew it would be the same as before—him demanding more than she could give.

"Do you think it wise to be out here in the open?" she asked.

A slight grin quirked the corner of his mouth as he pushed his hair back on his head. "Then *you* do not trust the stable boy any more than I do?"

"I said no such thing." She chose her words so as not to anger him. Thus far their bickering had led to one thing—sex. Sierra turned away so she could not see the water shimmering on his naked chest.

"You are certain then? It is warm beneath the surface."

"Later perhaps," she replied. "When it is not so crowded." She heard him chuckle.

"Suit yourself. I will be up in a minute." He grinned and dived underneath the surface, offering her a peek at his lovely arse.

"More nuts and berries?" He glanced up at Sierra as she placed the handful of fruit on a bed of leaves.

"Woodcock seems scarce in these woods," she reminded him. He laughed and popped a berry in his mouth.

Sierra toyed with a stick, poking at the fire. "You know that by now that hunter will have gone back to the castle and informed Aeglech that we stole his horse and left him for dead."

Dryston nodded. "Do you think that he will not go to the ruins now because he suspects it is a trap?"

She thought a moment and shook her head. "No, he won't back down. For two reasons—my vision and his pride. The first is a vision of castle ruins that I gave him once."

"I remember," Dryston said.

"And the second is that he was betrayed by the one who gave him that vision, by the only person left in his life that he trusted. It won't matter what danger he must face now. His sole purpose now will be to seek revenge for my disloyalty."

"You make it sound as if he had feelings for you. Did he?"

Sierra shrugged. "I don't even understand the things stirring around in me, Dryston. How could I possibly know what he felt?"

"You are a *seer,* don't you *see* things?"

Sierra sighed. "No, not always. There are emotions—lust, greed, anger…fear—that can block my gift."

He was silent a moment and she knew he was mulling over her words.

"Can I ask you something?"

The intimate tone in his voice caused Sierra to shift uncomfortably.

"You can ask," she replied.

"How did you come to be at the Saxon burke?"

"If you don't mind, I am not quite ready to share that with you," she said, standing up to stretch. "I think I will go for that swim now."

He pushed to his feet to follow. Sierra stopped him. "I can find my way. There is no need for you to watch over me."

"What about Cearl and the guards?" he asked. "No, I'm coming with you." He started to rise.

"Dryston, if they had followed us, wouldn't they have made their move by now?"

He studied her and she knew he wrestled with the wisdom of letting her go alone. Finally, he sat down, picked up a small stick and looked at her.

"If you are not back by the time this stick burns to ash, I am coming for you."

"You would remove me from the water against my word?" she asked, her brow raised.

He shrugged and lit the end of the stick, holding it up to illuminate his devilish grin.

"Shite," she muttered, shoving the curtains of vines covering the cave's entrance aside. The man had a head as big as the moon and a confidence that she both despised and—

Shite.

Sierra stopped in her tracks as if given a blow to the head. Her breathing grew shallow, there again was that prickly sensation crawling over her skin.

Despised and...

Loved.

The word was not one she had allowed in her thoughts for years. Worse, she'd just used it in reference to Dryston.

She held her palm to her forehead. Was it possible?

Sierra followed the creek to the spring, a nauseous feeling growing in her stomach. Though the autumn moon provided ample light, the lake's beauty was now cast in shadows.

At the water's edge, she discarded her clothes and walked

briskly into the spring. Every sound of the night seemed louder, less friendly, challenging her calm. She kept her eyes on the bank, watching for any movement. "Thank you, Roman," she muttered, realizing that his mistrust of Cearl had planted the seed of caution in her head.

After bathing quickly, she ran her fingers through her wet hair and started to swim toward the bank. But her foot suddenly became caught, and she found herself being pulled beneath the dark surface.

She clawed her way toward the surface, trying to free herself. As she twisted her body around, flailing through the water, she saw Cearl's face a few feet away from her. He smiled at her. She did not know what to think, and reacted instead, kicking and hitting until at last she freed her leg. She took a deep breath and began to swim again toward the shore, unsure where Cearl had gone or if she imagined him.

"Sierra."

Cearl's head bobbed to the surface. The moon illuminated his face. He was no longer smiling.

"I had forgotten how beautiful you are, Sierra. If that Roman had not interfered, you would still be at the castle with me."

Sierra pushed through the water, swimming with all her might toward the bank.

"Mouse!" he called as he swam with ease after her, his long arms slicing through the water.

Sierra crawled upon the bank and scrambled to her feet, grabbing her clothes. "Where are the others, Cearl? Have you brought them with you?" Disoriented, she searched for the path that would lead back to Dryston.

Dryston.

What if the guards were near? Perhaps they had already

found him. Sierra turned to face Cearl. Her hand fisted the
fabric in her hand, finding her blade wrapped securely within.

"Where is your Roman?" he snarled. She sensed jealousy
and hatred in his tone.

Her heart pounded and she fought to think. "He left me,"
she lied, hoping she sounded convincing.

Cearl's gaze narrowed on her.

"He left you alone? Out here?"

She nodded, brushing the water off her face. "He was jealous
when he found me with you, and after he tied you up, he took
me deep into the woods and left me."

He shook his head. "I knew he was a Roman swine."

"You always were a good judge of character, Cearl." Her
instinct to survive took over. She dropped her gown and stood
naked before him.

As she knew he would, he assessed her hungrily and began
to remove his sodden breeches.

"I did not like the way he looked at you, Sierra." He spoke with
a softness Sierra recognized. It was the voice of her stable boy.

Even though she felt he was harmless, Sierra had to be
careful. Besides, someone must have had to untie him.

"I will make us a bed here under the stars," she said. "It will
be just like the stables back home." She spread her gown out
over the grass, creating the facade that everything was back to
the way it was.

He tipped his head and gave her an odd smile.

"Home? So, you still think of the castle as your home?"

She laughed, hoping to convince him. "Of course, Cearl. Do
you really believe I would have allowed this Roman soldier to live?
Nay, I only aided his escape so that he would lead us to his camp."
She reached out, threading her fingers through his blond curls.

"You speak the truth, Sierra?" he asked, searching her face.

"Could I leave you, Cearl? The first man who ever made me feel like a woman?"

His grin widened as he drew her against him. His rigid member brushed Sierra's thigh. She turned her head, searching the woods over his shoulder and wondering how far behind him the Saxon guards were. She endured his hands groping her, his mouth slobbering over her flesh.

Nausea rose in her throat and she forced it down. She had changed. Where once she had welcomed Cearl's touch, she now detested it.

"They said I could not bring you back," he spoke as he fondled her breasts.

"They? They who?" She swallowed, trying to stay calm. His innocent blurting of the information made it clear to her that he was not truly aware of the circumstances.

"The guards," he replied. "When they found me, I told them he was holding you prisoner and that you would listen to me. I told them we had been lovers for a long, long time."

"So you came for me alone?" she asked, brushing her hand over the back of his head. He nodded in the crook of her neck as he pressed her to the ground, parted her legs and invited himself between them.

Sierra looked up at the heavens and told herself that this did not matter, that she did it to save Dryston.

"Sweet Sierra, did he touch you like I do?" he whispered, kissing her breast.

"Nay, Cearl, never. What will happen to us now?" she asked, curious to hear his plan.

"We will return to the fort and explain everything to Lord Aeglech. He will be pleased, you will see."

Poor Cearl. He was so naive.

"I grow hard, Sierra. I need your warmth."

He trailed kisses over her stomach as Sierra reached for her blade, tucked underneath her gown. He did not understand; he was far too trusting. Whether he brought her back with him or returned alone, Aeglech's men had only used him to find her. Aeglech in his paranoid state, without Balrogan as buffer, would be a mad man, prone to worse torture than she'd ever seen. She could not send Cearl back to suffer at his hands.

Tears pricked the backs of her eyes as he entered her, his breath catching softly. "Sweet Cearl," she spoke, her lips trembling as she fought back the tears. He would never be disloyal to his king. Pain tore at her heart as she convinced herself of what she must do.

He braced himself on his elbows and looked down at her.

"I have never seen you cry, Sierra." Cearl smiled. His smiling face was what she wanted to remember.

"I am sorry," she whispered and, with one swift jab, her blade found the pulse at the side of his neck.

Cearl's look of surprise made the bile rise in her throat. She shoved him away as he gasped for air, his blood spewing over her naked flesh.

Unable to speak, he reached blindly for her, a strangled groan coming from him.

Sierra struggled to her knees, trying to back away from him. He clawed at the grass, trying to get up, fumbling at the blade protruding from his neck.

"I did not want it to be this way," she cried, caught between running away and staying to help him, even though she was the one who had inflicted the wound.

Sierra was stopped by an obstacle from behind, and she

looked up in time to see Dryston lunge forward with his sword. She turned her face, shaking her head as Cearl came at her, his blade raised high.

A sickening sound followed and his body slumped against Dryston's sword. He slid to the ground and his blond head came to rest in her lap.

Sierra stared at the back of his head. Blood oozed over her legs. She held her hands poised to touch him, but she could not move. Suddenly, she was back in the dungeon. The smell of sulfur and death clogged her throat, suffocating her. The ghosts of the dead surrounded her, reaching for her with skinless hands.

She lifted her eyes to the pale moon and in her mind she saw her motherless, lifeless body. Sierra fisted her hands over her ears and shut her eyes, trying to make the images go away.

"Sierra!" a voice called from somewhere, but the din of her ghosts was too loud. Her body felt tired. She felt broken and bruised. Lost.

"Sierra!" the voice called again and Sierra began to shiver uncontrollably. She was pulled from the dark abyss, two arms pulling her back to earth.

Purging her stomach of the vile evil roiling within her, she rid her mind of the blood, death and hate. Someone held her until she could vomit no more, rocking her gently. "I am here, Sierra. I am here," the voice whispered.

Finally, the opaque void consumed her.

Smoke blinded her eyes and screaming filled her ears, followed by laughter, evil laughter that chased her. She dropped to her knees, covering her ears to block out the sound. All around her, fire licked at the walls and she searched for a way to escape the heat searing her flesh. She stumbled and tried to run through the haze. She could barely breathe…

Sierra bolted upright in the pitch black. She did not know where she was.

"Sierra?"

A hand touched her arm and she screamed, backing as far away from it as possible.

She heard a tap-tap and then a spark caught her eye, erupting next into a small flame.

"You are safe, Sierra," a man's gentle voice spoke. It was not her brother or Cearl.

It was the Roman warrior.

"Do you know who I am?" he asked, eyeing her closely.

Events from Sierra's past tumbled forth in her conscience. Her lips stumbled over her words as she tried to speak. "They violated her and hung her from a tree, those filthy Saxon bastards. They took us to the fort and my brother was taken, stolen from my arms and given to a guard, with orders that he be killed. I found the guard's knife and cut his leg, but they gave my brother to another guard. I begged and pleaded, but the king would not listen." She looked up and met the Roman's gentle green eyes. "He was just a boy, just a little boy. I hated my mother for leaving us. I hated my life." Sierra's shoulders slumped.

"Mother of God," the Roman muttered, but he did not move. "It was you."

She searched the ground, scratching her head as if the gesture might jar loose more of her memory. "Cearl. Cearl was my friend. He gave me food and his body could make me forget. We called it our time, our 'escape.'"

"I have seen so much suffering, so many slain. I cleaned up their blood, their flesh on Balrogan's tools. Aeglech made me dress like a boy." She touched her hair. "He kept my hair short and forced me to watch as he took a woman and slit her throat." Her thoughts ran together, haunting her with gruesome images.

She saw the Roman—had he told her his name?—ease around the fire and inch toward her. She scrambled away from him.

"I will not harm you, Sierra. As long as I have a breath in my body I will protect you."

She shook her head. "You cannot." Her eyes welled so that she had to blink to see clearly.

He did not come any closer, but looked at her with compassion.

"There is none of that here now. It is all in your past," he offered gently.

"Nay, he comes for me. I have seen him in my dreams. I can hear him laughing." She needed to warn this man. Her gaze searched frantically around her.

"Sierra, do you remember what just happened at the spring?" the man asked.

She looked around her, at the vines that hung loose over the opening, at her pouch that lay by the fire. Next to it lay her blade, glittering in the firelight.

The occurrence at the spring flashed in single pictures in her mind, one after another in horrible detail.

She met the man's gaze. "Cearl. Is he dead?" She remembered, but it did not seem real.

"Yes." The Roman moved closer. This time she did not back away.

"He came at you with your knife. Do you re—"

"Aye." Sierra nodded. "I do. I do." Tears spilled down her cheeks and she thought her heart would split wide open from the pain. She looked at the Roman and saw the arms that had pulled her from the darkness.

"Dryston?" she whispered. He nodded, wrapping her in his strong embrace.

Finally, she was safe.

Sometime later, Sierra awoke to the sound of a gentle rain. She did not know what time of day it was. The fire was out.

Asleep beside her was Dryston, his arm tucked around her, holding her close to his side. Careful not to awake him, Sierra eased out from beneath him and walked to the cave's entrance. She closed her eyes and let the rain wash her tearstained face. She pushed away Cearl's image and opened her eyes, filled with a new emotion—gratitude.

She filled her palm with rainwater, drinking her fill to appease the rawness in her throat. Her ribs ached from retching. The hatred that once imprisoned her no longer held her captive, but in its place was mostly emptiness, except for one glimmer of hope.

Sierra looked back at Dryston and in the misty light she watched the rise and fall of his chest. There were many reasons she had to thank him although she knew that her journey to healing was not yet completely over. He had shown her, however, that she did not have to walk the path alone.

She made up her mind that when they rode into the Roman camp together, she wanted no secrets to exist between them.

More than anything, she needed to know about the boy she saw flash in his memory.

She allowed the rain to splash over her head and neck, but she knew it would take more than water to wash away the memories.

"Sierra?"

Sierra turned and found Dryston standing behind her, eyeing

her with kindness and concern. How could she not be drawn to such a man?

She faced him, touching his unshaven jaw, and he covered her hand with his.

"Did you rest?" he spoke quietly brushing his hand over her hair.

"Yes, thank you," she said, and kissed his cheek. She did not presume that after all she had put him through, he would feel any more for her than a sense of duty to follow through on his word to take her to his camp.

"There is much you need to know," she started.

"I know," he whispered. He pulled her close and she leaned against him, her broken spirit absorbing his strength.

"Are you hungry?" he asked.

"Aye, but 'tis not for food." She waited, certain he would reject her with the same kindness that she had come to know from him.

His fingers grappled with the hem of her gown and he pulled it over her head.

"Tell me you do not pity me," she spoke. It would kill her to see pity in his eyes.

"What I feel for you is not pity," he replied. He took her face in his hands and kissed her with such tenderness that her body trembled.

"You are shivering. If this is not what you want or what you need, I will understand," he said quietly.

She saw the passion, not reckless and wild, but intense, in his steady gaze. "It is what I want more than the air I breathe," she said, realizing that her admission came from somewhere deep inside.

His touch was gentle; he offered Sierra all that her weary soul yearned for. They had no need of fire to warm their flesh. Feverish desire simmered between them and it was more than enough.

They explored each other as if for the first time. His mouth worshipped her, giving her pleasure. She gave of herself equally, touching his body, caressing and tasting every part of him. She came back to his face, touching his brow, his mouth, looking into those eyes that held her from the first day he looked at her.

His hands slid over the curve of her back, moving unhurriedly between her legs as she lay atop him. She opened her legs, straddling his hips, offering him access to her warmth. His long fingers stroked her, stirring the smoldering heat deep inside her.

"Why me?" Sierra's fingers teased the tight nubs of his chest. "I am not beautiful like other women."

He rested his warm callused hands on the tops of her thighs and his eyes searched hers.

"I was told once that I was always rescuing the hearts in need—"

Pride assaulted her. "I am *not* ne—"

He put a finger over her lips.

"You are the most courageous woman and the most brave that I have ever met. You have no need of rescuing."

He cupped her neck and pulled her close.

"It is you that has rescued me, Sierra." He stared deeply into her eyes.

No man had ever spoken such words to her, nor said anything that meant as much. He kissed her slowly and thoroughly as she took him inside her. This time their joining was different. There was a wholeness, a connection. No longer did she view the act of joining as an escape. Nay, with him, it felt like coming home.

She kissed Dryston hard. He sat upright, tucking her legs

around his waist. She curled her arms around his waist. They held each other tightly, their foreheads braced against each other, looking down to where their bodies joined. Slowly and fervently, they rocked each other to the edge, their breathing coming as one.

"Sierra," he groaned against her shoulder, releasing his seed.

"Dryston," she called out in the silence of the early morning as waves, not of darkness but of joy, washed over her. For the first time, she offered him more than her body—she offered him her heart.

Chapter Eighteen

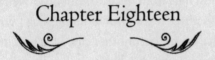

Dryston was glad to see Sierra's appetite return. The camp was not far now and when they got there he would see to it that she was given a proper meal.

"These berries are sweet. Did you try some?"

She held out a handful to him.

"You eat them. I will just enjoy watching you." It was the first time he had seen her blush. Her expression sobered and she swallowed, licking her lips as if trying to find the right words to speak.

"Are you having regrets about…what happened?" he asked her.

"Not at all. I'm still trying to sort things out. Give me time." She smiled at him.

He took her hand. "I understand, but if you need to talk, I am here for you. I want no more secrets between us."

She nodded in agreement. "Tell me again about the image of the boy I saw when I used my sight upon you. The one in the log in the woods."

His gaze held hers. "You think he may be the one you heard the story about?"

"Aye, perhaps it is the same boy. Who is he? What does he have to do with you?" she asked.

Surprised by her question, he realized they had never pursued the story. He cleared his throat. "When I was but a boy myself, I found a boy hiding in a hollow log. I remember his skin was pale gray, almost blue from the cold. But he looked up at me and I knew he was alive. It took some doing, but I got him to my horse and once home, my mother cared for him. It took weeks for him to physically recover, but his will to live was very strong."

"Aye, go on," she urged.

"By summer of that next year, he was walking again, and eating, but he still would not speak. It was as if something or someone had taken the ability from him. He was a quick and fierce fighter when we would all pretend we were in battle. In fact, even though he was mute, the other boys respected him because of his warrior's skills. I was the youngest in my family, with two older sisters, so it was good to have him at my side. We did everything together. We still do. He is the only brother I have ever known and I would give my life to protect him."

Her eyes softened as she looked at him. "Does he remember how he came to be in the woods? Does he remember anything about his family?"

"I thought the legend you told me about claimed they were killed." Something in her eyes heightened his curiosity, but he continued. "He does not have a memory of his family. Alyson—"

"Who is Alyson?" Sierra interrupted.

"Alyson is…from what I have seen, and if I know my brother—"

"Are they lovers, then?"

Dryston hesitated. "I would venture to guess that they are, yes." He grinned.

"And how well does this Alyson know your brother, beyond being his lover?"

He realized then that her concept of relationships was not vast. "Well, they talk frequently, on many subjects. She teaches him things—"

"Like what?"

"She believes in the ancient ways."

"Like me?" she asked.

"She does not have the gift of sight as far as I am aware of. She is a healer and has knowledge of herbs and potions. She reads the runes."

Sierra nodded and he could see her considering all that he had told her. But her insatiable curiosity puzzled him.

"Why do you ask about my brother?"

Her eyes fixed on his.

"Do you remember the girl in the legend I spoke of?"

Dryston nodded, a sense of realization forming in his gut. "The one you said had died?"

"Aye." She hesitated. "That girl was me, Dryston." She waited a heartbeat before she continued. "Our mother tried to save us. She hid us in a pantry." Her gaze drifted away from his, as if picturing the moment in her mind. "They did unspeakable things to her and then hung her as a traitor. But I can remember her last words. She said, 'You must think only of your brother and yourself. You must keep each other safe.'" She turned her eyes to his. "I failed in that, Dryston. And they took him away. I could do nothing but watch. For a long time, I held on to the hope that maybe he was alive, that somehow he had managed to survive."

He wanted to hold her again, ease her tortured memories. "I remember last night, when you spoke of this. I am so sorry for all that you have suffered."

"What I said about the legend was true. In many ways, that girl did die that night."

"Do you think my brother might also be your brother?" Dryston asked. The very idea staggered his imagination.

She offered him a brief smile. "I do not know and if it is, will he remember me? Here, I have something to show you." From her satchel, she pulled the wristlet he'd earlier found.

"This is a wristlet that my mother made for my brother when he was young. It was intended to protect him. He was wearing it the last time I saw him."

She hesitated and he knew she was mustering the determination to continue.

"The guard who took him. He summoned me the day of your hanging. He was dying and he wanted to give it to me. He told me that he wanted to die in peace. He asked my forgiveness, gave me this, and told me that when he left my brother in a snowbank, he was still alive. Still, I could not forgive him."

Dryston turned the woven wristlet in his hands. "I found it earlier when I was making your poultice. I thought Cearl had given it to you."

"That day, on the way to the gallows, remember I asked where to send word of your hanging?"

Dryston smiled. "That's not easily forgotten. Yes, I do."

"You spoke a name, but I do not remember *hearing* it."

"It's all right, there was much happening that day. For a long time my mother called my brother Duncan, after my great-grandfather, because he would not speak. Then, we were out hunting one day and we came upon a giant oak tree, standing alone at the top of a hill covered in flowers. And suddenly, he turned to me and told me he remembered something.

"I was so happy to hear him speak that I almost forgot to ask what it was he remembered. It was his name."

"And what is his name?" She leaned forward, her eyes intense.

"Torin," he answered.

Tears welled in her eyes. "Torin was my brother's name."

He watched in confusion as she tugged her gown up over her head. Dryston's eyes fell instantly to the gentle sway of her breasts.

She lifted her arm over her head, and pulled taut the flesh above her elbow.

"Has he a mark like this, under his left arm?"

He had noticed it when they made love. But the symbol was often found on earlier generations of Celtic children.

"The Awen symbol," he stated, shoving his heated thoughts aside. He turned her elbow to study it.

She took his chin in her hand and brought his face to hers.

"Does your Torin bear this mark?"

Dryston nodded, studying her features with renewed interest. He saw now a few similarities, the intense brown eyes, perhaps the same full lower lip. Torin's hair was darker— Dryston considered the idea carefully, not wanting to dash her hopes. Was this possible? Was he on the verge of discovering his brother's past?

"The symbol is the Celtic deity, it means—"

"Truth, beauty and love." He ended the sentence for her. "Torin asked an old monk while in Rome once what it meant. He did not know how he got it." Dryston sat in stunned silence. "If what you say is true—"

"I give you my oath, every word I have said is true," she said.

"So you believe that *my* brother is your brother." He spoke the words slowly, the implications settling in his brain. It was not so easy to swallow.

"'Tis an amazing thing, to be sure," she responded.

If it was truly so and Torin was her brother, Sierra could help to fill in the gaps of Torin's memory, and she, in return, would be reunited with her kin. To that end Dryston could not be a happier man.

For him though, it meant facing his brother, his best friend and commander, and admitting that he had slept with his sister more than once. It was possible that Torin would accept the news with his usual sense of calm, but then again, he might not. She was, after all, his sister. This was one thing Dryston was certain of, however—his brother would want to know his intent regarding his sister.

And that was a whole other kettle of fish.

"It appears to me, we should not waste any more time here. We will be able to resolve this great mystery when the two of you meet." Dryston stood, shoving his head through what little was left of his torn tunic. "I will go fetch the horse. The camp is not far now. We will follow the creek to the base of the mountain. There is a path that winds up the back of the mountain to the camp."

"Aye, I will see to it that it looks as if no one stayed here," she offered.

He stepped to the cave's entrance and glanced up at the sky. There would be more rain before they reached the camp. With any luck it would slow down the guards that he suspected were still looking for them.

"Dryston?"

"What if he does not remember me?"

"We do not know yet, for certain, if he is your brother," he cautioned.

The look in her eyes prompted him to draw her into his arms. He kissed the top of her head. "Do not worry, Sierra. We will find the answers in due time. We need to stay keen until we reach the safety of the camp."

"I want it to be him," she whispered against his chest. "I want him to be happy to see me."

"I cannot believe he would not be elated."

"He should hate me for not protecting him better."

"There is nothing you could do. Sierra, all that you have suffered and lived through is nothing short of a miracle. Torin is a smart man and a fair one. I am counting on that." He placed one last kiss on her forehead. "Now hurry. We need to get moving."

Her eyes suddenly widened. "Where is Cearl's body?"

Shite. Dryston did not want to get into this now. "He is at peace, Sierra. Let it go."

She leveled a look at him that told him she was not about to do any such thing.

"In the pool, the deepest part—he is at peace," he added, hoping that she would not suggest giving him a proper burial.

She nodded. "Aye, I thank you for that. You must know he was, deep inside, a good man. He was loyal to a fault, unable to see that Aeglech had used him. I did not want him to suffer the torture I knew he would be put through upon his return."

Dryston nodded, unsure if he agreed with her about the man's noble character.

"Go on now," Sierra said. "I will finish up here."

He untied the horse and walked him back to the cave

entrance. Sierra appeared, placing the satchel over her shoulder. She picked up Dryston's sword from where it leaned against a stone.

"Come on, I will give you a leg up." He bent down, clasping his hands for her. "Sierra, we—"

She pointed the sword at his neck. "Do not act like there is anything wrong," she uttered in a low voice, pinning him with her eyes. "There are two Saxon guards on the ridge above us."

"Get on the horse, Sierra," Dryston ordered quietly. "Play out the ruse. Pretend you are escaping from me. They are the same guards from the gallows. Chances are they do not know any different."

"There are only two. We can take them together," she said as she hoisted herself on the steed.

"Listen to me," Dryston explained. "You said yourself that Aeglech will march to the castle ruins. That is close to where Torin is to meet up with General Ambrosis. If my brother is not told of the change in plans then they will be caught unaware. It is vital that you ride as fast as you can. Follow the creek to the base of the mountain. Tell Torin about the plans being changed. Will you do that for me?"

"I do not want to leave you," she said.

"Any more than I want you to leave. Now handle that sword like you mean it," he said. "I will lead them away."

"Then take the seax from my leg," she offered. He removed the blade from the strap on her thigh.

"Do not come back, promise me. Get to the camp and tell Torin to send his men to the falls in the valley. He knows where I'll wait."

"Be careful." She planted a foot in Dryston's chest and sent him reeling backward.

"Saxon shite!" Dryston called up to them.

They turned their horses toward the trail leading down the ravine. Dryston smiled and took off like a rabbit being chased by wolves.

Chapter Nineteen

Sierra rode like fury through the pelting, cold rain. She tried not to think of leaving Dryston behind.

She noticed the terrain growing rugged, and she knew she was nearing the foothills. Relief flooded her body. She did not know how long she had been riding—only that she had not stopped, determined to get to the camp as quickly as possible to find help for Dryston.

She pushed the horse forward relentlessly as she found the path that trekked up the steep mountainside.

"Halt!" She heard a man exclaim as she flew past him. Sierra glanced behind her, seeing the man running after her.

She faced ahead of her and saw another man, his sword drawn, blocking the middle of the road.

To her left was the ledge. The camp had to be around the next bend.

The man, clearly of Roman persuasion, raised his sword.

And so, she raised Dryston's.

She did not slow down, but held Dryston's sword straight over her head, hoping the man would see that it was Roman. Her arm ached from the weight of it and when she reached the man, she dropped it to the ground, sending the man scrambling after it.

She rode full speed past him, dust and rock flying in her wake.

Ahead more shouts warned of her trespassing, but Sierra was determined not to go down without seeing the much-revered captain Dryston spoke of. The man who might well be her brother. She charged the remaining hill at breakneck speed.

A small crowd of men had gathered, blocking the top of the hill. Behind them, coming down from a tent overlooking the valley, walked a tall man, his expression stern.

She pulled slowly on the reins so as not to startle the horse. He relented to a canter as Sierra crested the top of the hill.

The man she had seen pushed through the crowd.

His expression was grim as he took her in with his dark eyes. He wore the clothes of an army commander, but he would not have needed a uniform to distinguish his position.

He had not drawn his sword, but the men surrounding her horse had. What seemed like a thousand eyes glared up at her.

"Stand down," the commander ordered.

The sound of swords being put away followed.

His dark eyes glittered fiercely as he studied her. She was too tired to move, afraid if she dismounted, she would not be able to stand.

Her horse pawed and pranced anxiously on its powerful legs. Sierra stared at the man. Was this her brother? His broad chest was covered by a molded-leather breastplate on his wide shoulders, he wore a red cape fastened by an ornate brooch.

"Who are you and how did you find this place?"

She began to speak but no sound escaped her parched throat.

"Get her water," the man ordered, not taking his eyes off her.

A scruffy-looking man with a shock of white hair hurried to her, lifting a cup of water to her lips.

She nodded her thanks and took a sip, welcoming the cool drink.

The guard who had tried to stop her on the path brought her sword to his commander. He took it and his gaze narrowed on her.

The old man glanced at the brand on the horse's hindquarters and muttered, "Saxon."

"Where did you get this sword and your horse?" the commander demanded.

Sierra dropped to the ground and stumbled to her knees. The commander reached down and hauled her up to her feet.

"I asked you a question."

After all the years she had hoped to find Torin, she was suddenly afraid to face this man she believed could be her brother. She closed her eyes. There would be much to explain if she told him who she was. And it was Dryston who they needed to focus on, not her.

"Dryston sent me. He needs your help."

"How did you get his sword?" the man fired back.

"He gave it to me," she responded, lowering her eyes to the ground. His tone was not unlike Aeglech's when he was angry.

"Gave it? You expect me to believe you?" He looked at her incredulously.

"You must. He asked me to tell you to send your men to the falls in the valley. He said you would know where to go."

He studied Sierra with the practiced eye of a military man. Then he nodded to the guard who had brought him the sword and called out to several others. They mounted their horses and rode down the path she had come up.

A young girl touched the commander's sleeve. She might have been Torin's age when Sierra last saw him. The commander knelt, placing his arm around the child's shoulder as she whispered in his ear.

Sierra watched, mesmerized by the change in the commander's demeanor. But his mouth quickly returned to its tight line.

"This child claims she remembers you from the Saxon fort. She says that you are the executioner's apprentice. Is that so?"

Sierra's eyes widened as she stared at the girl. She might have been one of many children Balrogan had left fatherless.

"I have never seen this child," Sierra replied.

The crowd grew restless, closing in around her.

"I was held prisoner for many years. Your brother, he helped me escape. You have to believe me." Sierra turned to the child. "I am so sorry. I know what it is like to lose your family."

More jeers came from the crowd. The commander held up his hand and drew immediate silence.

"Dryston wanted me to tell you that he set a trap for Aeglech and his men at the castle ruins. He wanted you to know the plans have changed."

"My men will check the validity of your words. But for your sake, this had better not be a trap. And if one hair on my brother's head is harmed, I will hold *you* personally responsible.

"Guards!" he shouted and two men dressed in Roman-legion garb stepped forward.

"Take her to the brig until we have Dryston safely back. I will want to speak with her. See that she is given food and drink. And just in case she's lying, I want the women and children moved immediately to the designated place. Take a few men and see to it."

"Aye, commander," they replied in unison.

The men nodded.

Sierra looked up at the Roman leader, willing him to notice anything familiar about her.

When nothing registered in his eyes, she thought of Dryston and prayed silently that he was alive and well. Until his safe return she would remain under the cloud of her past.

Sierra had passed the remainder of the day in an open-sided wagon. She was a curious spectacle to some, invisible to others as they passed by. Small groups of tents dotted the hillside, and small fires began to appear in the twilight. Most of the men at the camp were villagers, common folk—and from all parts of Britannia, judging from the varied languages she heard spoken. Yet they had one goal, and the solidarity of their mission both humbled and inspired her to join their cause. She thought of how they had come together under the leadership of Dryston and his brother, Torin. And she pondered again the words of the dying guard who had summoned her to his side the day of the hanging.

She wondered what the guard had told Aeglech that had angered him so. Had he told him that he had left her brother alive in the snow?

She looked up to one of the Roman guards approaching with another meal, her third since she had arrived, and still there was no sign of Dryston. She tucked the wristlet back into her sleeve and hoped if she showed it to the commander, it might jog a familiar memory.

Chapter Twenty

*S*hite. Just as he thought there was rain and plenty of it, it began to pour even harder, making keeping ahead of the Saxon guards trickier than Dryston thought. The leaves beneath his boots were slick and the rain beat down so hard that at times he had to stop to see where he was going. The bright spot, if there was one, was that the Saxons were still hot on his trail, and not Sierra's. Dryston knew these woods and he was grateful even more for the time he had spent here creating grand adventures. Never had he imagined seeing them come to life.

He stopped a moment to catch his breath, listening for the sound of horses. By the grace of God, he had been able to lead them near full circle, taking them through all the secret places he played in as a child.

Dryston lifted his eyes to the heavens and let the rain wash over his face. He opened his mouth to drink deeply of the tepid water. It was the horse's snort he heard first followed by the Saxons' yell that caused him to bolt from his hiding place. He leaped over fallen logs, dodged low branches and followed again the same path. If the guards were as dense as he thought, he hoped to keep them following him in circles until Torin's men arrived.

"Over there!" a voice growled from behind him as he started sideways down a steep hill. Below him was a path leading through the woods. Dryston did not recognize it, but he was becoming desperate. His boots slipped, and he balanced himself by grabbing on to exposed tree roots, vines, whatever he could find, until at last, his feet hit flat ground. He looked up to see one of the guards looking down at him. He wore no expression, nor oddly did he try to come after him.

His calm demeanor did not settle well with Dryston. He glanced to his left. A short distance away was another hill, steeper than the one he had just climbed down. To the right, on what should have been the path of his escape, sat the other Saxon guard on his horse, staring down at him. A slow grin formed on his ugly face.

Up? Left? Right? Behind him rose another cliff, leading straight up and with nothing to grasp in his climb.

So left it was.

Dryston charged for the hill, praying the guard would think him daft and refuse to follow. He slid to a halt, teetering on the edge of a sharp slope. His foot slipped again on the wet leaves, causing him to tumble over the side sooner than he had planned.

Over the edge of the ridge, he saw the guard coming at him full gallop and Dryston prepared for him to sail through the air, right over his head to the falls below. He glanced down over his shoulder to a narrow ledge. Covered with bramble bush, it was all that lay between him and the drop to the falls below. If by some miracle he could make it down to the ledge, there was a good chance that the horse would fall, crushing him on his way down. If he let go and did not stop at the base of the hill, his chances of surviving the drop were at least a fraction greater than if he turned and faced the guard with only Sierra's short blade.

It was a great deal to think about in the span of a few heartbeats.

Dryston looked up a few feet above and the Saxon's face appeared with a menacing grin over the side of the ridge.

With a deep breath and discarding all thoughts to the contrary, he began a slow descent down the steep, mud-covered hill, grasping at slimy exposed tree roots.

Dryston slipped and he dug his fingers into cold, thick mulch, slowing himself as he sought for a foothold. A protruding stone saved him from sliding farther.

A whooshing sound swept over his head and he looked up to see the Saxon hanging on to a branch and swinging his battle-ax like a pendulum. *Fuck him. If he lived through this he was going to kill every last one of them with his bare hands.*

Whoosh.

Dryston looked up. His fingers were sore and numb and he began to lose his grip. He searched right and left for something to grasp on to so that he could ease himself down to the ledge below.

Whoosh. The blade sliced the top of his scalp. Dryston decided then, that if he was to die, he wanted it to be with his head attached.

He closed his eyes and let go. With any luck, he would land on the ledge. His feet hit first and the rest of his body followed. He dared to sigh a breath of relief as he looked down and realized that he had landed not on the ledge but on a protruding branch. Like a bird, Dryston teetered a moment, before his mud-caked boots slipped, and he toppled backward, free-falling through the air.

His arms flung out at his sides, he watched the guard looking down at him grow smaller. He did not need to look down to know the water was coming up fast. As if rammed by a charging bull, the water smacked him from behind, forcing all the air from his lungs as the cold green abyss closed over him.

Dryston opened his eyes and pain immediately rushed his brain. The clang of blades in battle and the angry yelling of men in hand-to-hand combat drifted in and out of his consciousness.

He wanted to believe that by some miracle, he had been spared death. He lay still, as though dead, so as not to welcome a Saxon sword. Water splashed on his face as men fought around him. He remembered falling into the water, so either he had drifted to the sandbar or someone had fished him out. As the battle around him raged on, he noted that it did not feel as if any of his bones were broken.

Dryston's head throbbed, and because of the pain, he knew he was alive.

A hard thwack sounded above him, followed by a groan. Then a large body landed on top of him, causing his eyes to open wide.

One of the Saxon guards was sprawled on top of him. He had to weight over three hundred pounds, were he to guess. His eyes were dull and glazed over.

Dead.

"See to Dryston." He heard a voice bark. Dryston would have answered, but he could not breathe for the weight of the man on top of him.

A familiar face stood over him and grinned wide.

"He's alive, sir."

"Barely," Dryston whispered.

The two men rolled the Saxon off him and air rushed Dryston's lungs, bringing a fresh sensation of pain with it.

His savior's face fell as he glanced at Dryston's left arm.

"Captain," the Celt guard called over his shoulder.

Dryston was tired. He had no way of knowing how long he had lain there, how long he had spent running from the Saxons. It was all a blur.

He tried to smile when a captain of his brother's army appeared at his side.

"What is it?" Dryston whispered through the insistent throb in his head.

He knelt and checked him over thoroughly before he spoke.

"Can you hear me, Dryston?"

He nodded, trying to focus on the man's blurry face.

"Your arm is broken, maybe your shoulder. But you may also be hurt internally. We are going to get you a pallet and bring you back to camp."

Dryston blinked, too tired to speak. He tried to check his arm, but when he turned his head, pain exploded into a thousand pinpoints. He felt the rain falling on his face and saw the captain's face hovering over him, but he could hear no sound. Finally, the captain's face faded into a tranquil darkness.

"Who is this angel?" Dryston's eyes opened to see Alyson, Torin's beloved, tending to him.

"Good evening, brother." Torin came to Dryston's side and stood peering down at him. "You look like hell," Torin said.

"A fall of fifty feet will do that to you." Dryston tried to smile. Even that hurt.

His face grew grim. "I have greater concern for the marks you bear on your back."

Dryston glanced at him, but this time he chose not to respond.

"We managed to set your arm without any problem, but you fell unconscious when we reset your shoulder," Torin said.

Alyson stood next to Dryston, dabbing his head with a cool, herb-soaked cloth. "You had us worried," she spoke with tenderness.

He smiled groggily up at her. "What time is it?"

"It is evening. Quiet now. It is important you rest."

Dryston looked at his sour-faced brother. "You are not nearly as beautiful to wake up to," he mused.

"Torin, can you get your brother to lie still? He shouldna be thrashing about until we know the extent of his injuries."

"Where is she?" Dryston asked.

Torin glanced at Alyson. She shrugged.

"Here, drink this," she urged, holding a cup to Dryston's mouth.

He made a face. "That tastes like shite." He swallowed the horrid mixture and looked from one to the other. "Sierra? Anyone want to tell me where she is?"

"You have to finish this, Dryston. It will aid you if you have internal injuries." Alyson placed the cup to his lips.

"I am fine. Do you think I would leave this important battle to this man alone?" Dryston joked.

"We will discuss that matter later when you have had time to rest," Torin cautioned.

Dryston eyed his arm, covered with a sling. "How long do I have to wear this?"

"Until your arm heals, you stubborn mule." Alyson blew a

wayward strand of hair from her face. She squeezed the cloth between her hands.

"Let me see that cut on your head," she ordered.

"I would listen to her, brother. She is liable to place a spell on you."

Dryston lay still and let Alyson see to his head. "What do you think of her?"

Torin glanced at Alyson. He took her hand. "That is something I wanted to discuss with you. I wanted to wait until you were better—"

"I do not mean your intended bride—" Alyson's mouth opened at his presumption "—of that I am quite certain by now. No, I mean Sierra. She *did* make it here? Who else would have told you where to find me?"

His brother let go of Alyson's hand and stared down at him. "She did not give us a name. I need to speak to her, Dryston," Torin said. "A child identified her as the apprentice to the Saxon executioner."

Dryston frowned. "That was true once, but not anymore." He sighed, slapping his hand on the bed. "She helped me to escape, Torin. She asked only that I bring her here."

"And you didn't question why she would ask you to do that?" Torin replied.

"You will have to ask her," Dryston stated.

"Oh, I have every intention of asking her."

"She did not tell you, then?" Dryston asked his brother. His head was beginning to throb again.

Torin patted Dryston's good arm. "You rest now. You have been through much. We can talk later."

"No, dammit. I swear to you, she can be trusted!"

"How do we know that she was not sent as a spy?" Torin urged stubbornly.

"Because *I* sent her. Ask to see the wristlet. Perhaps that will convince you." Dryston grew tired. "I want to see her as soon as you have spoken with her." It was clear Sierra's name had not sparked any familiarity with Torin. Perhaps hearing her story would.

"Very well, but bear in mind the fact remains that she is guilty of heinous crimes against innocent people."

"She is Briton, Torin, just as we," he muttered quietly. "And she did not choose her life, until she chose to help me."

"That may be true, but if she has lived in a Saxon burke, there is no way of knowing how she has changed."

Dryston fought to stand, swinging his legs over the pallet bed. Alyson gave him a look of warning that he had better find a way to calm down.

"Dryston—"

He stopped her with his upturned hand. "Promise me that no harm will come to her, Torin. Promise me." He leveled his gaze at his brother, clenching his jaw from the pain.

"Lie down, brother," Torin spoke, glancing at Alyson.

"I care about this woman very much. What she has been through, what she has seen, what she has done—she never wanted any of it. It was a life forced on her and she accepted it in order to survive. She wanted to live because deep down she hoped one day to find you alive. What she has confided in me might well help bring back your memory, Torin."

Dryston reached for Alyson's hand.

"So you will be able to freely go forward with your future," Dryston stated, his gaze steady on his brother.

"You care for her, you say? These past few days must have been quite trying for you," Torin remarked.

Dryston glanced at him with an uncertain look in his eye. "What do you mean?"

"I mean, perhaps she has charmed you into believing her, Dryston. My apologies, Alyson, but it is not outside the realm of possibility for a woman to sometimes use whatever means necessary to gain what she wants." Torin looked at Alyson, who raised her brow and went back to her work.

Dryston's gaze swerved to the floor and back to his brother.

"Be clear about one thing, Torin, if one hair on Sierra's head is harmed the person who hurt her will answer to me. Are we understood?"

"You truly care for her?"

"Have you not been listening?"

"And does she…this woman, who just happens to be an executioner's apprentice—does she return these tender feelings for you, Dryston?"

Torin's eyes held Dryston's.

"I do not know," he finally responded. "But I want the chance to find out."

Torin sighed. "Have you found another heart in need of rescuing? Fine, I will speak to her. You rest now and do as Alyson says. She is a wise and good woman."

Dryston complied by lying back on the pallet.

"So, too, is Sierra. You will see," he said.

Chapter Twenty-One

They had not been unkind, but Sierra still did not know of Dryston's condition. No one spoke to her, but twice they had brought her food—bread, water and part of an apple—which she gladly ate.

She looked up when the commander came to speak to the guard standing watch.

"Bring the Saxon to the command tent," he spoke with grave authority. Was she to be freed, then? Her wrists were still bound, but she was able to stand. She waited for him to finish so she could ask about Dryston, but his stern expression caused her tongue to remain still. If this was Torin, *her* Torin, he was much different than she expected.

Apart from his intimidating height and build, this man was very serious and confident. His hair was much darker than she remembered and his eyes were no longer filled with the wonder and delight they once were. Until she spoke with him, she could not even be certain this man was her brother.

"Come on then, let's get you out of there. The commander wants to have a word with you." The guard reached up and grabbed her arm. Sierra jumped down the few feet to the ground and wobbled unsteadily.

The guard assessed her from head to toe, leaning forward to sniff at her. "We should at least wash yer face so the commander can have a good look at ye."

He led Sierra past several small clusters of men, most who watched her in guarded silence, to a tent set up with a barrel of water and a hole dug in the ground, covered by a crude seatless chair. The stench made her gag as he dragged her to the barrel, took her by the back of her neck and pushed her head into the murky water. She came up coughing and sputtering, barely able to ask to catch her breath before he repeated the process a number of times.

Afraid she would drown, she spewed the water from her mouth and blinked away the water dripping into her eyes.

"There. That should do it then."

Sierra lifted her bound hands and brushed water from her face, but didn't complain. How could she after all that she had seen in the Saxon oubliette?

A villager spat at her feet as they wound their way back through the scattered tents and groups of men. Many of the camp's inhabitants were already asleep, tucked in under the makeshift lean-tos. Others sat around the various fires, cleaning their weapons.

Sierra and the guard stopped outside of a large tent secured to the rock wall of the mountain. Inside, a soft glow from a small fire cast a reflection on the tent wall.

"I have the prisoner, Commander," the guard spoke, glancing at her as he awaited direction.

"You may enter," a gruff voice from inside answered.

The guard held back the tent flap and ushered her inside. The commander was seated at a table. She immediately dropped to her knees before him. He glanced up from his maps, gestured at her to stand and pointed to a small boulder.

"Sit down."

He rose from his chair and paced in front of her, his hands clasped behind his back. It was clear to Sierra that he had much on his mind.

He stopped and looked at her directly, his eye twitching at one corner as he stared at her. She wondered if she was seeing the image of his father. There was little trace of their mother in him.

He tapped his hands behind his back as he began to pace again.

"My sources tell me that you came from Aeglech's Saxon burke. Is this true?"

"Yes, milord."

"And is it also true that you are the apprentice to his executioner?" he asked, glancing at her.

"Yes, milord. I *was* apprentice to Aeglech's executioner." The implications of her answer concerned her. Without Dryston to back her up she was not certain this man would believe her story. Sierra bit her tongue, wanting desperately to ask of Dryston's condition.

"Was? What do you mean by that?"

"I mean the day your brother was to be hanged—"

"You escorted him to the gallows?" he interrupted.

"Yes, I was with the guard unit assigned to escort him to the gallows."

"Quite the honor, I suspect, for an apprentice. You must have been quite proud, I would think?"

Sierra remained silent. He was determined to accuse her and, in truth, she was not sure she deserved his compassion.

"You must have impressed Aeglech with your skill?"

She raised her eyes to his. If she told him the truth, about her promotion to master executioner, it would most certainly be her neck.

"Milord, I beg you is there any word of Dryston's condition?" The question was ill timed, but she had not slept in hours and needed to know. The commander stared at her, his anger evident in his dark eyes.

"How was it that you came to have the honor of escorting my brother to the gallows instead of your master?"

She pressed her lips together. If the man did not hate her enough, she was about to seal that fate. "He was dead," she replied quietly. Perhaps he would not catch the implication.

"So you were promoted to your former master's post. Aeglech must have been *very* impressed." His brow rose.

"Yes, Aeglech offered me this perverse reward because I pleased him," she answered, growing more frustrated as he continued to attack her character.

"I see, and in what way did you please him?" he asked.

"It was not by way of any sexual favors, if that is what you are thinking," she responded. "It was because I was able to gain the information he wanted from your brother."

His gaze narrowed.

"And what means did you use to garner this confession?"

She averted her eyes from his, reliving the horror of what she had done. Would she have done anything differently if she had to do it all over again?

"I am waiting, Saxon."

Sierra's eyes snapped to his. "I am *not* Saxon. My mother and father were both Briton."

"You have not answered my question!" His deep voice thundered through the stillness of the tent.

"I took a skelp to him," she whispered.

"A skelp? You used a skelp on my brother? That explains why his flesh bears the scars of a thrashing. *That* is *your* doing?"

"Your brother ordered it," Sierra stated quietly, knowing the moment it left her lips how daft it sounded.

The commander offered a short laugh. "Yes, of course, and did he also ask you to sever his finger?"

He bent over her, speaking directly in to her face.

Sierra covered her face with her hands, unable to bear any more. If Dryston could not recover from his wounds, then she had not kept her oath. And she would have lost the only man who had ever believed in her. She deserved whatever the fates had in store.

She rocked against her hands, her mind filled with torment—the sorrow of never seeing Dryston again, the look of hatred in this man's eyes. It was too much…

"Turn now, daughter, and face your destiny."

Her mother's words caused Sierra to look up and meet the commander's hardened gaze.

Swallowing what little pride she had, she held out her bound hands and pleaded with him.

"If you would untie me, I could you prove to you I am Briton. My mother was an ancient. I had a brother, but he was taken from me and I was led to believe he was dead. I was held as Aeglech's apprentice to his executioner against my will and forced to do unspeakable things." She caught his look of disdain. "Things that I am not proud of."

He looked away.

"Please, I beg you listen to me," she pleaded.

He picked up her blade, the one she had given Dryston before they parted. He turned it in his hand as he stared at her. She could see that he was contemplating her fate.

"Do as she asks, Torin."

Sierra looked toward the entrance where she heard a female voice.

"Alyson, she is my charge, please be so kind as to—"

"Let you make a mistake that you might regret the rest of your days?" A beautiful woman entered the tent. Her bright auburn hair spilled over her linen kirtle and her skin was pale and perfect. "I dinna think so, Torin. I believe we should listen to what she has to say. And 'tis all the better if done with an open mind," she added, offering him a stern look.

He sighed. "I do this for you, Alyson, not because I think it is right."

Kneeling in front of her, he severed the rope and she rubbed her wrists, her skin marred red from chafing. The woman came to her, and drew a small tin from her pocket. She opened it and inside was a strange-smelling ointment. She dabbed some on her fingers and touched Sierra's wrist, massaging where the skin was raw. Immediate relief followed. Sierra did not understand the woman's kindness, but she welcomed it.

"How is it that the two of you managed to escape?" the woman asked gently.

Sierra glanced at the man who bore the same name as her brother. "I was impressed by his courage. I had seen many men come through the Saxon dungeon and none of them had his strength. I knew only a man of unusual courage would be able to escape the place no one had ever escaped before." Sierra watched the woman's delicate fingers, so perfect and feminine next to her filthy callused hands.

"He said that if I helped him, he would bring me to his camp. I hoped that when I arrived I would find the boy whom Dryston found hiding in a log."

Alyson looked up at her. "He told you about this?" She glanced over her shoulder at the commander. He was staring at Sierra intently.

"I saw an image when I laid my hands on him. Aeglech wanted me to use my powers of sight on your brother to find where your camp was located. Among the other images, there was a boy. It did not last long, but the image stayed in my head."

"You have the gift, then?" Alyson asked.

"Aye, from my mother, but I have not used it much, as I do not trust what I see. That is why I wanted to see for myself if the boy was truly still alive. It is the very reason that I devised our escape. It is the truth, I swear on my mother's soul." She looked from the commander to the woman. "Do you believe me?"

The beautiful woman smiled at her, kindness shining in her eyes.

"I believe you," she responded.

She moved to Sierra's side and clasped her filthy hands in her warm grasp.

"Tell me about the day you were taken from your family."

"I was about ten and two years. My mother was bound to Aeglech as his Druid adviser. He used her skills to protect himself from outsiders. It was just the three of us, my mother, my young brother and me. We did not know our fathers—I knew only that mine was a Celtic warrior, but we did not know about Torin's."

She stopped and glanced at the commander. His dark gaze remained steady on her.

"My brother was born just before the Saxon invasion, and

when Aeglech came into power he slaughtered all the male Briton children in our village to assure that there would be no Briton lineage to contest his reign. My mother would not allow Torin to be seen in the open, especially in the village. We made a game of it, hiding him whenever the Saxon guards would come around to summon her to the castle. She would have to go every day, and soon Aeglech began summoning her at night, leaving me in charge of Torin.

"One day while she was at the keep, I needed to go fetch some water from the well in the village. Torin begged and pleaded for me to take him along, but I knew my mother would not approve. So I dressed him to look like a little girl, telling him he must pretend to be one while we were in the village."

Sierra took a deep breath, remembering the events. "I had tied a kerchief to his head, and dressed him in one of my old kirtles. As sweet as his face was, he could have been my sister." She smiled at the memory as it resurfaced after all the years, seeing his dark eyes filled with adventure.

"None of us knew that day that a guard watched from the shadows, his eye on my mother. She was on her way back from the castle when my brother saw her from afar. Before I could stop him, he had bolted from my side and headed straight toward her. At first she did not recognize him, but in his haste to run to her, his kerchief flew off his head, leaving his dark curls exposed for all to see. My mother's face went white as she grabbed the scarf and tied it quickly back over his head. She snatched Torin up and hurried home. I grabbed the bucket and followed her, feeling guilty for bringing Torin to the village."

"What happened next?" the woman asked, studying her.

Sierra paused, unsure if she could continue with her retelling of events. But she knew that to leave anything out now might cost her. "The Saxon guards came that night. By the time my mother was aware of their coming, it was too late to change the fates." A sob choked Sierra's throat.

"It is all right. We are here." The woman patted her leg and Sierra remembered her delirium back in the cave, when Dryston had said the same thing to her.

She kept her eye on the commander as she struggled with the rest of the story, hoping to see some spark of recognition on his face. "She made us hide together in the pantry, told us to take care of each other, kissed us once and then closed the door."

Tears streamed down her cheeks, the brutal sounds of that night flooding her memory. "They violated her, bound her hands and hung her from the tree outside our home." Sierra blinked from her trancelike state, pulling her thoughts back to the present. Her heart twisted. The commander, his mere presence able to make men shudder in their boots, had tears running down his face.

"It was dark," he spoke. "But someone was with me, holding her hand over my mouth. Someone kept telling me that all would be well."

As if awakening from a deep sleep, his body jerked and his eyes focused on Sierra. "You?"

She pulled her arm from her sleeve, lifting it so he could see the symbol they shared, inked on her skin. The guilt of that day washed over her anew and she wept.

His lip quivered as he fought to stay in control of his emotions. She wanted to hold him and tell him that she was sorry—sorry that she had not fought harder for him, sorry that she had hurt Dryston and been unable to deliver him, unharmed, sorry for so many things.

"I am your sister, Torin."

He pushed up his sleeve, revealing a muscular arm, and turned his elbow. There in the same spot was the Awen symbol.

The woman pulled her into a warm embrace. "Do you wish to see Dryston?" she asked in a whisper.

"Is he well?" Sierra asked as she pulled away.

"I think he will be better after he sees you. But first you will want to freshen up, I suspect."

She was telling Sierra in a kind way that she stank, but she already knew that. "A bath would help us all." She smiled, wiping her nose on her sleeve. She tucked her arm back in her sleeve and glanced at Torin, his head bowed, not looking at her.

She rose to follow the woman. Pausing at her brother's side, she did not know what more to say. She only hoped that in time, he would be able to understand she could not have prevented what happened.

She drew the wristlet from her sleeve and gently touched his hand. Filled with more emotion than she thought possible, she laid it in his large palm.

He looked up at her, his dark eyes searching her face.

"Why was I not killed?" he asked her quietly.

She studied him, trying to envision the face of the young boy she once knew. But time had taken that boy away and replaced him with a confident, charismatic man who was destined to do great things. "Because of Mother's curse. The guard who took you spoke to me on his deathbed, asking for forgiveness, wanting to meet his death with a clear conscience. He said he was afraid to harm you, choosing instead to let nature decide your fate." She closed his fingers over the wristlet and though she wanted to stay longer, she knew she needed to give him time to digest this news.

★ ★ ★

The woman named Alyson took Sierra to a spring hidden away farther up the mountain. She kept it a secret from the men, afraid they would ruin its beauty and magic. Sierra was not sure that she agreed with that decision, having smelled the men at the camp, but she was grateful nonetheless for the chance to wash off the dirt and sweat of her journey.

Alyson did not stay with her as she bathed, but when Sierra emerged a short time later from the water, she had returned and she handed her a full-length kirtle, the color of soft heather.

"'Tis your size, or close enough. We can soak your clothes in some lye soap to get them clean," Alyson offered.

"We can set them to ash just as well if you like." Sierra pulled the gown over her head. It was a bit long, and perhaps a bit roomy in the bust, but it was clean. She looked down at herself in the deepening twilight. *"Go raibh maith 'ad,"* she spoke with quiet humility as she brushed her hands over the smooth fabric.

"Ta' failte rom hat, Sierra. I am happy that you still speak the ancient language. Come, Dryston should be awake by now."

She took her arm and Sierra decided she would need to give herself time to get used to people touching her. For Alyson, a healer, touch was her skill. Sierra hoped that she would be able to help with her brother's pain.

Sierra could not understand the nervous flutters in her stomach. Alyson placed her arm on Sierra's back before they went inside the tent where Dryston recovered.

"You've no need to fear Dryston. The fates could not have chosen for you a man of greater character." She pulled back the flap of the tent and breezed in, immediately busying herself with checking his bandages and the sling on his arm.

Dryston opened his eyes and grinned when he saw Sierra. "So, finally, my stubborn brother listened to me?"

She nodded, offering a glance to Alyson. "He has much to mull over, but I hope that in time we will be able to be a family again."

"Och, not to worry," Alyson assured her. "I will speak to him. These are events that the runes spoke of. But we must let the course of things run as they should. It will take time, but have hope, Sierra. He will come around."

Dryston held out his hand as he pulled himself up and brought his legs over the side of the bed.

"Is this wise?" Sierra asked, looking to Alyson for approval. "Are his injuries life threatening?"

She gave a short laugh. "Not unless a sharp wit and brash tongue is considered deadly."

He looked at Alyson, then back to Sierra with a wicked grin. "If it were so, woman, I would be dead many times over."

They had a good kinship, Sierra observed. It would be one that she could learn much from, if she was so lucky as to stay.

"Could you excuse us for a moment, then?" he asked, rubbing his thumb over Sierra's knuckles. She was not used to these small acts of affection, but she did enjoy the feeling, of that she was certain.

"Only a moment?" Alyson teased as she paused at the tent flap. "I will be in Torin's tent should you have need of me." She smiled at Sierra.

"I will see to her, Alyson." He gave her a wink.

"Watch that one now—he is a clever scoundrel," she cautioned as she left.

Dryston turned his gaze to Sierra. "You look beautiful."

He scanned her from head to toe and her cheeks grew

warm. He pinched a bit of the fabric at her waist and drew her to his side.

"Are you better now?" Her body desired him, but she was just as content looking upon him, knowing for herself that he was well.

He searched her face as he drew his fingers through her short hair. Tingles swept over her scalp, rushing down her neck and shoulders.

"I feel strange, Dryston."

"Let us get outside if you are going to retch. I have seen that firsthand already," he spoke as he stumbled to stand.

"No, Dryston. Not strange like that. Sit down. I do not wish to be the reason you feel any more pain."

He sat back down and took her chin between his sturdy fingers.

"You are not the reason for any of my pain, Sierra. I do not wish for you to ever think such a thing."

"But the thrashing—"

"Which I ordered," he said as he held her gaze captive.

"'Twas the hardest thing I've ever done. Besides leaving you with those two Saxon guards on your tail," she said, tracing the angle of his shoulder bound by the sling.

"I am sorry I had to send you off on your own." He touched her cheek.

"I was worried about you," she replied.

"About me? *You?*" His grin caused her stomach to flutter. "That almost sounds like you might be starting to like me."

"Do not move too fast, Dryston. I am still trying to decide." She smiled.

He pulled away to look at her, his hand resting in her hair, fingering her short tufts. Sierra lifted her hand to his and brought it to her shoulder.

"Your hair will grow back, Sierra. But it does not matter to me. Short or long, it is attached to your head—"

He kissed her forehead.

"And that to your neck—"

He followed with another kiss to her neck, soft and lingering, causing her blood to heat.

"And that to your beautiful body—"

He trailed his fingers down the front of her gown, causing the soft tips of her breasts to tighten with arousal. No man had ever spoken to her with such flowery words. The stirrings they created inside were new and strange in many ways.

She touched her fingers to his lips, her gaze following her finger as she traced the outline of his mouth. "Your absence has left me empty, Dryston. I do not know what to do, how to fill this need within me. All I can think of is you inside me, making me whole, making me believe that all will be well. But I do not want to lie with you to satisfy my need only. I want to satisfy yours."

His lips curled into a wicked grin. "Nay, Sierra, I do not wish to simply lie with you. I want to take my time and love you as you deserve to be loved, touch you as you deserve to be touched," he whispered.

His breath smelled of mint from the medicine Alyson had made him drink to ease his pain. His mouth sought hers, gently letting her see that he was not interested in hurriedly sating his desire, but rather seeking to tempt her until she begged for more.

His kisses caused her lids to flutter, her heart pick up its pace, as if running to catch up with all that she had missed over the years. He held her face between his hands, moving over her mouth with slow reverence, drugging her with his kisses.

"What about your wounds?"

She turned her head, relishing the softness of his mouth and the contrast of his unshaven jaw against her neck. His hand slid down her back and he fisted her gown, drawing it up until his warm hand met her flesh.

"What wounds?" he asked softly, his breath hot against her neck as he caressed her thigh.

Sierra drew her palms over the sinewy flesh of his shoulders, careful of the tourniquet they had fashioned for his injured shoulder. She leaned down and placed a lingering kiss there, turning her cheek to his shoulder as he brushed his hand along her back, over her neck.

He faced her in the flickering candlelight. "It is not anyone's fault, Sierra," he said quietly.

She knew that much, but it was the expression on Torin's face that caused this guilt inside her. Despite all that had been revealed, their reunion had not been a happy one. He still did not trust her, and she did not know if he ever would. She had to live with that. He could not give what he did not have to give. She knew that well. Dryston had taught her that emotions were a special gift all on their own. But right now, she did not care if Torin believed in her. She knew that Dryston did and that was all that mattered.

Their entwined bodies cast intimate shadows on the tent wall and as much as she enjoyed watching their silhouettes she knew outside the tent could see them as just as clearly. Sierra leaned over and blew out the flame and a collective groan went up from outside.

"Go away, you bloody vultures. Do you not have anything better to do than spy on the injured?" Dryston called out.

"From what we could tell, 'twas not an injured body we saw

moving about in there," a teasing voice assured back, followed by raucous laughter.

"Nay? Perhaps not yet, but there will be if you do not go away," Dryston retorted with a smile on his face.

There was more grumbling and after a moment, only the sound of the wind.

His breath touched her face.

"I need to touch your skin, Sierra."

"Aye, 'tis the same for me, Dryston." She reached for his breeches and eased them down over his muscular thighs.

She slid her palms over the coarse hair of his calves. His skin smelled of the forest. "I rather enjoy your body, Dryston," she spoke and placed her mouth on his torso, kissing the tense buds of his chest.

"Feel free to take your time enjoying it." He laughed softly. "There is no need to rush." He held the back of her head, stroking her hair as he sat on the edge of the bed.

"So you do enjoy it as well—the pleasure your body gives me?" Sierra mused, teasing the spot just below his navel with her tongue.

"Aye, woman, see how well I enjoy your touch." He placed his hand over hers and guided her to his lap, where his phallus grew hard. Hungry to taste his mouth, she leaned forward and feasted on his lips, her hand stroking him, teasing him until she felt his tip glisten.

His breath caught as he eased her hand away. "Your gown, Sierra. I need to touch you."

He took her face in his hand, capturing her mouth in a searing kiss that sparked the need smoldering between her thighs. He kissed what flesh was exposed as he helped draw the gown over her head. "It is Alyson's gown, be careful where you lay it," she whispered against his lips.

He reached behind her and laid it on the table, never parting from her mouth.

"How do we manage this, Dryston?" She gasped as he crouched down in front of her and latched on to one of her breasts, lavishing her, drawing her pebbled tips between his teeth until her fingers curled at his shoulders. The juncture of her thighs burned with desire, desperate to join with him.

"Dryston," was all she could say as his hand brushed between her legs, his long fingers stroking her as his mouth continued to command hers. He turned her in his arms, running his hands slowly over her body, his face nuzzled at her shoulder. He cupped her breasts, weighing them, caressing them, as Sierra felt the strength of his cock brush the back of her thigh. She knew well the pleasure it gave her and hungered for him.

"I will die soon if I do not get inside you," he spoke against her neck.

She took his hand as she knelt on the bed and turned to face him. "What will happen now?" she asked, leaning forward, capturing his face in her hands and offering him a soul-searching kiss.

He smiled as she pulled away to look at him. "Do you mean immediately?" He chuckled. "I would think you might know that," he teased.

"I mean the future, Dryston. What will become of us?" she asked, fearing that she might not like his response, but she had to hear it just the same.

"We must still face Aeglech, Sierra. That mission has yet to be carried out. I believe that together with Ambrosis and his men, we stand a good chance of defeating the Saxons. But until Aeglech is dead, none of us is truly free." He kissed her gently. "I know that is not the answer you wished to hear."

Her heart ached and Sierra welcomed it because it meant

she was capable of such emotional pain and that she could now survive it. However, the pain of losing Dryston was something she could barely conceive of. But she understood his words and knew the truth of them. "It is well, Dryston. But tonight, let me stay with you," she whispered as she turned and stretched her body forward, lying over the edge of the bed so he could stand without further injury to his shoulder.

He stroked her from behind, stretching her with his thumb as he entered her, gentle in his movement as he inched deeper. He rested his palm on the base of her spine as he withdrew partway and entered her again. His sighs touched Sierra in a way she had not expected. Tonight she wanted to give him pleasure—it was less about what she received, and more about what she could give him, perhaps, to remember her by. She pushed back against him, forcing him deep inside her. He groaned, and Sierra lowered her head, giving herself over to him. His thrusts increased in their urgency.

"I cannot hold back," he growled, his hips moving with great determination. Sierra's body, tight with need, teetered on the brink of her release. One more divine thrust, and her body unraveled with delight. She heard a guttural sound escape from his throat as he pumped thrice into her, emptying his hot seed.

She lay down and he drew a blanket over the two of them as he tucked himself against her back. He gently kissed her shoulder and for a brief moment, Sierra allowed herself the fantasy of making love to him every night. It was a lovely dream, but a dream nonetheless, and Sierra drew a shuddered breath as she embraced the truth.

It was not long before she heard the sound of his slow and steady breathing and knew he was asleep. Just as he had his mission, Sierra, too, had something she had to do. She could not speak to Dryston about it because she knew he would try to stop her. And she could not speak of it to Torin because he likely would not believe her and so would try to stop her, too. Neither were they likely to allow her to ride into battle with them.

Sierra made up her mind to face Aeglech alone. It was not a task she was looking forward to. But it had to be done. This was about avenging the life of her mother, of Torin's mother, for stealing from them an entire life that could never be brought back or done over.

Sierra drew Dryston's hand to her lips, breathing in the musky scent of his skin, etching it in her memory, so that come what may, no one could take from her the memory of their few days together. She placed a soft kiss on his hand and slid from beneath his grasp. She dressed and watched him sleep until the first birds of dawn signaled it was time for her to go. "Rest well, *a ghra' mo chroi*," she said, kissing him on the cheek. "Thank you for setting me free."

Stealing Torin's sword had been much easier than taking back her horse. Sierra adjusted her brother's sword over her lap. She hoped that Alyson would not mind that she had had to tear her pretty gown, but the length was too cumbersome. Her next thought leaped to the grim notion that she may never get the chance to return the gown, torn or not.

True to Balrogan's name for her, quiet as a mouse, she had slipped into Torin's tent, stopping for a moment to get her bearings. Then, she had gone to the place where earlier she had seen him lay Dryston's sword, and there she found his as well. She hoped he would understand the reason for her taking his sword instead of Dryston's. In her mind, it would be as if they were there together, avenging their mother's death. With any luck, she would have a chance to return the sword and offer her explanation before Torin sent her to the gallows.

She kept low, holding the sheathed sword under her arm as she sneaked over to where the horses were kept. Using an apple she had tucked away, to keep the animal quiet, she led him down the narrow path to the secret spring that Alyson had shown her. From there, she made her way through a thick path of trees to the front side of the mountain, checking occasionally over her shoulder to see if anyone followed.

As the first tattered gray fingers of dawn crisscrossed the morning sky, Sierra found herself sitting on the Saxon stallion, looking down to the valley where the castle ruins lay. Dryston would be waking soon—would automatically reach for her and he would realize she was not there.

Torin, too, would be awakening to discover his sword was gone. She could see him in her mind's eye, his face dark with fury as he stomped to Dryston's tent, prepared to tell him that he had been right, his traitorous sister had escaped to join her new Saxon family.

Perhaps Torin was right, she thought. Perhaps she would never be capable of leading a normal life. Perhaps the path of her destiny was simply to ensure that Dryston had a future, that Torin and Alyson could live their lives in peace, and that the deaths of so many innocent Britons were avenged.

Sierra closed her eyes. Greater power than welding a skelp filled her soul. She reached her arms to the sky, lifting her face to the first morning breeze wafting across the valley. Above her the wind began to blow, bitter with the bite of an early frost. On the horizon, fat rolls of gray storm clouds darkened the sun's attempt to rise. The sky grew black, foreboding, as it draped the valley in a bleak wash of dusky gray. Flashes of lightning flickered in the dense clouds, and thunder rolled in the distance.

She sensed her mother's presence, even before she looked to the cliff rising high over her shoulder and saw the giant silver wolf staring down at her.

"I am not afraid," she called out to the wolf over the roar of the frigid wind. Fat raindrops began to smack Sierra's skin. The wolf darted from the edge of the cliff and reappeared in front of her, heading down the mountain. Sierra nudged her horse, urging it to follow the wolf.

Today she would meet her destiny.

Chapter Twenty-Two

He rubbed his cheek along her inner thigh, causing her to giggle. He had never heard her giggle before and was delighted to coax it out of her. She smelled of the woods and water lilies.

"There are more ways that I want to bring you pleasure, mo cridhe," he offered, kneeling between her legs. He kissed each breast; he was able to caress her with one hand only, but he had heard no complaints.

Taking his face in her hands, she kissed him and turned, placing her back against his chest. She reached between her legs, finding his staff at the ready and leaned forward, offering him her sweet opening. "Take me, Dryston," she whispered.

He entered her slowly, stretching her, urged deeper by her sighs. It was as if her body was made to fit him perfectly, and her desire to please him amazed him.

"Dryston," she said as their bodies pushed each other toward bliss. "Dryston."

Her voice sounded oddly like Torin's.

"Sierra?" Dryston muttered in his semiconscious state.

"Dryston? Where is she?"

"Torin?" He shaded his eyes to the brightness of the sun as his brother held open the flap of the tent.

"Sierra, where is she?"

Dryston glanced beside him, where he was certain she had been all night. "She was just here a moment ago. What are you yattering about?"

"When was the last time you saw her?" his brother asked roughly. He moved toward the bed, his large hands fisted at his sides.

"Calm yourself, Torin. Stop talking to me in riddles," Dryston stated, his head beginning to throb.

"She is *gone,* Dryston. I should have followed my gut and put her back in the brig last night. The Saxon horse is gone and so, too, my sword."

"Your sword? That is lunacy. What reason would she have for taking your sword, Torin? If she wanted one, why not just take mine? What did you say that would cause her to leave?"

"Dryston, I have not spoken to her since my interrogation."

Dryston hopped naked from the bed. "I need to go look for her." He tried with bumbling effort to place legs into his breeches. "What possible reason would she have to leave?" He struggled to dress with only one good arm. "Some assistance would be appreciated," he said to his brother.

"Have you checked with Alyson? Perhaps the two of them went for a morning walk?"

"With my sword?" Torin gave his brother an incredulous look as he yanked his breeches up around his hips. "Nay, she is not. Alyson is still asleep."

He took a step back and leveled a look at Dryston. "I know

this is hard for you, but do you know, without a glimmer of doubt, that she did *not* go back to Aeglech?"

In all of his life, Dryston had never wanted to bash his brother's head in, until now. What he said was absurd.

He held his head as if his brain might burst. "Yes, I am certain. That was our plan to get him away from his castle and come to us. Sierra had a vision of it, she told Aeglech about it and then she betrayed him by helping me to escape. Now it's a matter of pride for him and he won't rest until he sees her dead."

"You will not go alone," Torin spoke quietly. "We will go together as planned. The men are now assembled."

"But it does not concern you that your sister is out there alone? Your own flesh and blood?" Dryston's voice began to rise with frustration.

"You are every bit my own flesh and blood, Dryston. You know this. It was her choice, not mine, to leave," he spoke. "If the Saxons are indeed there, then we shall have our battle. If not, we ride on to the Saxon fortress. But you have to face the hard truth, Dryston. Why would Sierra leave, taking my sword unless it was to meet up with her king?"

"No." Dryston shook his head as he struggled with what he knew to be the truth. "She would not have left without waking me, not without saying something." Pain twisted his heart as he met Torin's dark eyes and saw in them the justice he had always admired.

"She did exactly that, Dryston. I am sorry."

He was right, of course, but the sting was no less painful.

"There is one thing I need to ask of you." Torin hesitated a moment before he continued. "I need you to escort Alyson up the hill to the safety of the caves."

"Bloody hell, my intent is to ride to Badon and fight with you."

Anger clouded Torin's face. He stepped forward and grabbed Dryston's good shoulder.

"I am not giving you a choice in this, Dryston. I need you to take Alyson up the mountain and keep watch over her and the others in the event that we are not victorious."

"Not victorious? Torin, you are one of the greatest military strategists I have ever known. Nay, send another man less qualified than me to take Alyson. I insist on being at your side."

Dryston searched for his shirt and hoped Sierra would show up soon. "Where is my tunic?" His eyes lifted to Torin's and he met reality. Was it possible? Could she really have left without saying goodbye? True, he had not given her the understanding that they would have a future together, at least not until Aeglech was dead. And it was clear that Torin did not yet accept her as she had hoped. Why would she stay? Still, she would have to know that to return to the Saxons meant certain death—unless it had been part of her plan.

"So you agree you may have been used?"

Dryston slumped to the edge of the bed. "I cannot believe she would go back to him…not to that murderous beast. You should have seen where she lived, Torin. God in heaven, the stench alone—" He stared at Torin, not wanting to believe Sierra would willingly go back.

"Aye, it is not easy for you to understand, but it is all she has ever known. Perhaps in some strange way, she finds comfort there."

"No, that is not your sister, Torin. You did not see her in the woods. It was as if she was learning to live again. Everything seemed new to her, an adventure to be embraced. No, I cannot imagine she would willingly choose to return. And worse, what will happen is he will kill her." He shook his head, reaffirming his belief that what they had experienced together these past few days could not have been an act.

"How can I just let her go knowing what is going to happen?"

"Dryston," Torin spoke calmly. "There is more you need to know." He sat on the bed beside him.

"Alyson is going to have a child, my child. I cannot stay with her. You and I both know that your arm prevents you from engaging in battle." He searched Dryston's face. "If anything should happen to me—"

He shook his head. "Nay, brother, speak no more. I will not hear it. Especially not now. You have no choice but to return to that poor girl and make her your bride."

Dryston was going to be an uncle—the fact had an energizing effect on him. He would see first to Alyson's safe return and then go to find Sierra. He only hoped he would not be too late. "Very well, brother, you win this time," he said, patting Torin's knee. "But do not think that you can leave me alone with your beautiful Alyson for too long." He forced out a grin.

"As if she would consider having you." Torin grinned in return.

Dryston's smile dissolved. "But I can tell you this, Torin. You are mistaken about Sierra."

"Time will tell, brother."

"Let Alyson know that I will come by your tent soon. And be warned, I have skills, brother, that you have not been privy to," Dryston teased. In his mind, however, Dryston was already forming a plan. If nothing else motivated him, he wanted to give Sierra the chance at reuniting with her family. He pulled his head through his tunic, and maneuvered it around his sling.

Torin slapped him on the back. "I will have Alyson get ready."

Dryston let him go on thinking he would not defy his

orders. His brother had enough on his mind. Torin was to be a father? And he an uncle? This gave him even more reason to find Sierra. She had a family here, and it was growing.

Dark clouds blocked the morning sun as Dryston rode into the mountains with his future sister-in-law. Neither of them had spoken much after they had watched Torin and his men load up and head down into the valley. They were to meet Ambrosis and his men and assemble before heading toward the Badon ruins. It was a cool morning for early autumn, but a grand day for a battle. The weather did little for his mood however.

"My heart goes out to you, Dryston, about your Sierra," Alyson stated quietly.

My Sierra. He glanced at her. She was indeed a beautiful woman and between her and Torin, his nieces and nephews would be handsome folk.

He kept his eyes on the road before him, swallowing against the lump in his throat. "Could I have been so blind, Alyson?"

"About Sierra?" She gave him a side look. "If so, then she fooled us all. I did not sense any deception or malice in her, Dryston. What would cause her to do what she did?"

"Torin maintains that this was her plan all along. He believes that she helped me escape in order to lead the Saxons to our camp."

They rode on in silence, but he could see that she was busy thinking, caught between her own beliefs and those of her future husband.

Alyson tipped her head and gave him a puzzled expression.

"If that were true, why then did Sierra not return to the camp with the Saxon army? Surely she would have by now?

Why would they wait for our army to ready and be on the move, before they attacked?"

Dryston yanked on his reins and stared at her. "Of course! Why had I not thought of that before?" He searched his mind for any other reason Sierra would leave, taking her brother's sword. And it hit him suddenly what she was doing.

"Mother of God," he muttered, realizing that she was going to meet Aeglech herself.

"What is it, Dryston? What did I say?"

"I have to get to the ruins, Alyson. Is there a shorter way from here?"

She turned on her horse, searching the area. "There is a narrow path, near the spring. It will take you around the other side of the mountain. Follow the ledge and it will see you down the other side. It meets up close to where Torin and his men are to meet Ambrosis."

"How far to the safety of the caves?" Dryston asked, bringing his horse around to face Alyson.

"Just around this last curve. What are you planning, Dryston?" Alyson asked, her horse prancing in place.

"We will have to talk later." He nudged his horse forward. "We must hurry."

"What are you going to do?" Alyson asked again as they rode into the camp.

He leaned over and kissed her cheek, calling a young lad to come help her off the horse. "See to it that she rests, and, Alyson, stay alert," he cautioned.

"Dryston?" she spoke in an exasperated tone. "What are you going to do?"

"What I should have done all along, Alyson. Trust my gut, and trust Sierra."

"Be careful of your shoulder," she called to him as he jockeyed his horse in the direction of the road and prayed he would get to the ruins in time.

If his hunch was correct, Sierra had gone to the castle ruins herself to meet up with Aeglech, not for the sake of strategy, but for revenge. If the Saxon king had believed what she had told him, as Dryston hoped, Aeglech's men should already be approaching Badon. Just over the hill behind the ruins was where Torin and his men were to be assembled.

As Dryston drew near the ruins, he kept to the forest's edge searching for Aeglech's men. In the distance, he could hear the insistent thrum of the Saxon battle drums, echoing across the valley, and realized they were not far behind. The crumbling castle came into view, parts of its outer walls still intact. There seemed to be no movement around the remaining castle bastion. He walked his horse slowly as he rounded the backside of the tower.

His heart stilled.

Two horses grazed in the tall grass, one coal black that he did not recognize. The other was Sierra's stallion. He did not have to guess who the horse belonged to, for his suspicions were confirmed by the two Saxon guards keeping watch from atop a nearby hill. Aeglech had apparently ridden ahead to affirm his battle strategy or—and he did not want to think it possible—Sierra had made plans to meet Aeglech there all along.

Whichever the case, Dryston was going to make sure that Aeglech's army was short by at least two men.

He rode his horse quietly through the dense trees and underbrush, coming up behind the guards looking out over the hill.

With his good arm, Dryston withdrew his sword and wrapped the reins around the wrist of his poor arm. He cleared his throat.

The two turned and one look at his sling caused them to glance at each other and smile.

Thunder rumbled on the horizon as a bank of storm clouds rolled into the valley.

"A fine day for a fight, gentlemen," Dryston said, returning their smile.

Chapter Twenty-Three

Sierra stood in front of the barricaded door and held her brother's sword over her head, poised at the ready. The man standing before her seemed to take a mocking delight in the view.

"You have changed, *wealh*. Your aggression is much more evident. I wonder if I should take credit for such a change, or of it should go to Balrogan, for all he has taught you. I am not sure, however, that you have thought this plan through as carefully as you should have." Aeglech spoke with a glint in his gaze. "What did your Roman prisoner think of your idea?"

Sierra knew Aeglech would want to scout out the potential battlefield himself, trusting the job to no one else. "The Roman has no idea that I am here."

Aeglech's brow rose. "When I saw my prize horse, I knew you were here, waiting for me." He paced back and forth in front of the window, glancing outside each time he walked by.

"Come away from the window," she spoke as she jabbed the

point of Torin's sword at him. He held up his hands in surrender and backed away. Still he did not reach for his sword.

Sierra edged around the castle tower room and shut one of the windows, blocking the dim light coming in. He kept his distance of her sword, and she held her ground, watching him as closely.

The wind picked up outside, blowing leaves past the remaining open window. There was little left of the abandoned castle, and at first sight, only tufts of straw, a chair and a Roman helmet in the desolate room.

But Sierra's eye caught the familiarities of her former home—the long black chain attached to the wall with its heavy metal shackles, the skelp partially hidden beneath the straw and the wooden trap door placed to one side of the room. Sierra knew the horrors that would have occurred down the winding stairs to the dungeon below.

"It is fitting, do you not think, that you should die in such a place?" she stated calmly.

His gaze swerved to hers, his brow cocked in surprise. "Die?" He offered a short laugh as he glanced at the helmet on the ground. With a swift kick he booted it across the floor, sending it clattering to her feet.

He mocked her with his heartless grin. It was meant to intimidate, this confidence he so pompously displayed. Sierra adjusted the grip on her sword and held his steely gaze, trying to predict his next move.

Aeglech chuckled under his breath as he tapped his fingers over the sword at his hip. "I trust your Roman has since recovered from your thrashing?"

"He is not *my* Roman." She did not want speak about Dryston. "Why do you not draw your sword, Saxon?" she asked, preparing her stance as she gripped the sword tighter. It grew heavy, causing her forearms to ache under the weight of it. That was one reason he delayed, she realized. He wanted her arm to wear out, then he would exact his revenge for her disloyalty.

"I find this courage of yours, though reckless, appealing as always, *wealh*. I knew then as I do now, that my decision to make you my executioner's apprentice was correct. Naturally, I had no idea that I would be promoting you to the position of master. That is, until I discovered your little secret."

"You are talking in riddles, Aeglech. They say that a man does that when he is losing his mind." Sierra kept a watchful eye on him as he walked back and forth. He was biding his time. She decided his army must be on its way. Which meant Ambrosis and Torin would also be gathering their men.

"Oh, but, *wealh,* you see, my mind is clear. Everything is clear. It is all under my control." He glanced at her. "Why do you think Balrogan died?"

Sierra stared at the man who considered human life so trivial. She knew he was goading her. He wanted her to lose control, so he could snatch it from her. She remained silent.

"Balrogan died because he was disloyal to his Saxon heritage. Unfortunately, he was more loyal to me than his lover. That was his mistake. He told me that his lover's father, one of my former guards, was dying, and confessed to Balrogan that the rightful heir to my throne might still be alive—and was rumored to be part of the rebellion. Had word gotten out about my executioner and his lover, it would have made a mockery of my court." He shrugged. "Of course, they had to die."

Sierra took a step forward, blinded by the anger exploding in her brain. It was his mouth curling into a crooked smile that halted her steps. She swallowed, reeling in anger. It was what he wanted, what he sought in all of his battles—a worthy opponent.

She stepped back and took note of his frustrated sigh. If she had any chance to survive this encounter she was going to have to think like him.

"Be cautious, *wealh,* of your anger. For some it is the elixir of power—for the weak, it sucks from them all that they have, making them weaker." He leaped toward her arms outstretched, and brought his foot to the floor with a primal yell, followed by hysterical laughter. "Besides, I am doing you a favor."

"I want nothing from you," she replied.

He shrugged. "Believe me, *wealh,* it is no trouble."

"What makes you think I would die for him or anyone?"

He smiled and leveled a look at her.

"Because, *wealh,* you were foolish enough to come alone. If you did not care so deeply you would not have risked so much."

Determined not to allow his words to affect her, she did not respond.

"Where is this Roman now? The man you risked everything for?" he demanded.

"It does not matter," she responded, holding his gaze to prove that he no longer held her in his mental grasp. "This is between you and me, no one else."

He crooked a blond eyebrow.

"Not even your brother?"

Sierra's heart faltered. How did he know about Torin?

"I see you are surprised." He shrugged. "The guard was rather forthcoming on his deathbed. Not only did he confirm that his son was Balrogan's lover, he had another bit of interesting news to share. He confessed to not killing your brother as he was ordered, and that alone was enough reason to break his neck. Still, I might have allowed him to live had he not, in a moment of weakness, mentioned that his former wench had secretly delivered your brother and she knew that the babe's father was Vortigern." He glanced at her with a smirk. "Like mother, like daughter—you are both whores." He sighed. "The poor man took a strange delight in thinking that my days as king were numbered, so I ended his suffering."

So that's what the guard had been trying to tell her. No wonder her mother was so protective of Torin. Yet everyone who knew the truth had been killed. She stared at Aeglech, finally understanding that it was not his pride that prompted his coming, but his need to find the only other person who might know the truth and so contest his supremacy. "You won't get away with this," she said. "I won't let you."

He smiled. "Tell me, *wealh,* what does your brother think of you? What makes you think he will accept you so readily after being my apprentice all this time?"

"I do not know my brother," she shot back. That much was true.

He hesitated, eyeing her Roman sword.

"Why would you go to such trouble to free the Roman prisoner?" he asked calmly.

"He offered me a safe place to escape your hell, Aeglech, nothing more," she snapped.

"Nothing more?" He folded his arms over his chest. "It's hard for me to believe that. After all, you never once tried to escape before. But a stranger comes along who offers freedom and you risk everything, even your life, to follow him? No, there is more to it than that, much more." He looked at her with a shrewd gaze. "I think you have met your brother, and I think you know exactly who he is."

The sound of Saxon drums carried on the wind blowing through the valley. Aeglech knew that he had the upper hand. In a short time, there would be hundreds of Saxons descending on these ruins, and Sierra's fate would be sealed.

"I have no ties to anyone," she snapped. It unnerved her that he could read her so easily. Her mind reeled with the very idea that Torin was the rightful heir to Britannia's throne and that right now, she was the only one left alive that knew it. At least it was to her advantage that he thought she was.

"Oh, I question that, *wealh*. The very fact that you came alone to meet me tells me that you are protecting someone. A noble move on your part, but very unwise. Tell me more about your brother."

"I told you, I do not know my brother," she answered.

"But that is his sword, is it not?" Aeglech asked, his eyes glittering with interest.

Sierra turned the handle of the sword over in her hands. Her palms were beginning to sweat. "I do not know whose sword this is," she lied.

"Your eyes give you away, *wealh*. That is a Roman sword and a fine one. Whomever it belongs to is a man of great power…a leader of men. It must be painful that your brother does not accept you as readily as you had hoped."

His voice grew quiet, soothing, the way it had that day in his chambers.

"But *I* accept you, Sierra. Just as you are." He walked to a chair tossed on its side and up-righted it, offering it briefly first to Sierra before he sat down like a guest in her house.

"Do your people accept you now, knowing what you have

done? Where will you go? We would be good, you and I. Our passion runs deep. I felt yours that day in my chambers. Do you remember how well our bodies fit?" He leered at her.

"Prepare to die," she said flatly.

"Come, Sierra, I appeal to your sense of reason. There is still time to reconsider. You have skills that I can use, more so now with Balrogan gone. You can have whatever you want. It is yours for the naming. I made the same offer once to your mother and I now offer it to you."

"I would rather die first," she tossed back.

The corner of his lip curled upward. "I thought that might be your answer. Now the only question you have to answer is by whose hand you wish to die. Your brother's or mine?"

"Draw your sword, Aeglech. Give me an opponent worthy of a fight."

"Then I am right in guessing that your brother was not pleased with what he saw? The Roman neither, perhaps?

"Truthfully, Sierra, can you find fault with your brother for not trusting you? After all, you have been an accomplice to the murder of many Britons. And as for your lover—"

"He is not my lover," Sierra shouted, her frustration growing with each additional moment that she looked upon the Saxon king's face.

"That is too bad." His eyes lowered, eyeing her cutoff gown. "Such a sweet body, too. I grow hard even now thinking of when you bathed before me. Do you remember, *wealh,* how my hand felt on your breast? How it felt when I stroked you deeply? You enjoyed it as much as I. You wanted me inside you, to feel my power thrusting between your thighs."

"No more, you bastard murderer, or I will kill you now."

He laughed. "You mother did not like it when I made her bathe for me, either." He pinned her with a taunting look.

"Draw your sword," she muttered between clenched teeth. He smiled.

A crack of thunder split the silence. Another loud rumble brought a flash of lightning closer to the tower.

Sierra flinched but did not take her eyes off him.

"Your mother was special, Sierra, just as you are."

"Your yatter tires me, Aeglech," she warned.

"I enjoyed her and I believe she enjoyed me—judging by her screams of pleasure."

Sierra's jaw ached from grinding her teeth in anger. The bastard knew exactly what he was doing.

"It may be true that your Roman satisfies you," he stated. "But not nearly as much as I would."

Sierra stood firm, forcing back her emotions. It was his way to torture the mind first, incapacitating his prey and then striking when they were vulnerable.

Outside the sound of thunder mingled with the beat of the Saxon drums growing ever closer. Sierra knew she was going to have to make her move before it was too late.

The hair rose on her neck and arms an instant before a bolt of lightning came through the open window and struck the Roman helmet on the ground, sending it flying across the room. Sierra ducked as it flew past her head and quickly turned her focus back to Aeglech. He was looking out the window.

Seeing her opportunity, she lunged forward, aiming for his unguarded side. Her sword sliced through his garments easily and entered his ribs, sliding through the muscle and sinew. His raging blue gaze snapped to hers as he grabbed at the sword, trying to pull it from her grip.

She stood less than a sword's length from him, his fury burning a hole through her as he fished for the sword on his hip.

"Damn you to hell, you Druid witch! You are ruthless and more like me than you wish to think."

She turned her wrist sharply, digging the blade deeper into his side as he cried out in pain. "Do not ever tell me that I am like you again." She jerked the blade once more, hearing the snap of one of his ribs.

"Bitch whore," he screamed, grabbing his side. His breathing was labored as he lurched forward and dropped to his knees.

Sierra drew the sword from his side and a river of blood began to pour from the gash.

"You think I am ruthless? Were you aware that it was *your* father who killed Torin's? Yes, 'tis true, your mother told me. And let us talk about Vortigern, a Briton king who was responsible for the deaths of hundreds of innocent Britons long before we Saxons arrived on these shores. Vortigern's greed was worse than any Saxons. He killed his own people. The only reason your mother was spared was because he needed her gift. Do you not see that you were already destined to this life of darkness before I brought you to my fortress?"

Sierra frowned, trying to make sense of what he said. Was this more of his lies and trickery?

He laughed. "Your father was a great Celt warrior. I coaxed that information from your mother. However, Torin's father was a greedy bastard ruler, no better than I. I can see why she would choose to keep Torin hidden."

"That is not the reason. We hid him from you and your barbarian ways," Sierra said, tired of his lies and torturous mind games.

The wind blew wickedly, whistling through the louver at the

top of the tower walls. She shoved aside Aeglech's words as she grabbed a shackle iron suspended from the wall and snapped it with a final clang to his ankle.

He fought against it as he sought blindly for his sword. Sierra bent down, grabbed it from him and ran it swiftly across the back of his heel, grateful for all that Balrogan had taught her.

His breaths now came in gasps as he dropped to one elbow on the floor. He tried to smile and the movement caused blood to trickle from the side of his mouth.

"Master Balrogan taught you well, *wealh*."

She could not hear his words for the thrumming in her ears. She looked out the window and saw on the horizon a multitude of Saxons marching to their drums.

She slammed the window shut, jamming the lock into place.

"Your fate is as good as mine, *wealh*. Stay here with me, and let me hold you as you die." He coughed, bringing up more blood.

She was not about to die at his side or even in the same room. She would rather have been bludgeoned by a thousand swords than to stay there with him.

Sierra shoved as much straw as she could find to the center of the room and pulled a flint from her pouch.

"What have you left, *wealh?*" He tried to force the words through a cough. "You are nothing and you came from nothing. No one will save you—you cannot fix what cannot be fixed. I was your only chance for a future, do you not see? Your only chance—"

"You damned me once to hell, Aeglech, and you will never do so again, to me or anyone!" she screamed.

Sierra tossed his sword across the room and crouched, striking her flint against the straw. A second later, it burst into flame. The dryness of the straw quickly caused the fire to grow and she knew that it would not take long for the smoke to rise and alert the warriors across the field.

She smashed the wooden chair against the stone floor and placed the pieces carefully on the fire to be sure the flames would burn long. The fire increased in size, flaring up with the debris scattered on the floor. She stood, free at last from the mental anguish and physical torture of her imprisonment.

Sierra was now ready to face her death.

She looked through the haze of smoke at the man who had kept her oppressed all these years, trying to break her will. She smiled, because he had not succeeded. She hoped her mother would be proud when they were reunited.

"Damn you to hell," she whispered as she watched his body slump over. Smoke filled the room, its tendrils inching their way to the louver above.

Sierra closed the door and started down the narrow steps to the ground below. She did not know what her fate would be as she stepped out into the pouring rain.

For a moment, Sierra stood still, letting the rain wash over her. Beyond the outer wall, atop the hill that led back to the camp, she looked up and saw a dark figure on horseback staring down at her. The man in her vision. Alongside him, on the crest of the hill, stood hundreds, maybe more, waiting for the Saxons to arrive. Thunder rumbled in the distance, matching the persistent beat of the Saxon drums behind her.

"Sierra!"

A shout drew her from her daze. Riding down the hill, full gallop, was Dryston. The Saxons saw him at the same time and a frightening battle cry rose from the horde. Discernible only to her ears was the sound of a man's scream coming from the burning tower.

Dryston reached her side and offered his good arm to her.

"I don't remember that this was part of our plan, Sierra," Dryston said, holding out his hand to her.

She handed Torin's sword to him and hauled herself up behind him.

"We need to discuss your military strategies, Sierra," he said as he nudged the horse up the hill to where Torin was waiting.

Her brother's gaze met hers as they rode up beside him. Dryston handed him his sword. "You have a battle to win. We are even."

He shook his head as he inspected his sword. Aeglech's blood still stained the steel. "You have avenged our mother's death. Now we battle to avenge the deaths of all of the innocents of Britannia who have died. You will stay with us, then?" he asked, his dark eyes searching hers.

Sierra nodded. After nine years, it was time to begin again.

"I will see to it that she does not wander again." Dryston patted Sierra's leg, his hand resting on her knee.

The brothers clasped arms in a moment of solidarity. As Dryston rode them out of harm's way, Sierra looked over her shoulder and saw her brother, sword raised, ready to lead his charge into battle.

She considered how to tell him that he was the rightful heir to the Britannia throne.

FROM THE BESTSELLING AUTHOR OF
DIRTY, TEMPTED AND *STRANGER*

MEGAN HART

One summer Bess Walsh was
taken, absolutely and completely,
by Nick, a fervent sexual
accomplice who knew how to
ignite an all-consuming passion
she had no idea she carried deep
within her.

Bess had always wondered what
had happened to Nick after that
summer, after their promise to
meet again. And now, twenty
years later, back at the beach
house where they met, taking a
break from responsibility, from
marriage, from life, she discovers
his heartbreaking fate—and
why he never came back for her.
Suddenly Nick's name is on her
lips…his hands on her thighs…dark hair and eyes called back from
the swirling gray of purgatory's depths.

Dead, alive, or something in between, they can't stop their hunger.

She wouldn't dare.

Available now, wherever books are sold!

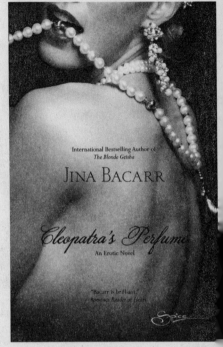

naughty bits

**WHEN ALL YOU
HAVE TIME FOR**
is **A QUICKIE...**

naughty bits is the first-ever compilation of
breath-hitching, leg-crossing, pulse-quickening
short erotic fiction from the editors of Spice Briefs.
Penned by some of the genre's favorite authors,
including Megan Hart, Delilah Devlin, Jodi Lynn
Copeland, Kimberly Kaye Terry and Sarah McCarty,
these fifteen provocative, flirty, haunting—but
always arousing—erotic encounters may be brief,
but each one is guaranteed to be the naughtiest
part of your day!

Available wherever books are sold!